Bones in the Belfry

Also by Suzette A. Hill

A Load of Old Bones

BONES IN THE BELFRY

Suzette A. Hill

Constable • London

Constable & Robinson Ltd
3 The Lanchesters
162 Fulham Palace Road
London W6 9ER
www.constablerobinson.com

First published in the UK by Constable,
an imprint of Constable & Robinson, 2008

First US edition published by SohoConstable,
an imprint of Soho Press, 2008

Soho Press, Inc.
853 Broadway
New York, NY 10003
www.sohopress.com

A copy of the British Library Cataloguing in Publication
Data is available from the British Library

UK ISBN: 978-1-84529-582-0

US ISBN: 978-1-56947-510-2
US Library of Congress number: 2007044072

Printed and bound in the EU

1 3 5 7 9 10 8 6 4 2

To Roger Hartley Lloyd: the joker in the pack,
in loving memory.

1

The Vicar's Version

When Nicholas Ingaza persuaded me to store his ill-gotten paintings circumstances had ensured that I was in no position to refuse. The year was 1958 and my situation as vicar of St Botolph's, Molehill, Surrey, was what you might call precarious. Six months previously I had had the misfortune to eliminate one of my parishioners by process of strangulation, and the whole business had been exceedingly trying for me. Not that I *was* tried, for through a blend of sheer good luck and the ineptitude of the investigating police officers I had somehow managed to escape detection and continue my parochial duties unencumbered by criticism or scandal. Then just when things were getting back to normal and I was starting to feel moderately safe, Nicholas cheerfully intervened and my long-sought peace was once more disrupted.

Among other things, and for want of a better term, Nicholas was an art dealer living a life of somewhat misty ambiguity in Brighton. He had not always been an art dealer. Once upon a time he had been a fellow student at St Bede's, the theological college where I had trained after the war; but events and his own predilections (notably the patronizing of a certain London Turkish bath) had directed him elsewhere – jail, to be exact – and we had long lost touch until his unexpected emergence in the bar of the Old

Schooner, Brighton, in the summer of 1957. As things turned out, it was an encounter which would prove both useful and dangerous.

To explain Nicholas Ingaza is difficult: he is one of those people whom one never really knows but whose capacity to both rile and charm can have an unsettling, even disastrous, effect upon those around him. Beneath the lazy banter and brilliantined suavity there lurks an anarchic spirit, a maverick obstinacy which had certainly created havoc with the authorities at St Bede's all those years ago – and which even now was jeopardizing the plans I had so carefully laid for my own future security.

At the height of the 'troubles' (i.e. the time when I was in maximum danger from police curiosity) Nicholas had provided me with an alibi, or rather he had corroborated a fiction I had been forced to concoct. He had done this without my having to confide the essential reason for the subterfuge; but his brief part in it had left him tiresomely inquisitive about an event in my life it would have been foolish to reveal. Consequently Nicholas had what you might call a hold over me; and, as he had lightly pointed out, I was in his debt – 'You owe me one, old cock!' being, I think, his exact words.

After a decent interval the owed favour was inevitably requested and I had reluctantly complied. Under the pretext of needing additional storage space for an absent client, he had delivered two large pictures to the vicarage. No mention was made of their provenance and the items were to remain in my 'safekeeping' until such time as his client required them. I asked no questions, undid no cords, and tried to pretend that they were not there.

The vicarage is small, the pictures large; and after a few days the absurd inconvenience was impossible to sustain. They would have to go elsewhere: either down in the church crypt, filthy and damp, and for some reason beloved of my dog Bouncer; or up in the belfry. The former was by far the more accessible but the conditions seemed less than ideal. The belfry was dry, airy and sufficiently remote to deter prying eyes or passing tramps. Thus it was up to the belfry that I somehow managed to lug the wretched things, watched enthusiastically by Bouncer who seemed to think that my oaths and panting exertions were some form of new game. Anyway, there I left them, returned to the vicarage, and putting them out of my mind tried to resume a quiet and untroubled life.

That, I think, might have been achieved had it not been for Mrs Tubbly Pole. As it was, her arrival in the parish caused considerable upset to the carefully placed apple cart, and its contents were sent cascading in a number of directions – principally mine. Later I developed a wary liking for Mrs Tubbly Pole and we became moderate friends, but at the time she was dynamite.

A couple of weeks after I had received the goods from Nicholas, a house became vacant a few doors down from the vicarage. Its owners were moving to Kenya on a two-year diplomatic term, and rather than sell they had decided to rent it out. The 'To Let' sign disappeared after only a week and I learnt on the grapevine that 'a very nice lady from London' had taken it for an unspecified period.

The nice lady's arrival was heralded by the usual spate of errand boys and delivery vans, but for a while I saw nothing of the new tenant – although her presence at the house was firmly marked by the appearance of an obese and brindled bulldog which spent much of its time lolling idly over the bars of the front gate. Of bulging orb and sabre tooth, this creature would wheeze and snuffle in a way that clearly unnerved passers-by, making them scuttle past with lowered eyes. Its name, I subsequently learnt, was Gunga Din – presumably something to do with the owner's colonial days in India (on which, as I came to know her, she would expatiate with nostalgic relish).

9

Inevitably, however, our paths soon crossed: at the local pillar box to be exact. There I waited my turn as a large female enveloped in musquash was busy ramming bulky packets into its narrow slit. Finally, muttering something about the inadequacies of the postal provisions, she turned and nearly bumped into me.

I raised my hat politely; whereupon, appraising my dog collar and clerical grey, she exclaimed, 'Ah, I'm new to this area. My name is Tubbly Pole, and *you* must be the Reverend Francis Oughterard – quite a public benefactor, I hear. I like a man of generosity, pretty rare these days!' And she pumped my hand vigorously. I was slightly non-plussed by both comments – confused by the first, embarrassed by the second. Was Tubbly her first name? And if so was that how she wished to be addressed? Surely not! But one never quite knows about these things . . .

The reference to my generosity was discomfiting; not so much on account of natural modesty as because, although I had indeed contributed to some of Molehill's worthier causes, the monies for such gifts were a large part of the legacy left me by the lady of whom I had disposed.

That legacy, far from being welcome, had been an embarrassing bombshell. In the circumstances the last thing I had wanted was for my name to be linked to the deceased in quite so public and intimate a way. At the time, Mrs Elizabeth Fotherington's dispatch had been a psychological necessity; and monetary considerations were far from my mind when I had been forced to put an end to her ceaseless chatter and coy innuendoes on that dreadful June morning in Foxford Wood.

For months she had been tiresome beyond endurance, driving me insane with her importunate attentions. This garrulous widow of uncertain years had become the bane of my life; and it was typical of the woman that even from beyond the grave she had still been able to exert a simpering control over my privacy and peace of mind. Leaving me that large sum was her *coup de grâce*, her final act of meddlesome intrusion. And, crucially, it was the one thing that might have connected me with the crime!

Thus I had done the only possible thing: abrogated all claim to the legacy by distributing the funds to various local charities. The public approval which this inevitably produced, while in itself unsought, had certainly helped my purpose of stifling suspicion. Nevertheless, it was a means to an end which I have always found faintly embarrassing – and which is why I now felt awkward at Mrs Tubbly Pole's fulsome praise.

So muttering something self-deprecating, I quickly turned the subject by asking how she was settling in, and made a great show of patting the 'handsome' bulldog. This was obviously the right thing, for she launched into a bubbling eulogy of the creature's finer points and complimented me on my shrewd judgement of canine quality. Our encounter was concluded by an exhortation to be sure to visit them; and wagging her finger imperiously, she told me not to leave it too long or else 'the mountain will be forced to come to Mahomet!'

As I walked home I pondered her words with not a little apprehension. Supposing she was going to be another Elizabeth! But on reflection I considered this improbable. Unlike that lady, Mrs Tubbly Pole seemed of a cheerful and robust nature and did not strike me as one to go ga-ga over an obscure parson twenty years her junior. Having little personal vanity in that particular sphere, I also thought that the chance of ever again eliciting such avid interest remote in the extreme! Thus reassured I returned to the vicarage to feed the dog and cat and give myself a light restorative.

A week passed, and what with one thing and another – squaring up to the Mothers' Union, parleying with the church heating engineers, and calming the organist's tantrums – it had been quite a strenuous day. However, it was over now and I could enjoy an evening of uninter-rupted quiet. There was a concert starting on the Third Programme which I had been rather looking forward to. So switching on the wireless, I settled back in the armchair, closed my eyes and prepared to relax to Heifetz and the opening bars of the Elgar Violin Concerto.

As the first notes were struck, the front gate clicked loudly. I cursed, and from the window saw waddling up the path the portly form of Gunga Din followed by his owner Mrs Tubbly Pole. Evidently I had been too tardy in paying the requested visit and, as warned, the Mountain had taken things into her own hands. The dog wore a tartan coat clamped to its ample back. His mistress was sporting some drapery of shaggy fur reaching down to her ankles, and a wide velour hat with upturned brim. The effect was a cross between the Queen Mother and Bud Flanagan. Reluctantly I went into the hall to welcome my guests. Her shape loomed through the glass panels of the front door, and even with it still closed between us I could hear her throaty tones echoing around the porch as she embarked on introductions.

'My dear Vicar, I hope you don't mind my intruding. Gunga and I were just passing and thought we might drop in and –' by this time I had opened the door – 'DISTURB YOUR PEACE,' she boomed in my face. I smiled weakly as dog and mistress shoved their way into the narrow hall and were shed of their respective coats.

I steered them into the sitting room, switched off the wireless and mumbled something about making a cup of tea. She sunk herself into the larger of the two armchairs while the bulldog flopped heavily in front of the fire.

'Well, it's half past five, you know – almost six o'clock. Not too early for a glass of gin, I'd say. Gunga and I like a little nip of an evening.' I brightened at this and went to fetch the bottle, assuming the reference to the dog to be a joke. 'A dash of ice and tonic if you don't mind,' she called, 'but he'll have his neat. A saucer will do.' The tone was genial but confident and I realized she wasn't joking.

Thus directed, I poured a few drops of my precious Plymouth into a saucer and gingerly pushed it under the dog's snuffling nose. He lapped it thoughtfully. Mrs Tubbly Pole lapped hers and started to appraise the room. Her eye fell on Bouncer sitting meekly in the far corner near the piano. There was an unusual stillness about the dog and it occurred to me that he was probably mesmerized by the spectacle on the hearthrug. Met his match there, all right!

'Oh, you've got a dog as well as a cat,' she enthused. 'Must be a fellow animal lover!' I explained that I hadn't exactly chosen them, that they had in effect installed themselves and somehow just stayed on.

'Ah, but they must find you deeply congenial. You obviously generate a great sense of security. I know all about animals – they won't stay with just anyone, they're very selective!'

I was flattered by her assessment but felt doubtful whether Bouncer and Maurice shared her confidence. At that moment there was a slight movement by the door and I glimpsed the latter poised on the threshold staring querulously at our guests. As he did so I heard her say, 'I fear my Mimi fell by the wayside two months ago. Gunga Din is only just recovering. He *so* loves pussy cats! . . . Don't you, little man?' She beamed down at him. Interrupted in drowning his sorrows, the little man stared up lugubriously and then with a sigh returned to his saucer. Maurice had disappeared.

'I expect you've been wondering why I've come to Molehill,' she observed. I hadn't particularly but composed my features into the appropriate look of enquiry. 'Of course, it's only a temporary arrangement, shan't need more than six months. You see, I'm one of those hack writers – and a pretty successful one too. My métier is the detective novel.' She grinned broadly, spread her plump

13

fingers on the arms of the chair and leant back awaiting my response as if all was revealed. It wasn't.

'Really?' I said. 'How very interesting. But I can't quite see –'

Before I could continue she had launched into a list of titles – *Mortuary Capers*, *The Case of the Vanishing Corkscrew*, *A Stiff in the Grass*, *Daggers over Dagenham*, *Blood in the Wind* . . .

'All good stuff,' she exclaimed, 'and jolly lucrative – they're never out of print, you know! I expect you're bound to have read some of them.'

'Well . . .' I began doubtfully.

'Now don't tell me that you of all people haven't read *The Mystery of the Curate's Curse* – should think that would be right up your street!' She gave a friendly snort and threw down some more gin. 'That was a real launching pad! All about skulduggery in Lambeth Palace. One of my most ingenious, though I suppose by today's standards a bit old-fashioned but it put me on the map all right!' She chuckled happily.

As a matter of fact it did rather ring a bell, and I thought that it could have been the book to which as a young soldier I had gratefully clung during the heavier bombardments. The events it had depicted were so bizarre as to make the nightmare of air raids and shell fire almost normal, and even at the time I had been struck by the author's seemingly off-beam ideas about the Church of England and its clergy – the clerical protagonists being not so much unhinged as completely barking! However, despite such patent unreality, the book had provided a welcome distraction from the war's own lunacy and I was grateful to the author for his inventiveness. I say 'his' because I was fairly sure that the jacket had carried a masculine name. Did Mrs Tubbly Pole write under a nom de plume perhaps?

'Of course I do!' she cried. And then changing her voice to a deafening stage whisper, she craned forward and announced, 'I am . . . *Cecil Piltdown!*'

There was a silence as I absorbed this piece of intelligence. She stared wistfully at her last drops of gin. I hastened to fill the glass, cleared my throat and said dutifully, 'Well, I never!' It sounded a bit limp but seemed to please her all the same.

'Oh yes,' she continued, 'Cecil is my alter ego – what you might call my guiding doppelgänger! We've been together for years. A most productive partnership, and earned us a nice little bob or two – as the vulgar would say!' She gurgled merrily. 'And now – and now we have come to Molehill!'

'Ah,' I ventured. 'That's very nice – but I still don't entirely see what has brought you . . .'

She tutted in mock exasperation. 'Surely that's obvious, Vicar. It's *your* murder! The corpse in the woods!'

My stomach muscles clenched with such violence that I thought I was going to bust a gut and I stared at Mrs Tubbly Pole in paralysed horror.

She went rollicking on. 'Don't tell me you're surprised – everyone knows about Molehill's unsolved crime: that beautiful June day, the harmless lady lying flat on her back amidst bracken and birdsong, the charming little dog who found the body and alerted his master, fields awash with cowslips . . .'

Even in my discomfort I was struck by her writer's instinct for lyrical hyperbole, and wondered grimly at Elizabeth's so-called harmlessness and Bouncer's 'charm'. Neither description was what you would call accurate.

'Splendid material,' she enthused, 'and I'm going to base my very next novel upon it – and *you* are going to help me!'

Unlike Gunga Din I am not used to taking my gin unadulterated, so when in panic I groped robot-like for the bottle, poured a liberal stream and downed it in one gulp, I was unprepared for its explosive effect. Throat burning, eyes awash, I listened in a state of glazed catalepsy as she unfolded her plans.

She explained that as a stranger to the area she had scant grasp of its 'special character', i.e. its essential features, inhabitants, topography, local customs and social practice. If she were to produce a plausible novel with plenty of local colour she would need an insight into such matters. As it was, she had merely an outsider's view – not without its use of course, but only of partial value. What was needed was *inside* knowledge – which was where I came in. As erstwhile friend of the deceased and pastor of the parish, I was apparently ideally placed to supply an authentic whiff of Molehill life and thus play a crucial role in her literary project. My assistance would be invaluable; success was assured.

'Why, you will be my partner in crime!' she laughed gaily. (Was Cecil to be supplanted? I wondered.) 'With my imagination and you supplying the local detail – who knows, we might even crack the original case itself!' And she literally rubbed her hands together in glee.

Naturally I made what protests I could, emphasizing that I was virtually a newcomer myself and not nearly as well rooted in the community as she seemed to think: that despite the press reports, my involvement with Elizabeth had been more as acquaintance than friend; and that since my feet (I resolutely lied) had never trodden the paths of Foxford Wood, as guide to the murder site I would be less than useless, etc. etc. All was ignored. Fate it seemed had selected me for special treatment, and the Hand of Destiny in the form of Mrs Tubbly Pole held me in its grip.

At last, after a barrage of intemperate reminiscence, scurrilous tales of rival writers, and a lavish toast to her current literary mission, mistress and dog prepared to leave: the one jubilant, the other in a state of drooling torpor. As for myself, once they had gone I cut supper, downed a handful of pills and crawled up to my usual refuge. Too tired even to light a cigarette, I fell into a mercifully dreamless sleep.

2

The Dog's Diary

I'm really settled into this place now and don't even miss my old master any more. In fact I'm probably better off without him, though at the time it seemed pretty disastrous when he left me all on my own and rushed off to Brazil with half the bank's dosh. They still talk about it now – 'That dreadful Mr Bowler's bezzlement,' (or some such word) 'we never liked him.' (Yes they did! Always giving him bottles of sherry and such – though I suppose that was just sweeteners for their overdrafts.) 'A disgrace to the bank, shouldn't have been allowed!' they squawk. Well, allowed or not, he did it: took the money and buggered off leaving everyone in the lurch, not least me! There's a new manager there now – rather a weedy one by all accounts. Doesn't look as if he'd say boo to a cat. At least my old master had some nerve ... Which brings me on to my present owner: the vicar, Francis Oughterard (or F.O. as it's easier to call him). That's a bit of another story, make no mistake!

He's got nerve too, I suppose, though most of the time you wouldn't think it. Always seems to be in a flat spin – crunching those humbugs and smoking his head off; either that or lying on his bed throwing down pills with a cold flannel over his eyes. Still, you have to hand it to him – it's not every human who can do away with one of their own, hold the rozzers off his trail, *and* keep the church going (well, sort of). Sometimes I feel quite proud of him: I bet there's no other dog around here who can boast of having a murderer as a master. Maurice, the cat that I share F.O.'s house with, says I've got to keep *very* quiet about it otherwise we shall all be in the can. He's right of course (one of the few occasions), and I haven't told a soul, not even O'Shaughnessy, my best friend the Irish setter – which is probably just as well as he *is* a bit of a blabbermouth, though jolly good fun. Maurice says he's goash and glumfing though I don't really know what those words mean, but then there are a lot of Maurice's words which sound peculiar.

Anyway, all of that stuff was last year and things have calmed down now – although my special sixth sense tells me that it won't last. For someone hell-bent on finding peace and quiet, the vicar always seems up to his neck in some mess or other. Which is maybe why I like living here: it keeps a dog on its toes! There's the crypt and graveyard too, my most favourite places. The crypt is best because it's dark and restful and neither F.O. nor Maurice ever go down there. The vicar is too lazy to go anywhere that isn't essential and Maurice is secretly nervous of the mice. They're fiercer than his usual type though they seem all right with me.

The other place, the graveyard, is cracking fun! When I'm feeling a bit bored and want some extra life about me I always go off there. It's *much* bigger than Bowler's old garden where I used to play when I belonged to him, and is full of funny nooks and corners (good sniffing areas), and grassy paths where I can race up and down. There's even a small rabbit colony which comes in very handy when I'm in sporting mood as it saves me the trek to Foxford Wood (that place where he did the old girl in). Sometimes I do make just a teeny bit of a noise – you know the sort of thing, clearing my throat and testing my lungs – but that's all right, except when Maurice happens to be there lounging on one of the tombstones. He gets awfully ratty, hisses and spits and uses words which I *do* know but didn't think *he* did!

All in all it's a good life – which is why at all costs Maurice and me must PROTECT THE VICAR!!

3

The Cat's Memoir

Since the not unfortunate demise of my mistress, Mrs Elizabeth Fotherington, I have been living at the vicarage of St Botolph's. It is a smaller and less salubrious establishment than the one to which I had been accustomed, but its incumbent the Reverend Oughterard, although somewhat trying, is kind and generally inoffensive. The smothering blandishments of my former owner had driven me almost to distraction and there were times when – had I the strength and the means (and were less dependent on the good food she provided) – I could have readily strangled her. But fortunately the vicar did that instead.

He and I share the same need for peace and quiet. She gave it to neither of us, and in the end he could stand it no more. As things turned out, his lapse worked to my advantage and I am really more than moderately content in this clerical abode. However, nothing is painless, and so there is of course the problem of the dog: Bouncer. When his master, the local bank manager, absconded with the bank's funds I generously made arrangements to install him here in the vicarage (as detailed in my earlier Memoir). I do not regret this gesture, for fundamentally Bouncer is a good-natured creature; but being a dog, his raucous temperament can jar the nerves. Indeed, there are times when I have to assert myself quite strongly and instruct him in the arts of etiquette and savoir-faire. It is a thank-less business.

One unusually warm day in late January I was sitting cleaning my paws on the vicar's crazy paving, when Bouncer appeared from behind the tool shed toting his rubber ring. He looked edgy.

'What's wrong?' I enquired.

'Nothing much,' he growled, 'except that those big parcels that he's put up in the belfry have fallen against my bag of secret marrow bones and now they're all bloody jammed underneath and I can't get at them.'

'Well, that's something to be thankful for,' I exclaimed, adding sharply, 'but kindly refrain from swearing. You know I don't like it!' He was quite unabashed and started to chew his foot. I left him to it, and slipping through the hedge made my way over to the church and up to the belfry.

He was right. The parcels, which had been rather care-lessly deposited, had become dislodged and fallen across the bone bag making it quite inaccessible to the dog's ferreting nose. One of them was lying very close to the opening of the trap door and the slightest shunt could send it toppling down the steps. I could see where he had been scratching – shreds of brown paper and chewed string littered the floor, and protruding from one of the parcels was the corner of what seemed to be a picture frame. Typical of F.O., I thought, to want to put his paintings in the belfry. Any normal person would hang them in the house! But then of course . . .

As I gazed at the ripped paper it occurred to me that if the vicar were to visit the belfry to inspect his parcels or check the bells he would see the debris, move the pictures and discover the wedged bones. There would doubtless be a palaver, the bones would be confiscated, and Bouncer would have to devise yet another storage space – and probably one closer to the house. I recalled with a shudder their previous hidey-hole – and my appalled shock when I encountered them there. At least in the church belfry they were well out of harm's way, or at any rate *my* way. I don't know which I dislike more, the sound of bells or the sight of bones. Both are obnoxious.

As I pondered the question there was a loud scrabbling noise a few feet below. Covered in dust and bits of flaking plaster Bouncer emerged into the chamber panting heavily. 'Cor!' he exclaimed. 'It doesn't get any easier!'

'If you curbed your peculiar passions,' I answered coldly, 'you wouldn't have to resort to such exertions.'

He grinned vaguely and started to sniff at the parcels. For one distasteful moment it seemed as if he was going to lift a leg, but instead he turned and said, 'You know, Maurice, we're going to have to shift those things. I've taken a great deal of trouble rebuilding my collection after that business with the piano stool, and there's one or two in that sack which I don't wish to be without – *delicacies*, you would call them.'

'I most certainly would not!' I cried.

He looked pained but added amiably, 'Besides, if he comes up here again and sees that mess he's bound to get twitchy and then we'll all cop it. He's already working himself into a lather over that Tubbly woman!'

'Not to mention her gin-sodden bulldog,' I exclaimed indignantly. 'Enough to give anyone a turn!'

He laughed raucously. 'Your face when you came in and saw him lying in front of the fire, especially when Tubbly said, "Oh, he *loves* pussy cats!"' And Bouncer put on what he fondly imagined to be an imitation of Mrs Tubbly's darkly expansive voice. It was a disagreeable noise and I was not amused.

'I am glad you appreciate the trouble your antics may cause. Why you had to start interfering with those parcels I cannot imagine!'

'Well, you know how it is when you want to gnaw something rather badly – you haven't time to pussy-foot around.'

I told him what I thought of his gross appetites, not to mention his crude terminology; but after a quick sulk I resumed my usual geniality and started to apply my wits to the problem. The two parcels were square and very large – much bigger than us – and looked quite heavy. Getting them away from the open trap door, withdrawing the sack of bones and concealing the general mess was going to be a taxing task and would require all my ingenuity. The rope securing one of them had got hitched up on a nail protruding from the surrounding balustrade and would clearly further hinder removal. I pondered.

'I tell you what,' said Bouncer, 'the fellow we need is O'Shaughnessy. I'm sure he could fix it.'

I flinched. 'Certainly not! The last thing we want is that great creature floundering about up here – he would do untold damage!' (O'Shaughnessy was Bouncer's special friend, a wild Irish setter who had recently come to the neighbourhood and for whom Bouncer had developed an inexplicable hero-worship.)

'Oh well,' he said moodily, 'it was just a thought.'

'Look,' I pointed out, 'I know he was helpful when we had that problem with the vicar's cigarette lighter in Foxford Wood, and I appreciate his bringing that piece of haddock for me at Christmas, but what we have here is an extremely delicate situation which requires equally delicate handling. That is not something which comes within O'Shaughnessy's sphere.'

'If you say so,' he growled.

'I do say so. The object is to ease the bones from underneath the parcels in such a way as not to give ourselves a hernia and without causing conspicuous damage to the goods or sending them hurtling to the floor below. As you say, if F.O. discovers something has been at these parcels *and* sees your mangy fossils strewn around them he'll become fraught and fragile again and it will be we who endure the fallout. It doesn't take much! He is also bound to confiscate the bones. You wouldn't like that, would you? The task requires finesse and a certain – how shall I put it? – feline subtlety.'

'You mean you want to have a go,' he said.

I sighed. 'It would be safer!'

Picking my way carefully, I strolled to the far corner of the belfry from where I could get a better perspective. The whole thing needed meticulous appraisal and I spent some time in assessing the dimensions of the parcels, the circumference of the trap door, the tension of the securing rope, and the weight of his dreadful bone bag. Bouncer watched, grinning inanely.

Finally I returned slowly to the middle of the chamber, settled myself comfortably and proceeded to sleek my paws and touch up my ears.

'Well?' said Bouncer. 'What do you think? Chop chop!'

'What I think,' I replied coolly, 'is that the task is not without difficulties but is perfectly possible. All that is required is a steady nerve, a dextrous touch, and a quick tweak of the rope. That will slacken the tension, ease the bigger parcel and facilitate withdrawal of the bone bag with minimal disturbance. It is quite straightforward really.'

He stared at me with his mouth half open and head tilted slightly on one side. He normally does that if he is feeling sceptical or bloody-minded. But in this case I think he was impressed by my powers of analysis.

'Ah,' he said, 'so you're going to do that, are you?'

'Most certainly.'

'Right-ho.' And he took up a position close to the open trap door.

Despite my words of assurance to Bouncer, I wasn't *quite* sure how I was going to proceed, for in the course of my inspection I had noticed a further complication – a long corner of the sack with its strands of hessian was closely entwined with the parcel's string binding, and detaching the two would not be easy. However, it doesn't do to look flummoxed. My left paw is particularly adroit in such matters and I judged that with concentrated patience the bits could be unravelled. That done and the rope gently tweaked, the dog could give a quick tug with his teeth and so pull the sack from the overlying pictures. I explained this to him and directed that he be poised for the ready.

Extending a claw I started to pick tentatively at the muddle of string and sacking. Gradually it began to unravel, and thus emboldened I intensified my efforts and then applied my teeth. The additional pressure was a mistake: the top parcel trembled slightly, its rope fell from the nail, and then suddenly, as I was so delicately teasing the string of the one underneath, it started to slither towards the open trap door. In the nick of time I leaped back as the great thing slid past me, and then bumped and trundled its way down the belfry steps. There was a great deal of noise which made my ears go quite numb.

We stared down in dismay and saw the picture with its wrappings ripped apart lying face up at the foot of the stairs. From our angle it looked like something abandoned in a junk yard.

'Well, you've properly put your paw in it there, haven't you!' Bouncer observed.

Despite the shock I naturally had my wits about me. 'You may recall that it was *your* bones that were responsible for this absurdity in the first place. *I* was merely pandering to your appetites and trying to help you out of a tight corner. My theory was excellent but theories occasionally go adrift – through no fault of their devisor!'

'Oh well,' he grumbled, 'those who can, do: those who can't, teach!' I could see from his smug expression that he was pleased with that, and tired of his insolence gave him a prod with my unsheathed claw. It had the desired effect and he looked suitably contrite.

'I suggest you start to remove those confounded bones to some recess where F.O. is unlikely to chuck his lumber! While you are doing that I shall assess the damage.' So saying, I picked my way down the narrow stairway to the loft below and proceeded to survey the picture.

Apart from a few scrapes and minor splinterings of the frame, there didn't seem to be any obvious damage – or at least none that F.O. was likely to notice – and I turned my attention to the subject itself. This I found peculiar and distasteful. The background was unattractive – all dark and grim and murky with great swirls of pallid mist and streaks of muddy orange. But it was the front part that really made me shudder: a vast conglomeration of human bones and skulls – white and glistening and nasty! I am a cat of delicate sensibilities and, as you have probably gathered, do not share Bouncer's partiality for things osseous. It is bad enough having to endure the sight of his gnarled trophies, but they at least are smaller both in dimension and number; and to face such a stark and sudden panorama was more than I could stomach. I emitted a long mew of disgust which brought the dog floundering down the steps.

'What's up? What are you making that racket for? It's enough to wake the dead!'

'They *are* woken,' I said. 'Just look at that!' And I gestured with my tail towards the canvas. He sat down in front of it and stared for a long time.

Eventually I asked him what he thought. 'I suppose you like it, your sort of thing presumably – all those bones!'

'No,' he said slowly, 'I don't, as a matter of fact. I think it is SILLY. They're not proper bones at all – like plastic, too white and no meat. They don't look anywhere near real.'

'They look real enough to me!' I exclaimed.

'Ah, but you're not a conners whatsit. I am.' I graciously accepted his connoisseurship in the matter but still preferred to avert my eyes, and suggested that since there was nothing else we could do about the painting it was time to return to the vicarage and to supper. On the way back I observed that if that was an example of what the humans call 'art' I didn't think much of it.

'Don't suppose he does either. That's probably why he shoved them up there. Wanted to get 'em out of the way!'

'You could well be right,' I acknowledged. He wagged his tail vigorously.

4

The Vicar's Version

The next day I was sufficiently distracted by my parish duties to forget, or at least ignore, Mrs Tubbly Pole's bizarre proposal. I had a wedding on my hands in the afternoon and it turned out to be an occasion of such excruciating embarrassment that Mrs T.P., Nicholas and his tiresome pictures all paled into temporary oblivion. The bride, a seemingly earnest but bovine local girl, had started to come to me some weeks earlier seeking pre-nuptial counsel and preparation. Never having been married myself I take rather a pride in my calm objectivity in such matters, and like to think that I gave her sound spiritual advice regarding her new status. At any rate she seemed quite impressed with my discourse and showed a proper appreciation of the occasion's solemnity. However, she confessed that there was one thing that was bothering her acutely – her virginal, or rather non-virginal state. I assured her that a proper contrition would of course speedily resolve the matter and that she could approach the altar with a clear conscience. To this she replied that it wasn't her conscience that was the problem but her dress.

She must have seen my perplexity for she explained, 'You see, my gran always says that if you've been a bad girl you can't wear white and that if you do you'll be smitten and have bad luck for ever after. But if I don't wear white my mum will have a fit and call me every name under the sun – she's very particular like that.' I asked her what her young man thought. There was an embarrassed giggle, and then she said, 'Oh, Trev, *he* said he'd like me in my birthday suit!'

Inwardly I cursed her gran and mum, not to mention the lewd Trev, but said lightly that perhaps a delicate shade of ivory might suit all interests and always looked nice, adding jovially that if I were in her position I would sport scarlet!

'Would you, Vicar?' she asked gravely.

'Oh yes,' I laughed, enjoying the joke, 'Give it to 'em good and proper!'

The day came – and the bride wore scarlet. The brides-maids were in gold lurex, sequinned mascara, and black mock-ostrich feathers. The groom, his hair combed into the slickest D.A. you have ever seen, was attired in a teddy-boy suit of impeccable cut, and with drainpipes so tight as to make me wince in vicarious agony. Resplendent in puce and pink, Mum and Gran sat stiffly in the front row, the one glowering, the other bun-faced. Across the aisle, festooned with Kodaks and mammoth silver-foiled carnations, Trev's parents lolled bibulously. I recall that one of them – I think it was the husband – had a cigar thrust behind the ear, and I spent the first ten minutes nervously awaiting it to be lit up in the middle of my address. As things turned out such an eventuality would have mat-tered not one jot . . .

Despite her visibly pregnant paunch (starkly outlined in the vibrant satin), the bride Madeline had chosen to wear stilettos of such spectacular elevation that she not so much teetered as staggered up the aisle, gamely supported on the arm of some diminutive kinsman. He seemed bowed down by his burden and looked distinctly the worse for wear, and I thought it unlikely he would last out the ceremony.

Indeed, dazzled by so rich an array of lurex and scarlet I rather wondered about my own chances – but, beaming encouragement, waited for the procession to complete its faltering course to the chancel steps. Bride and escort finally made it, and she was delivered into Trev's smirking care. Taking a deep breath I commenced the service, and slipping into the familiar rubric began to feel that despite the threat of the cigar all might possibly be well ... It wasn't of course.

As we neared the apex of the ceremony my attention was caught by the white face of Mavis Briggs at the back of the church. As far as I knew, Mavis had no connection with either the bride or the groom, but she is one of those parishioners who contrive to be everywhere and always. From bible classes to bazaars, wakes to enthronements, Mavis is invariably there; and should I ever be required to conduct an exorcism I am convinced she would somehow get in on the act. It would have been less bad were she not given to reciting execrable poetry at the drop of a hat. Much of this is of her own penning which makes it all the worse. Funerals are her speciality, and at such times it takes enormous skill to pre-empt some maundering and pious recitation. Seeing her now increased my gloom as I wondered vaguely what bits of doggerel lay in store for us at the reception. But it soon became clear that it was not doggerel that she had on her mind.

She stared at me fixedly and then started to make the most peculiar movements – contorting her features, opening and shutting her mouth, and gesturing with upturned thumb towards the door behind her. Naturally I took no notice and tried to concentrate on what I was saying. However, out of the corner of my eye I noticed that the gestures were getting increasingly frenzied, and fearing that she might be drunk or worse, I speeded as fast as decorum permitted to the crucial exchange of vows. I never got there.

Suddenly, pandemonium was loosed. The door Mavis

was standing in front of burst open, and the sidesman Davies and the churchwarden Colonel Dawlish came crashing in grappling with two young men. 'Young men' is perhaps a rather charitable term, for they looked distinctly ruffianly and were emitting shouts and words not usual to wedding guests. Felling Davies and thrusting the Colonel to one side, the larger one began to advance grimly down the aisle. For one dreadful moment I thought he was making a beeline for me (Elizabeth Fotherington's avenging angel?) but his eyes were on one quite other: the girl in red satin. The startling nature of the intrusion had brought cries of alarm, but as the youth got nearer to the bride the noise was replaced by a stunned silence. Madeline, though still patently unsure on her pins, regarded him with calm and indulgent eye.

'So you've come then, Fred, have you? Not before time neither.'

He muttered something incomprehensible, and grabbing her by the wrist proceeded to drag her away from the chancel steps and back up the aisle. In fact the only reason she needed dragging seemed less to do with reluctance than with her footwear. Hitching up her voluminous frock, and with much stumbling and giggling, she followed him past the gawping pews.

And then the air was rent with banshee shrieks as Mum and Gran, furiously puce and pink, started to make their position clear. Clutching the hapless Trev they thrust him after the departing couple, exhorting him to honourable retrieval. He seemed disinclined and hung back twitching. Not so his father, who with a bellow of rage lunged forward in pursuit, tripped, and was then promptly given a black eye by the kidnapper's henchman. From that moment chaos reigned.

Among the congregation were the boyfriends of the bridesmaids (presumably dragged along to admire their girls' finery). These seemed divided re the merits of Trev and Fred, and their lack of consensus led to a mêlée of

31

unfortunate size and intensity. I looked on in horror as fists flailed and hassocks hurtled. Collars were discarded, hats cast aside, hymn books lobbed, and handbags wielded with practised ease. The wedding party was in its element.

The chief protagonists appeared to be Mum and Gran who were fighting with a zest I had never previously witnessed in anyone, but it was difficult to discern their particular affiliation as each seemed ready to take on who-ever happened to cross their paths. I kept well out of range, and glancing up saw Tapsell peering down from his organ loft, waving his arms and shouting the odds in a state of rampant ecstasy. Wretched fellow, I thought, could he never conduct himself with dignity? His job was to play the organ, not be a tick-tack man! He must have seen me scowling for at that moment he sat down and launched into a violent rendering of the march from *Tannhäuser*. The noise was deafening – yet only marginally more so than the row raging from beneath.

Amidst all the mayhem I glimpsed one still and solitary figure: Trev, sitting on the pulpit steps smoking a cigarette. I felt a momentary pang of envy as I could have done with one myself. However, I went over to him and said gently that smoking was not really allowed in the church and could he possibly wait until later. He nodded obligingly and stubbed it out in Mavis Briggs's tastefully placed pot of trailing ivy. Feeling sorry for him I started to marshal words of sympathy.

He cut me short and with a slow smile said, 'That's all right, mate. I never really liked her and it weren't mine anyway.' It was difficult to know what to say to that, and while I was racking my brain, he added ruminatively, 'Just goes to show, don't it: if yer keeps yer fingers crossed long enough somethin's bound to turn up in the end.' I was impressed by the tenacity of his faith. And thus fortified, I left him to his peaceful contemplation and set off to quell the revellers.

Eventually of course, things died down, though I think

that was less to do with my efforts than with the combatants' desire for beer and buns. Thus, averting my eyes to avoid confronting the state of the church and firmly locking its door, I herded them into the parish hall where they set about the wedding tea with the same relish as they had shown in beating one another up. Of the runaway couple there was no sign, and the last I saw of Trev was a spindly-legged figure sauntering nonchalantly across the canal bridge in the direction of the Swan and Goose. He looked enviably free.

The next morning there was a complaint from the cleaners and a request that I go and view the fallout from the festivities. Obediently I walked over to the church and surveyed the damage. It was a daunting sight. The grey flagstones had become a kaleidoscope of spilt confetti and shredded flowers. Hymn books, service sheets, broken vases, articles of apparel – gloves, scarves, collars, the bride's veil – all lay strewn in loose abandon. Unaccountably the Mothers' Union banner had been ripped from its socket and was slumped limply over the back pew, its blue and gold embroidery looking raddled in the morning light. It may have been my imagination but there even seemed the faintest whiff of stale ale, and I cast a wary eye around for signs of a broken bottle.

My gaze was intercepted by the baleful face of Edith Hopgarden as she and her fellow polishers stood relishing my dismay. Clearing my throat and tut-tutting loudly, I grabbed the nearest broom, rolled up my sleeves and started to sweep vigorously. One by one, and with grudging grace, the ladies joined in and were soon hard at work complaining primly and swapping anecdotes about Madeline and her questionable companions.

After a while I thought I might safely slip away but was waylaid by Edith who, taking me to one side, said that she hoped the previous day's events were not going to set a precedent for future weddings at St Botolph's. I assured her this would not be the case, and then asked solicitously after the health of Mr Hopgarden. This generally does the trick in forestalling further offence. Ever since I had once stumbled across Edith in flagrante delicto with Tapsell in Foxford Wood her attitude to me has been one of reproachful petulance. However, the one thing that gives ballast to our relationship is a shared allergy to Mavis Briggs. Thus in addition to Mr Hopgarden, reference to the former is invariably useful in defusing bouts of Edith's simmering hostility. So I asked her if Mavis was all right after being so nearly trampled in the skirmish at the church door.

She sniffed and said tartly, 'Well, she's making a great *fuss*. Thinks her arm's broken but it's pure imagination of course. I don't know what she was doing by the door in the first place.' I was inclined to agree but said nothing and, leaving her brooding on the ninnyish Mavis, made my escape.

On the way back to the vicarage I saw Mrs Tubbly Pole and Gunga Din in the distance but they didn't see me and I slipped into the house unmolested.

5

The Vicar's Version

Rather unexpectedly a card from Nicholas bearing a French postmark had arrived by the early post; but having more important things to do than decipher his obsessively tiny script I had delayed giving it my attention. Now, with a few spare moments, I was able to do so.

It began by sending me fulsome 'Greetings from Le Touquet' and went on to describe the delights of its municipal gardens and the casino. Why he thought I should have been interested in either I could not imagine. However, what did interest me – or rather irritate – was the postscript to the effect that he hoped the pictures were 'behaving themselves' and that he might be over soon to remove one and replace it with another. That Nicholas might simply take the two of them away altogether and leave me in peace was clearly a fantasy of absurd devising! I sighed wearily, and seeing Maurice glide past was tempted to tweak his tail, but fortunately prudence prevailed.

The morning had not been helped by bumping into Mavis Briggs – last seen at the wedding going gently berserk in front of the church door. Recalling Edith Hopgarden's scornful reference to the allegedly injured arm, I was not surprised to see her sporting a large sling and a martyred expression. I tried to look sympathetic, and together we tut-tutted about the mores and alarming peculiarity of modern youth.

Eventually I was able to disentangle myself, but not before she had warned me about the state of the floor-boards in the lower loft of the belfry, observing in pained tones that it would only take the merest stumble for a bell-ringer to be laid flat out, or worse still, losing control of the rope, be hoisted to the rafters! Accidents were so common, she observed, glancing pitifully at her bandaged arm.

I assured her I would go and investigate immediately; and assuming an air of worried concern set off briskly for the bell tower. However, since it was nearly lunchtime and I was feeling rather tired, I decided to postpone the matter till the afternoon. Doubling back on my tracks and keep-ing the dwindling figure of Mavis in sight, I got home unobserved in time for the one o'clock news, a cigarette and a bit of shut-eye.

Later that afternoon and moderately refreshed, I set off once more to inspect the floorboards. Despite the irritation of the Le Touquet postcard, I must have been feeling in lighter mood, for as I started to mount the first flight of stairs my mind was beset with images of Mavis Briggs swinging spectacularly on the end of her bell rope, watched by a ring of gaping colleagues as she spiralled slowly and remorselessly skyward . . .

Savouring these scenes, I emerged into the lower cham-ber. The mirth stopped: across the bottom rungs of the belfry staircase, its coverings split and loosely trailing, sprawled the larger of Nicholas's pictures.

I gazed dumfounded. I could have sworn blind they had been stacked safely against one of the rafter posts. How on earth could this one have found its way to the bottom of the steps? Surely on top of everything else I was not now to be plagued by some deranged poltergeist. It was too bad! I stared at it bitterly, cursing Nicholas and wondering how I was going to summon the energy to heave the wretched thing all the way up again. However, it certainly couldn't be left lying there – so up it must go. Taking off my jacket and crunching a peppermint humbug for strength, I commenced my labours.

It was only when the picture was once more resting against its post that I started to take a proper look at it. I wasn't exactly impressed. The principal colour was a sort of dingy bluey-black intermittently slashed with streaks of ochre with here and there splodges of grey – rather like ragged balls of sock knitting-wool. It was difficult to make out whether they were meant to be clouds or just random bits of decoration. In the foreground, and rather unpleasantly, I thought, were large heaps of white bones and skulls. Could it perhaps be intended as a protest against the current spate of cemetery vandalism? Nothing so simple, I suspected. Doubtless it held some dark preternatural significance which for the moment entirely escaped me. It all seemed decidedly gothic and morbid and I couldn't imagine why anyone should want to hang it on their wall.

I wondered about the smaller one, now also dislodged and lying on the floor though still in its wrappings, and was tempted to undo the string and take a look; but I was pressed for time and thought that if it looked anything like its companion such fumblings were hardly worth the effort. Nicholas had implied they were valuable, but judging from the first specimen I rather doubted this. He had always dramatized. If this other one was of the same style – dismal and pretentious – it seemed unlikely that anyone would really go to the trouble of stealing them. So perhaps after all, my nagging suspicions were groundless and the tale of simply needing extra storage space was entirely genuine. There was, I supposed, just a remote chance that he had been telling the truth. And clinging to that thought I began to feel better.

But there was still the curious matter of their displacement. Could it have been rats, cavorting squirrels, a sudden gust of wind blowing in from the roof vents . . .? Or perhaps it was just one of those times when inanimate objects, poised more precariously than realized, do fall down on their own. I remembered an incident from child-hood, when right in the middle of the night my cricket bat, propped against the nursery wall, had suddenly slipped to the floor with the most dreadful clatter. It had given me a terrible fright and I had woken the whole house with my wails.

Yes, there was obviously a perfectly simple explanation – but I really hadn't the time to pursue it further. The Vestry Circle was meeting later that afternoon and had asked me for suggestions about their next month's agenda. As I hadn't a single notion it was time I thought of something to say. And with that wearisome challenge in mind I clambered down the stairway and hurried back to the vicarage.

6

The Vicar's Version

I was sorry about the wedding fracas – not just because of its ghastly embarrassment and the mess it had made in the church, but because I had quite liked Madeline and had rather looked forward to assisting her in tying the knot with some nice young man. I am generally good at doing weddings and enjoy them almost as much as I do funerals, so felt vaguely cheated that this one had not worked as well as it might.

Christenings, on the other hand, are not my métier: I am sensitive to noise, and the infant squalls invariably put me off my stroke. I am also (despite a certain skill at the piano) rather maladroit, and there have been one or two occasions when the subject of the ceremony has slid head first into the font. Surprisingly it is not so much the parents who have been bothered by this, as the godparents. They seem to get unduly exercised and can create a fuss. I think this is probably something to do with the novelty of their new spiritual status: they feel constrained to demonstrate their fitness for the job. Still, it does make it all a bit nerve-racking.

There was also a further reason why the wedding bothered me: the press. At the time there had been such a shindig going on that I had not really registered the clicking of flashbulbs, but thinking back remembered them only too vividly. Slung with cameras, a bevy of local reporters had been assembled on the grass ready to snap the happy pair when they emerged from the nuptials. They had got more than they bargained for! The ennui of waiting had been miraculously curtailed by the arrival of Fred; and his entry upon the church had left its doors agape, graphically exposing the horrors within. I imagine it was what Fleet Street would call a 'scoop'. And scoop the photographers certainly did – gleefully and relentlessly.

Once safely home and sprawled on the bed, I dwelt on this aspect of events, but convinced myself that although St Botolph's could do without such publicity it was essentially a local matter and unlikely to hit the national papers. I could not have been more wrong. Two days later there were articles plus photographs not only in the *Daily Sketch* and *Mirror*, but also in *The Times* which seemed to take particular relish in describing the affair. Naturally I was dismayed – but I was also deeply worried: the cause of my anxiety being less to do with ridicule from the public than with the reaction of my bishop, Horace Clinker.

The previous year when the Elizabeth Fotherington business had been at its height Clinker had taken it into his head to transfer me from my current appointment in Molehill and make me chaplain to some obscure and moth-eaten Home for Retired Clergy. He had been keenly set on this and seemed to think I should be grateful to quit a parish becoming notorious for its 'Glade-in-the-Woods Murder'. I was in fact appalled at the prospect as I had grown very fond of Molehill, and the bishop's glowing descriptions of the new posting were so awful as to make me desperate. It had been a delicate and complicated matter: but put briefly, to force Clinker into having a change of heart I had resorted to getting him spectacularly drunk.

Amazingly the ruse had gone without a hitch, and soon afterwards, shamed into passivity, he rescinded his decision and left me severely in peace. Indeed, the silence from the Bishop's Palace was so pronounced that I had begun to think I might never be bothered by episcopal diktats again. However, this latest turn of events might well ruffle the calm! Years ago when I had been an ordinand at St Bede's Clinker had been the temporary dean, so I had some knowledge of his habits – one of which was an obsessive daily perusal of *The Times*. I had no reason to assume that things had changed.

Mercifully, the next morning I had a dental appointment in Guildford. 'Mercifully' because my absence from the vicarage would at least temporarily foil any telephone contact from Clinker or his gauleiters. In my job one is grateful for such respites.

Escaping from the dentist unscathed and wanting to prolong my freedom from Clinker for as long as possible, I dawdled over some household shopping; and then, having skipped breakfast, decided that elevenses were in order. I bought a newspaper and headed for one of the darker recesses of the Angel Hotel, and settling into a capacious armchair ordered coffee and a couple of cream buns. I have rather a sweet tooth, and in times of stress – which with Clinker doubtless in the offing I considered this to be – will occasionally indulge myself. I had just finished the first confection and was debating whether to light a cigarette before embarking on the second, when my eye was caught by an intriguing headline: WHAT PRICE THE STOLEN BONES? The article that followed gave me more than pause for thought. It practically gave me a heart attack.

The item involved the description of two paintings by an artist of whom I had never heard – one Claus Spendler – which had recently disappeared in transit from a gallery in the Hague to a Mayfair establishment for inclusion in its exhibition of early twentieth-century oils. Apparently their loss had created quite a furore in the art world, for Spendler – a hitherto obscure Austrian artist – had been recently 'discovered' and was not only enjoying a spate of earnest attention from the cognoscenti but also commanding increasingly high prices among sharp-eyed dealers.

41

At the advanced age of eighty-two, the artist was fast becoming an international celebrity. The smaller of the missing pictures was apparently entitled *On the Brink* and had as its subject a nude youth standing upon a rock-strewn shore poised to plunge into dark and swirling waters. According to the writer of the article, its sub-title should have been 'The Leap in the Dark' for its Kierkegaardian links were, he opined, 'only too apparent'. I am sure he was absolutely right.

However, what made my blood suddenly run cold was his account of the other picture, *Dead Reckoning*: '. . . a lowering canvas of midnight glooms and yawning lunar scars contrasting starkly with myriads of polished skulls and cairns of desolate bones . . . A painting of such stunning metaphysical power that the viewer quakes before its appalling depths.' Recognition was instant. It was undoubtedly the oppressive thing which I had uncovered only three days ago! My original suspicions about Nicholas and the reason for my custodianship were horribly confirmed.

Worse was to come: 'When asked to put a price on the pair, a spokesman for the Art Dealers' Association of Brighton and the South Coast, Mr Nicholas Ingaza, suggested a sum in the region of £14,000,* adding that of course the longer they remained untraced the more this figure was likely to increase. He also said that it was highly improbable they were still in Europe, let alone England, but were by now doubtless residing in some collector's den in Tangier or Boston.'

Tangier? Boston? . . . They were in my blithering belfry!

No longer attracted by the cream bun, I left money for the bill and re-emerged into the sunlight of the High Street. And then, just as I had started to wander back to the car

---

* Approximately £200,000 in today's values

park bearing my parcels and my fears, I was suddenly grabbed from behind and a voice boomed in my ear, 'Ah, the Reverend! Just the man I wanted to see!' It was Mrs Tubbly Pole. She clutched my arm and I dropped the parcels.

'Good morning,' I said from a crouching position on the pavement. 'Fancy meeting you!'

'Yes, well met, wasn't it! Now, I have an urgent matter I need to discuss and if you've nothing better to do this evening I think you had better pay me a visit. Don't suppose you *have* got anything else lined up so I'll expect you about six o'clock.' She grinned encouragingly, and before I had staggered to my feet was pursuing her stout course down the hill.

Wonderingly I watched her go. And then, thinking my absence from the vicarage that evening might further delay speech with Clinker, and since, as she had correctly surmised, there was indeed nothing scheduled, I resigned myself to spending another alarming session with Mrs T.P. and her bulldog drinking partner. It might, after all, take my mind off other matters.

When I got home the first thing I did was to rush up to the belfry and wrench the wrapping from the other picture. I suppose I hoped that it might be something quite other than the one described in the newspaper. After all, being a receiver of just *one* internationally acclaimed painting would be only half as culpable as fencing for two ... wouldn't it? However, as things turned out, such Jesuitical niceties proved immaterial, for the second picture was exactly as the paper had described – although wherein lay its worth I was still unclear.

Like the first, it too was of tenebrous hue, but unlike its companion it featured a human figure: an androgynous youth whose naked buttocks seemed disproportionately large for his slender frame. As the article had stated, he was standing on a pebbled shore gazing out at a tumescent sea. Whether he was indeed about to launch himself upon the waters, as the commentator had declared, or was merely enjoying the fresh air, I was undecided. But neither possibility was especially interesting. To my untutored eye the painting seemed flat and crude, and the dark seascape generated none of that subtle drama or mystery which will sometimes envelop beaches at twilight.

Still, whatever their quality, these were the missing pictures all right! And what had been a dreadful but untested suspicion had now become an only too concrete reality . . . Bugger Nicholas!

7

The Vicar's Version

As directed, I arrived at Mrs Tubbly Pole's shortly after six o'clock and was ushered into the large drawing room. I had visited the house once before when the Cohens were still in residence, and as they had let it partly furnished recognized a good deal of the original rather stylish contents. However, these had been largely overlaid by several imported and ramshackle sets of shelves crammed to bursting with box files and books, journals, sheaves of newspaper cuttings and papers of all sorts. These last, stuffed randomly among the interstices, gave the shelves a look of wild dissolution – in keeping, I thought, with the rest of the room.

The Cohens' carpet – a large Tiensin rug of impeccable design and provenance – was littered with wads of used and unused typing paper, the intervening areas largely occupied by an assortment of briefcases and bulging waste-paper baskets. The Chippendale sideboard, once elegantly adorned with Regency candlesticks, was now the repository for two large typewriters, a discarded shopping bag, and a remarkable array of gin and liqueur bottles – placed with what can only be described as care-free abandon. A couple of knee rugs, Gunga Din's tartan coats, and unfinished bits of knitting were draped haphazardly over backs of chairs; and everywhere there was a conglomeration of fading photographs. Apart from sepoys and elephants, these seemed mainly to feature a little man with fearsome moustache, glaring angrily from beneath a sola-topi. In front of the sofa was a large dog basket; and whether the liberal sprinkling of surrounding cake crumbs was connected with the absent occupant or his owner, it was difficult to tell.

I surveyed the scene with interest, feeling that my own domestic bedlam was rather paltry in comparison.

'What will you have?' she asked, propelling me towards one of the few empty chairs. I intimated that a small Scotch would be welcome, and from the sideboard she fetched two bottles, one whisky and one gin, and dumped them on the nearby table.

'One for you and one for me,' she announced. Tumblers, a pail of ice, and some rather dusty-looking biscuits followed. Then, having poured two generous measures and settling herself opposite, she raised her glass in my direction. I suppose I was expecting something hearty like 'Bung Ho!' or possibly even 'Bottoms Up!' Instead, in a voice that was a fair imitation of Humphrey Bogart she said, 'Here's looking at you, kid!'

The phrase was familiar of course, but certainly no one had ever toasted *me* in that way before. In fact, as I came to think of it, no one had ever toasted me at all. I was both pleased and flustered. 'Er – your good health,' I responded feebly. There was a pause as we sipped our respective drinks. At least, I sipped mine; she, I think, made a rather bolder assault.

'Well now, Vicar, what have you been up to lately? Had a bit of a dust-up in the church, so I hear. Quite a little party!' She chuckled. 'Must have been fun!'

'It wasn't,' I said glumly. 'It was awful.'

'Oh well, I shouldn't worry. It's bound to blow over!'

'I doubt it,' I replied. 'I think the bishop could be on my tail. He was my boss at training college which makes him keep an officious eye on me . . . And you see, there was a small upset last year which was slightly embarrassing, so I think this wedding business might re-stir his concern about Molehill and my future prospects here. Wouldn't be surprised if there was another visitation at any moment!'

'You can cross that bridge when it comes,' she said briskly, 'and it probably won't anyway. He'll rant a bit and then do nothing. It's part of the pattern.' I must have looked sceptical for she added, 'Besides, if he does try anything, leave him to me: I know all about bishops!'

'Do you?' I said in surprise.

'Oh yes,' she replied airily. 'My late husband –' and she gestured towards the photographs – 'had at least two on his side of the family: rather tiresome cousins. I soon settled *their* hash.'

'Goodness!' I exclaimed.

'Yes, they're like gun-dogs, you know. Handle them firmly and they soon come to heel. It's simply a question of your will against theirs.'

I rather suspected that Mrs Tubbly Pole's will was considerably stronger than mine, but made a mental note that should the worst come to the worst I might well employ her services.

'Now,' she said, refilling the glasses and eyeing me intently, 'we must get down to brass tacks. What I *need* is to get into your belfry!'

I recoiled. 'Whatever for?'

'Because,' she replied patiently, 'I require special information which I can only gain by inspecting the church tower and its bell chamber.'

'What sort of information?' I asked faintly, as images of the purloined paintings danced before my eyes.

'Oh,' she replied vaguely, 'you know – position of the bells, dimensions, the general feel of the place . . .'

'But *why*?' I protested.

'It's my novel: there's been a slight change of plan. As I told you, it's to be based on your murder –'

'The *Molehill* murder,' I interjected quickly. (How I wished she wouldn't be so free with the possessive case!)

'Yes, yes – the one in Foxford Wood. I've decided it would be more interesting to have the corpse discovered not in the wood but in the church belfry. Not new of course – Dorothy Sayers did it years ago – but I think I can put a pretty good twist on the original!' She grinned confidently.

'I am sure you can,' I murmured, 'but you don't really need to go up there, do you? I mean, there's nothing much to see and I can always describe it to you.'

'Certainly not,' she said severely, 'that wouldn't do at all. Never in all my career have I relied on second-hand data. I must test things for myself – a question of professional pride. After all, my readers expect it of me. Never let it be said that Cecil Piltdown didn't know exactly what he was talking about!'

She stressed the point with another slug of gin, while I racked my brain for excuses. None came and I was reduced to babbling ineffectually about the dust and debris, the narrow rickety steps, even the smell. She was undeterred and pressed me for a date and a time.

'That's settled then,' she cried triumphantly. 'Saturday night it is! Now, time to get old Gunga in . . . he's been in the garden quite long enough.' So saying, she disappeared into the hall where I heard the front door being wrenched open and the sound of much whistling and yoo-hooing. This was replaced by bellowed endearments as dog and mistress were reunited, and together they returned to the room.

Gunga Din looked reasonably sober, and evidently recognized his guest for he plodded over and ceremoniously licked my hand; and then breathing heavily sat down at my feet and gazed up in solemn scrutiny.

'He *likes* you,' she declared. 'Give him a little of your whisky and he'll be your pet for life!' I was unenticed by this prospect but dutifully poured a drop into the proffered saucer and set it before him. As with the gin at our last meeting, he lapped it slowly, and then with a contented sigh rolled over and began to snore gently. I was reminded momentarily of Bishop Clinker who six months earlier, and also as a result of my ministrations, had been in a similar position.

Fortunately the entry of the dog had diverted my hostess from her novel and questions about the death in the woods. Instead she talked amusingly about her days in India and the exploits of her late husband, Jacko – who at five foot two and of uncertain temper had evidently been the scourge of the Indian Civil Service.

'Oh yes! They talk of him even now ... he was awful, you know. Quite, quite *awful*!' And she gurgled in happy reminiscence. Glancing again at the figure in the photographs I could well believe her.

We chatted a little longer, and then glancing at my watch I realized it was far later than I had thought. 'It's been a delight, Mrs Tubbly Pole, and thank you so much – but I have an early service in the morning and really must be going!'

'Well, if you must, you must – but surely one for that long road!' And despite my protests she poured another generous libation. 'I *also* think it is time we were on Christian name terms,' she announced. 'You must be tired of addressing me as Mrs Tubbly Pole and I am perfectly prepared to be called by my first name.'

'Ah ...' I said, not sure what else was required.

'Yes, it's high time,' she said. 'The name is ... *Rosebud*.' She must have seen my look of consternation, for grinning slyly added, 'Didn't think you would like that, nobody does! Don't worry, I have a middle name – *much* better: Maud.'

'Ah,' I repeated in some relief. 'Yes – yes, I think perhaps that does suit you better: clear and to the point with a sort of no-nonsense ring.'

She beamed. 'Exactly, Francis, exactly. I knew we were on the same wavelength!' I very much doubted whether I could ever be on the same wavelength as Mrs Tubbly Pole, but smiled obligingly, cleared my throat, and rather precariously got to my feet and moved towards the hall. Oblivious of my departure, the Pet-For-Life continued its fireside slumber.

Hooting words of encouragement, my hostess waved cheerily from the porch as I unsteadily negotiated the gate and began my way home – not sure, in more senses than one, whether I was coming or going.

8

The Cat's Memoir

He saw me and came racing over amid much sound and fury and announced, 'I could kill that bog-eyed basket, kill him I could!'

'I thought you felt sorry for Gunga Din.'

'Not any more I don't. Flirty Gerty is making a beeline for him and he's bound to take advantage, the basket!'

'I doubt it,' I said, 'he's not very observant. She won't get far.'

'Yes, but she always likes a challenge,' he answered grimly.

'Well, she's got one there all right!'

I must explain that Flirty Gerty is a pert and foxy Pomeranian who has been giving Bouncer the run-around (and most of the other male dogs in the neighbourhood) for some considerable time. She's a contrary little creature of whom I disapprove (one of many in that category), but Bouncer being less discerning is of course susceptible.

'It wasn't so bad being seen off by a bit of posh like William,' he grumbled, 'but to lose out to that short-legged fathead is a bit much!' (William was a rather distinguished Great Dane who for a brief spell had entertained a mild fancy for Flirty but had moved on to higher things – a Russian borzoi, I seem to remember.)

'Try ignoring her,' I suggested. 'Withdraw your favours, that might do the trick.'

'Chance would be a fine thing,' he growled, 'can never get near enough to give her any!' And despite his misery, he leered.

Ignoring the coarseness I continued kindly, 'The thing is, Bouncer, you're too good for her. There are plenty more fish in the sea, you know.'

He looked puzzled and started to say, 'But you know I don't like fi—'

'A mere *façon de parler*,' I said patiently. He seemed even more perplexed and I tried again. 'Flirty by name, flighty by nature! You should look elsewhere. I am sure there are many ladies who would be only too ready to appreciate your ... *rugged* charms.' Yes, when necessity requires even I will – to use one of Bouncer's own terms – lob the flannel.

He seized it eagerly. 'I say, do you really think so? They'd like my rugged charms, would they?'

'Yes, yes,' I said quickly, not wanting to go too far down that questionable path. He began to look smug.

'So you think I should ditch her?'

'Emphatically. She's not worth the biscuit.'

I could see he was rapidly recovering, and was not surprised when he barked, 'Biscuits! Where *did* I leave them? Under F.O.'s bed, I think.' And wearing his special foraging expression he hurtled off towards the vicarage.

Later that afternoon, safe from the distractions of the vicarage, I was basking on my favourite tombstone, enjoying some rare moments of tranquillity. Then stretching languidly I sensed a slight movement from below, and glancing down found myself confronted by the upturned face of Gunga Din. Naturally, I fixed him with a hostile glare and prepared to make a scene, but before I could do so he said solemnly, 'Hullo, I've come to play.'

I was in no mood for playing, and least of all with that inebriate. However, being a cat of impeccable manners I said graciously that I was feeling a little tired but knew a good game that he might like and in which I would join him later. He pondered and then asked what sort of game.

'You see that tree over there?' I said, flicking my tail in the direction of a large chestnut. He nodded. 'Well, it's quite fun competing to see how many times one can run round it without feeling dizzy. Bouncer and I often do that. You go and practise and I'll be over soon.' He wheezed off towards the tree and I watched as he slowly proceeded to circumambulate its trunk. A few seconds later I had slipped off the tombstone and was making my way back to the vicarage.

Halfway there I bumped into Bouncer who said, 'I've just seen old Gunga. He hadn't got his harness on – must have escaped from Tubbly. What's he up to?'

'Walking round a tree,' I replied.

'What's he doing that for?'

'Seeing how long it takes him to feel dizzy. It's a new game.'

'Doesn't sound much of a game to me,' growled Bouncer. 'Still, I'll go and take a look,' and he trotted off towards the graveyard. I continued on my way, thinking that with Bouncer thus occupied and F.O. about to go off to one of those dire bell-ringing sessions I might manage a quiet nap.

I woke to the sound of him chewing his rubber ring. 'How did you get on?' I asked with interest.

'Quite well,' he replied. 'It's not a bad game.'

'Really?' I said in surprise. 'I should have thought it was a trifle boring.'

He grinned. 'Not the way I played it. Bit his arse.' And with one of his coarser guffaws he bounded off into the

53

kitchen. Just occasionally Bouncer makes quite a diverting companion.

At that moment F.O. came mooching into the room and folded himself into the armchair. He was clearly in one of his twitchy moods and I surmised the bell-ringing hadn't gone too well or something had happened to shake his nerve. It doesn't take much. Mind you, dispatching one of your parishioners must be quite an onerous matter and ideally would require a disposition of steely sangfroid. This our master does not possess. Nevertheless, though lacking the qualities of a competent murderer, he had so far managed to elude suspicion (partly due to my ingenuity with the cigarette lighter, as detailed in my previous Memoir) and the case had conveniently tailed off.

So what was causing his current state it was hard to tell – unless of course it had something to do with the advent of that Tubbly woman and her dropsical bulldog (the latter enough to induce a decline in anyone!). I remembered that their recent visit had indeed seemed to send him into one of his spins, and that after her departure he had retired abruptly to bed without even the courtesy of preparing my usual milk. Yes, it was clearly something to do with Mrs T.P. – and quite possibly those pictures in the belfry brought over by the questionable type from Brighton. Because of Bouncer those things had caused me insufferable trouble, so perhaps they were also in some way responsible for the vicar's edginess. It wouldn't surprise me. I hadn't liked the look of them one bit.

As I pondered these things I noticed that F.O. was gearing himself up to make an assault on the piano. You can always tell when this is about to happen: his fingers start to drum on the arm of the chair and he rotates his left ankle. The urge to play seems to hit him at moments of extremity, i.e. when in either a good or a bad mood. That night it was evidently the latter and I hastened from the room just in time to escape the opening chords.

In the hall I nearly collided with Bouncer for whom,

unlike myself, music has a peculiar attraction. He invariably appears when the vicar is playing, and sits listening with a glazed and vacant expression. For a dog with such philistine tastes this so-called 'musical sensibility' never ceases to surprise me. But it takes all sorts, I suppose, and of course Bouncer *is* a very peculiar sort.

Anyway, I gave him a brisk jab with my paw and told him this was no time to be mooning over the vicar's piano-playing as I had important matters to discuss, and if he wouldn't mind detaching himself from the sitting-room door we might find a place of peace where I could apprise him of my thoughts. Naturally he grumbled, as he invariably does, but was sufficiently intrigued to leave the door and pay attention.

'Look,' I said, 'there is something afoot. I have been putting two and two together and –'

'Made zero!' exploded Bouncer amidst yelps of mirth. I narrowed my eyes, arched my back and fixed him with a stiletto stare. That quietened things.

I continued. 'He was all right over Christmas and most of New Year once all that police business died down; relatively balanced you might say, but since then he's become edgy again and I think there's something on his mind which, as you know, will rebound on *us*. If he is in jeopardy it will upset the –'

'STATUS QUO!' boomed Bouncer. 'And we shall be out on our ears!'

'Precisely,' I said quietly, closing my eyes to blot out the din.

In fact I had been going to say 'the apple cart' but the dog is both fond and proud of the term 'status quo' having somehow picked it up during his long sessions in the crypt where he noses about among the old tombs and ossuaries sniffing the past, and in his weird canine way absorbing the Latin inscriptions. For a creature of normally such crude and limited vocabulary he has an uncanny knack of producing the most bizarre phrases. In this case, however, he was right. We had spent the whole of the previous summer trying to protect our master and preserve our own domestic interests. It had been a delicate business and had imposed a considerable strain. The last thing we now wanted was further threats to the vicar's – and indeed our own – status quo!

'There is something going on,' I warned, 'and we shall need to be vigilant. Keep your nose to the ground, Bouncer. And if you've got any sense you will make amends to Gunga Din. Show solicitude about his backside; he could be very useful in telling us what his mistress is up to. I just hope she's not going to prove dangerous to F.O.!'

'So do I,' he replied. 'Otherwise she may be for the high jump like the other one.'

9

The Vicar's Version

I reflected on Mrs Tubbly Pole's proposed inspection of the belfry and wondered whether she would bring the dog with her. I hoped not: the prospect of hoisting both Gunga Din and his mistress up those narrow steps was not a happy one. I still couldn't really make out what she hoped to *do* up there. She had said something about 'breathing in the atmosphere'. Some atmosphere! Woodwormed joists, bat and bird droppings, cobwebs the size of small sheets, and above all freezing cold. Too many breaths and she would surely choke or catch pneumonia. No bad thing perhaps, at least it would keep her at bay for a while!

There was one benefit, I supposed: at least her fascination with the belfry would stop her snooping in Foxford Wood. It had been bad enough having to return there on my own on that abortive mission to retrieve the cigarette lighter, but to be accompanied by Maud Tubbly Pole playing Sherlock Holmes would have been intolerable. Tiresome though it might be, introducing her to the dubious delights of the belfry was a less unsettling prospect than showing her the place of Elizabeth's end.

However, there was still the problem of the pictures. With her novelist's obsession for 'authentic detail' she was bound to spot them, and I doubted whether draping them in dustsheets would deter either her probing eye or her curiosity. The only other place for them was the crypt, but that meant yet more exertions – and in any case, ten-to-one she would demand to explore down there next! They *had* to be got rid of – not just because of her visit but for my peace of mind generally. Now that I had concrete proof of the things being undoubtedly 'hot' their continuing presence was unsettling in the extreme.

The problem was how to dispose of them without provoking Ingaza. To renege on our tacit compact – me to store the paintings in payment for his help during the previous year's police enquiry – could well be dangerous. At theological college he had always treated me with a careless geniality. But we had never been close, and on occasions I had observed the steely and inventive way in which he had handled those whom he had found 'tiresome'. Fortunately I had not seemed to belong to that category, but were I to upset his current project I might just become one of its number. It was a risk I could not take. At the time of my unfortunate incident Nicholas had colluded in a tale I had spun to the police, and though distinctly curious, had asked no questions. To lose his indulgence now might prove disastrous. I lit a cigarette and brooded.

Out of the corner of my eye I saw Bouncer watching me with that half vacant, half intent expression that he often has, and not being in a mood for his quizzical attentions I told him to buzz off p.d.q. He loped away to the kitchen from where I could hear the faint rattle of his bowl and the querulous miaowings of the cat. They are a peculiar pair, but in a masochistic way I find them oddly companionable and do not regret taking them in.

With the dog out of the way, I settled seriously to the problem of what to do with Nicholas's ill-gotten goods. My sister Primrose had telephoned earlier in the day, and although we had chatted only briefly I suppose she must still have been in my mind. Anyway, in mind or not, I suddenly saw what might be done: I would get *her* to store the wretched things!

58

Inhabiting a sizeable house and being an artist herself, albeit of a very different kind from Herr Spendler (and, at least in my estimation, of better quality), she had plenty of space in her studio or a spare room where they could lie safe and undetected until such time as Nicholas was ready to reclaim them. That would surely solve everything: not only get me off the hook but, more immediately, save them from the prying eyes of Mrs T.P. It was the obvious solution and I couldn't think why it had not occurred to me before. And then of course I realized: Primrose.

On the whole I am fond of my sister, and compared perhaps with some siblings we have quite a good relationship – good in that we lead entirely separate lives and have only sporadic contact. This suits us both, for on the few occasions that we do meet our time together, while not exactly warm, is invariably cordial. However, Primrose is five years older, and right from childhood has treated me with a mixture of pained exasperation and wry indulgence. Sometimes she can be exceedingly bossy, although I am not the sole target in that respect. For the most part, however, she is placid – provided her arrangements are not disturbed or will thwarted, when she can turn distinctly awkward. It was this latter trait that might prove a problem ... If it did not suit Primrose to house the paintings she would make that abundantly clear and no amount of wheedling on my part would shift her. In any case, she was bound to ask questions, and since for some reason she always seems dubious of my activities, parrying those would not be easy.

Still, I reflected, nothing venture nothing gain. And after all, even if she did turn me down there was nothing to lose – except possibly my sanity were I lumbered with the goods indefinitely! The sooner they were away from the vicarage the better – and if I were to feel remotely at ease with Mrs Tubbly Pole during her crazy belfry project then they would have to be got rid of within the next five days.

There was no time to lose, I would have to telephone Primrose immediately.

I paused, struck by the delicacy of the task. Much would depend on her mood and my tact. It seemed easier to pour a glass of delaying whisky which at least would give me time to consider my strategy and steel my nerve . . .

An hour later, with half the bottle gone but strategy and nerve prepared, I dialled the Sussex number. Primrose answered straightaway and I launched into my spiel. As spiels go it ran quite smoothly, most of what I said having at least a grain of truth – albeit with certain rococo embellishments.

I told her that an art dealer friend whose storage facilities were hopelessly inadequate had accepted my offer to house a couple of his paintings. Normally he would have tried to place them somewhere nearer home; but driving through Molehill shortly after Christmas he had dropped in to wish me a happy New Year, and as we chatted, happened to mention the new acquisitions which he had just been to collect from a seller in Northamptonshire. (I had never been to Northamptonshire, which is perhaps why it came into my head.) I told her he had grumbled about his lack of space, and that in a thoughtless moment I had suggested he leave them in my safekeeping until needed. Despite his protests I had been insistent, and he had gratefully agreed . . . But after only a few days of their presence I realized I had taken on more than my small house could cope with, especially as I was now having to accommodate some of the props for the bible class's Nativity play. Embarrassed by my rashness but not wanting to let my friend down, I was in a bit of a quandary. Could Primrose by *any* chance . . . might she conceivably be willing to . . .?

There was a long silence at the other end. And then she said, 'Did I hear you mention your safekeeping?'

'Yes,' I said.

There was a further pause, and then came what can only be described as a snort of derision. 'Don't be absurd,

60

Francis, you've never kept anything safe in your life! Always losing or ruining things. You're the last person to entrust a pair of paintings to!' I was taken aback by that and felt quite indignant.

'I call that very unfair,' I exclaimed. 'Don't you remember the infinite pains I used to take over my stamp album, not to mention my marbles collection!'

'Perhaps,' she replied doubtfully, 'but what about the rocking-horse and your Hornby train set!'

I blushed. They had indeed been unfortunate incidents, and even now I can hear my father's angry tones as he berated me for buckling the precious Hornby and thus denying him his fondest pastime.

'They could have happened to anyone!'

'No, only to you,' she said firmly.

I sighed. Clearly Primrose was in no mood to be soft-soaped, and glumly I resigned myself to abandoning the plan. However, her next words took the wind out of my sails.

'Obviously you must bring them down here immediately – the sooner they're out of your clutches the safer! And while you're about it, you had better stay for a couple of days: the garden is getting so overgrown and there's a large patch I need clearing.'

Stung by the allusion to my imputed incompetence, I was nevertheless delighted at the ease with which she had complied – though rather less pleased with the reference to the garden. Still, in the circumstances I could hardly decline. There was also a slight snag about the length of my stay. My original hope had been to nip down to Sussex, hand over the pictures and get back to Molehill the same day. Parish matters had been slightly more pressing than usual and I really couldn't afford to take the time off. But clearly Duty would have to bow to Expedience for I certainly couldn't risk offending Primrose! Some arrangement had to be devised.

The neighbouring parish had just taken delivery of a new curate, a fresh-faced tyro endearingly eager to please but, I gathered, somewhat lacking in initiative. Perhaps I could borrow him for the duration: such an opportunity surely providing him with admirable practice.

My luck must have been in, for St Hilda's rector, possibly wearying of his protégé's dependence, seemed only too eager to co-operate and asked rather plaintively if I was sure I didn't want him for longer. Thus the matter was settled, and after drawing up a set of instructions for the newcomer I started to prepare for my visit.

The first thing to do of course was to rewrap the pictures. This was a laborious task as deftness is not my forte and it was maddening having to grapple with so much recalcitrant paper and twine. But I finally managed it and sealed the things with as much sticky tape as I could find. (The last thing I wanted was their being vulnerable to Primrose's inquisitive probings!) Then came the chore of lugging them down from the belfry and into the car; an exhausting business, and what with that and some preliminary packing I felt quite overcome by fatigue, and slumped thankfully into an armchair.

I was just dozing off when there was a scrabbling at my knees: Bouncer, reminding me that it was long past his supper time. Seeing him there reproachful and insistent, I suddenly realized that in my concern with the pictures I had made no provision for the animals. What should I do? Leave them with the new curate? Possibly, but perhaps better not. From what I had heard of Barry – as I gathered his name to be – the additional responsibility of a wayward cat and dog would doubtless prove too much. Two days ministering to Tapsell's tantrums and the likes of Mavis Briggs was chancy enough for anyone, let alone a nervous novice! There was nothing for it but to take them with me.

10

The Dog's Diary

Of course he grumbled all the way down there – hissing, spitting, mewing. No chance of getting a kip. Not that I wanted one really, because I like looking out of the window and seeing all the cows and trees and sheep go by; and you never know when you might see another dog whirling past in his master's car, and you can make faces at it and look very fierce.

Mind you, Maurice was in a different position from me – in his cat-cage on the back seat. So I suppose you can understand him being a bit cheesed off. He hadn't been in a car before so I don't expect that helped either. Of course, *I've* been in one *lots* of times and know all about them. But Maurice doesn't like me knowing things he doesn't, so that had put him in a pet from the start. The moment F.O. shoved him in that cage and I saw him scowling out through the wire I knew we were in for a bumpy ride. Not that the vicar noticed – too busy singing hymns and puffing his fags. (With that amount of smoke swirling around I'm surprised he could see out!) Human beings don't have a good baying technique like us dogs, and when they sing their voices can sound pretty queer – and F.O.'s is one of the queerer. Not in the first league, you might say. The piano is his thing and he'd do better to stick to it.

Anyway, for some reason he was in one of his cheerful moods – something to do with those paintings he'd stuck in the boot, I think. As a matter of fact, I felt quite cheerful myself. With those stupid things out of the way I could get at my bones in the belfry again without any more upsets!

When we arrived Maurice was let out, went ear-splittingly berserk, and with bullet face scooted off into the bushes. Didn't see him for a long time and meanwhile I was allowed into the house. There was this woman – Prim something, I think she was called – and I noticed she had the same smell as F.O. I suppose they're connected in some way. Anyway, they got on all right but I think she was surprised to see me.

'Whatever's that!' she said, and didn't seem to know whether to frown or laugh. In the end she roared with laughter which annoyed me a bit, but I sat quietly – thinking that if I was GOOD they might lob some grub in my direction. They didn't, of course. Too busy getting those pictures out of the boot and burbling on about them. I got fed up and went into the garden to explore and take a sniff around. I can tell you, there were some very peculiar things out there – *very* peculiar indeed . . . But that's another story and I'm beginning to feel a bit snoozy now so it'll have to wait.

11

The Cat's Memoir

There are some things in life which are putrid. And crammed in a cage in the back of the vicar's clapped-out banger while he warbles his way down to Sussex is one of them. The journey was a nightmare: my nerves shot to pieces and dignity in shreds. To make matters worse there was that oaf of a dog sitting up on the front seat nodding and beaming as if he was the Queen Mother. It took me quite some time to collect myself, but I can assure you that when I did, I gave it to them with knobs on – one of the best productions I've mounted for a long time. Even Bouncer looked a trifle sheepish. And I could hear that tall sister berating F.O. for bringing me with him. Very satisfying.

When I had fully recovered and was disposed to being gracious again, I took an evening stroll around her domain and was agreeably impressed by its size and undergrowth. In the course of these perambulations I encountered Bouncer crouched in front of a large wooden crate with his head thrust up against its wire-mesh screen. I asked him what he thought he was doing.

He didn't answer at first, and then said slowly in a sort of muffled *sotto voce*, 'You want to take a look at this, Maurice. Give you another turn, it will!' I ignored that sally, and pushing my way past him sat down and peered in.

My eyes were met by two gigantic fluffy heads, one white and one grey; heads with long drooping ears, wild staring pink eyes and an inordinate growth of twitching whiskers. I have to admit to being startled but naturally wasn't going to let *him* see that.

I flicked my tail and in a casual voice said, 'Ah yes, rabbits.'

'Rabbits!' he exclaimed. 'My arse, they're not rabbits, they're monsters!' And thus saying, he pushed his snout more tightly against the wire.

After a while he muttered, 'They don't say much, do they?'

'Well, I shouldn't think they do,' I replied, 'not with your great face bearing down on them. Enough to dumbfound any creature!' He didn't seem to hear and continued staring in as if mesmerized. Having better things to do with my time than gape at freak rabbits I left him to it, and wandered off to make further assessment of our temporary abode.

When I returned it was supper time and the three of them were assembled in the kitchen: F.O. gulping down red wine as if it was his last day on earth, and Bouncer gnawing a brand new ham bone – presumably a product of the sister's misplaced charity. I elected to keep a dignified distance, still somewhat peeved at my treatment in the motor car and having no wish to make their amends easy. Time enough for apologies in the morning. However, before sampling my milk I did ask Bouncer if he had made any progress with the rabbits.

'Have they spoken yet?'

'The grey one did – sort of.'

'What did it say?'

'Sod off!'

'And did you?'

'I was in two minds. I mean, I wasn't going to have that carrot-chomping Jumbo telling me what to do! But I was beginning to feel a bit peckish and thought that if I went indoors and played my biscuits right I might get that Prim person to give me a nice titbit . . . which she did.' And grinning smugly he attacked the bone with renewed and noisy relish.

I felt it time to seek a quieter and more congenial setting and repaired to the drawing room where, tired from the rigours of the day, I curled up and slept the night through in moderate comfort.

I was glad to get home. The new scenery, though not without its interest, was quite enough for two days; and pleasant though the sister's garden was, it lacked the breadth and majesty of the graveyard. There is a great deal to be said for tried and tested surroundings – as indeed for people. The vicar certainly tries me often enough, but I have tested him sufficiently to know that, although defective in a number of ways, he is on the whole a congenial host. Primrose, the sister, I found less so. Not of course that she was impossible like my former mistress Elizabeth Fotherington – let alone that gallumphing daughter – but she has what you might call a certain *spikiness* which is inimical to my kindly urbanity. Needless to say, because she had given him that disgusting ham bone, Bouncer thought she was 'JOLLY GOOD'. The dog never learns.

He also seems obsessed with her moronic rabbits and has talked of little else since our return. Indeed, only this morning I overheard him telling O'Shaughnessy about them and exaggerating their dimensions out of all proportion. The setter seemed entirely receptive to his lies and I could see him egging him on, flailing that duster of a tail and grinning from ear to ear. I don't think the Celtic influence is very good for Bouncer; he is fey enough as it is.

From what I could make out, the vicar's mission was successful, in that the sister had seemed prepared to house the gross pictures with (absurdly in my view) few questions asked. I watched them heaving the things up into some sort of attic, and gave thanks that this at least would be one thing off F.O.'s mind, and trusted we might now be in for a spate of repose.

In the vicarage, however, such periods are of only relative calm. On the evening of our return, for example, I had to endure a particularly painful re-enactment of Bouncer's bedtime rituals. In the unfamiliar surroundings of the Sussex house these had been largely curtailed, but once back on *terra cognita* they were resumed with a vengeance.

The ceremony is elaborate and unattractive. First there is the matter of his playthings which have to be retrieved from various corners and dragged into his basket: the mangy rubber ring, one of F.O.'s old socks, invariably a chewed Bonio or two, and of course the awful ball with its jangling bells. This process will take some time; after which, evidently thirsty from his exertions, he laps loudly and clumsily from his bowl. Then once in the basket, the ablutions and scratchings begin and his head goes down to explore his nether regions. This involves much snorting and shifting about. Finally, after making several scrabbling pirouettes and emitting a loud groan, he flops down dead to the world. At that point I breathe a sigh of relief.

But as you might expect, the vicar is little better. One can hear him all over the house – thumping about on the landing, opening and slamming the bathroom door, gargling and coughing, pulling chains, turning on taps. An ear-splitting palaver! I often think that there's not much difference between dogs and humans: both are noisy and largely insane.

12

The Vicar's Version

It had been a pleasant journey down; partly because I enjoy driving but mainly because I felt a blessed relief that the pictures were to be safely transferred. Primrose greeted me kindly, but at first seemed a trifle put out by the presence of Maurice and Bouncer. In my preoccupation with the paintings I had entirely forgotten to alert her to their coming, and the omission had not been helped by Maurice being particularly bloody when he was let out of the car. However, by the time we had hauled the parcels out of the boot and gone into the house for a drink she had calmed down, later even supplying Bouncer with an exceptionally meaty bone – a gift to which he applied his usual full-throttled attention.

I like my sister's house. It is solid and spacious and occupies a sheltered position facing the South Downs. It gets a good deal of sun and the garden is pleasantly secluded. She had moved into it about six months previously, and when I had first visited her, just after my dire event, it had seemed an almost restful haven. I say 'almost', because being Primrose she had inevitably prepared a number of chores for me (although these, given the circumstances, did have their diversionary use). But the brief visit had nevertheless allowed me to collect my thoughts and stiffen my nerve for the return to Molehill and the overtures of the local police.

At that time she had also just taken possession of a rather sinister pair of chinchilla rabbits whom she had dubbed Boris and Karloff. Their appeal was what one might call esoteric, but knowing that Primrose had grown attached to them I now dutifully enquired after their welfare. She regaled me at some length about their quirks, habits and dietary preference; but even when the topic was finally exhausted I couldn't help thinking that their charm was subtle rather than manifest.

At one point I did ask whether perhaps she was thinking of substituting chinchillas for sheep in her sketches of downland churches. This didn't go down terribly well and I was told with some asperity that I clearly hadn't lost my knack for the facetious. I was slightly put out by this as I had genuinely wondered whether her celebrated (and lucrative) little churches might not benefit from a change in their accompanying fauna. However, since the buying public's enthusiasm for scenes of church, sheep and Sussex Downs showed no sign of flagging, she was probably right to keep to the winning formula.

Tactfully I started to change the subject, but before I could she said briskly, 'Now, what about *your* paintings? As said, I don't mind storing them here for a while – at least they're better off with me than with you – so long as they're not those ghastly Spendlers of course! Goodness, what a fuss the papers are making about that business!' She laughed derisively and started to open another bottle.

I smiled palely, proffered my glass and tried to think what line I might spin about the contents of their frames. In my eagerness to offload the things it had not occurred to me that she might ask direct questions about their subject or provenance. Now, looking at them resting wrapped and stacked against the kitchen dresser, I could see she might be curious.

'Chance would be a fine thing!' I replied jocularly. 'Those

pictures would set me up for life all right!' And I began to laugh loudly but catching Bouncer's startled eye adjusted my tone and said something to the effect that my colleague had talked so much during his visit that I hadn't really given the details my full attention, adding vaguely that I thought they were some sort of modern abstracts but couldn't be sure.

'Really, Francis,' she expostulated, 'you are hopeless, never listen to anything! Daddy was quite right – a head stuffed with nothing but sea air!'

Yes, he had said that quite often, I recalled – indeed, right up to the day before his death in the nursing home when I had absent-mindedly poured Lucozade into his whisky glass. He had been so incensed we thought he might rally, but capricious to the end he fooled everyone. I seized on the memory of our parent as a means of diversion from the pictures, and we spent a congenially masochistic time dwelling on our life with him.

What with the wine and the family reminiscences, the problem of the paintings started to fade and I began to feel pleasantly relaxed. But Primrose has inherited from our father the uncanny knack of stirring things up just when you think they have simmered down; and suddenly, apropos of nothing, she said, 'Of course, they'll never drop that case, you know. They never do, not fully. They'll let it go dormant for a while and then sometime – even years later – start gnawing away again. You mark my words, it won't be the end of it.'

It had been quite a demanding day and I suppose I was feeling sleepy, for the import of her words didn't really register and I said lazily, 'What case? Don't know what you're talking about.'

'The Molehill Murder of course! That woman parishioner of yours, the one that left you all the money – though why you had to go and give it away like that I simply can't imagine. Sometimes I think I have a complete idiot for a

71

brother!' Even in my welling panic I reflected that Primrose had always been mercenary.

'Oh well,' I mumbled, 'it seemed a good idea at the time. Hadn't got much use for it really. You know how it is . . .'

'No, I don't, as a matter of fact,' she rejoined tartly. 'I don't know at all. Sometimes I think you live in another world, Francis! But still,' she relented, 'I suppose it could be worse. After all, you might have turned into a drunkard – or a bishop.'

I enjoy a good tipple, but having a rather uncertain stomach and being prone to headaches, thought the first option almost as unlikely as the second. Then recalling the episode of Bishop Clinker and the White Ladies I also wondered why Primrose should in any case have made the distinction. The two fates, I had learned, were not mutually exclusive.

Grasping the topic of bishops as a means of steering matters away from Elizabeth and my inexplicable bounty, I said hastily, 'Talking of bishops, I think old Horace may be gearing up for another visit. There was a bit of a shindig at one of my weddings a couple of weeks ago and I think he's got wind of it.'

Primrose was surprisingly sympathetic; and, the Molehill affair safely circumvented, we spent some time mulling over the officiousness of high office. My sister addressed the subject with characteristic pungency, being herself currently embroiled in some complicated dispute with the burgers of Lewes. From what I could make out, it revolved around the rival claims of the town's High Street and her Morris Oxford, although the finer points of the saga rather escaped me. Suffice it to say, she was in one of her litigious moods and I felt a glancing sympathy for the municipal authorities. I could have done with Primrose to help me with Clinker, but then with a pang of trepidation remembered that I already had an ally in that sphere – Mrs Tubbly Pole.

The next day, with Primrose's curiosity fortunately

faded, the pictures were consigned to her spare room where, amidst the general clutter of trunks, cardboard boxes and other accumulated debris, they melted into reassuring anonymity. Then, having finally completed my prescribed tasks in house and garden, and, as instructed, having bade a ceremonious farewell to Boris and Karloff, I was free to return to Molehill – considerably lightened in one way but with the shadow of Clinker still looming in another . . .

In fact, when I arrived home, there was surprisingly no sign of Clinker's shadow. I had feared that at least one missive would be awaiting me from the Palace, but the post proved mercifully bland. Neither was there a telephone call that evening nor indeed the next. I began to wonder whether, despite its extensive press coverage, the wedding matter had somehow escaped his notice. It seemed unlikely. And even if it had, the oversight would surely have been amply remedied by the diocesan grapevine. However, there was no point in meeting trouble more than halfway and I had better things to do than fret over a hypothetical barrage from the bishop. There was, for example, the belfry tryst with Mrs Tubbly Pole.

With the paintings out of the way this was now a less daunting prospect. Nevertheless, the thought of devoting much of Saturday evening in assisting her – and presumably Gunga Din – to negotiate the belfry's perilous stairway did not exactly inspire delight. It also occurred to me that the gin was low. On my own I could have eked it out until the following week, but knowing their joint capacity there was nothing for it but to put hand prematurely in pocket. I thought grimly that had I foreseen Mrs Tubbly Pole's arrival in Molehill I might have retained rather more of Elizabeth's legacy than I did!

13

The Vicar's Version

It would be nice to draw a veil over Mrs Tubbly Pole's belfry inspection. It is not an episode I care to dwell upon. However, certain things arose which for the purpose of narrative I am forced to recall.

She arrived at six o'clock sharp, accompanied as feared by Gunga Din. Both wore the appearance of bulldog resolution and I realized that my vague hope of diverting them by drink was a non-starter. Sartorially they were clearly prepared for the venture: the dog – presumably to ease its scramble to the top – was now divested of his usual coat and harness, while his mistress was encased in a pair of serge knee breeches making her look not unlike a portly Pantalone from the *commedia dell'arte*. She carried a large walking stick – whether for prodding the dog, fending off bats, or merely as a symbol of mountaineering endeavour, I could not be sure. It proved a more than tiresome encumbrance.

She was in high spirits and we set off briskly and volubly up the lane to the church. As we went she discoursed graphically on the writer's duty to set the scene so the reader could 'breathe in the atmosphere', imbibing its very taste and smell. Atmosphere, she assured me, was half the novelist's battle. There would be plenty of that, I thought grimly, recalling the mouldering rafters and cobwebbed mice droppings. I asked her what the other half was.

'Plot,' she intoned, 'plot, plot, plot! Which is *why*, Francis, it is so vital that you supply me with your views of the original crime so that I can work them into my narrative pattern.'

'I'm not sure that I have any views,' I said nervously, adding by way of distraction, 'But what about character – surely that matters?'

'Not a bit,' she observed. 'Readers don't want character, they want *action*!'

'Really? You surprise me. I thought perhaps ...' My voice trailed off as she wagged an admonishing finger.

'Now, Francis, don't teach your grandmother etc.! Do you think that Cecil Piltdown and I got where we are today by wasting our time on character? After all, think of the great queen!' She grinned triumphantly. I didn't know who or what she was talking about and said as much.

'Why, the great Queen of Crime of course, Agatha Christie! Her characters are as flat as pancakes but nobody complains – and the books sell like hot cakes. As do mine! Now, tell me all about that dark wood. I've read the newspaper reports of course, but there's nothing like getting it from a local horse's mouth!' She gave a hearty snort of laughter but by this time we had reached the bell tower and I was able to evade answer by addressing the matter in hand: the ascent of the steps.

This, as I had feared, proved a slow and demanding process, made all the more tricky by Gunga Din's obvious reluctance to participate. I had been right in my assumption about the walking stick – its principal function was indeed the persuasive prodding of the dog, and despite his mournful protests he was eventually manoeuvred to the first floor. His mistress followed laboriously and I brought up the rear, wishing ruefully that I could be back in the vicarage slumped with a gin and a good book.

The lower chamber looked its usual dank self, and I felt almost apologetic for there not being a greater air of mystery. What she would get out of it I couldn't imagine! But the visitor seemed more than happy trundling around touching the walls, eyeing the bell ropes, even producing a small notebook in which she seemed to be noting down dimensions. Such was her absorption that I began to hope that further exploration up the rickety steps to the next stage would be unnecessary ... Foolish Francis, as my father would have said.

'Excellent,' she exclaimed. 'Excellent! Now, let us proceed.' And giving Gunga Din another prod she turned towards the narrow staircase and the open trap door.

'Are you sure you really want to go up there? I mean, it's awfully dirty and I can assure you there isn't much to see!'

'I'll be the judge of that,' she said firmly. And seizing the dog by the scruff of his neck she began to propel him on to the bottom stair. He was clearly disinclined, and with bulging eye sprawled stubbornly at the base.

'He's not too keen,' I said, stating the obvious. 'Wouldn't it be better to leave him down here? He'd probably be far happier.'

'No fear!' she answered. 'You don't know him. As soon as Mummy's back is turned he'll be off down those stairs and going God knows where! He's a wily old bird.' I looked at him. He didn't look the remotest bit wily, just morose and bloody.

'There's nothing for it – *you'll* have to carry him. Now up you go, the pair of you, and I'll follow!'

I gazed askance at Gunga Din and he stared back lugubriously.

'Well,' I said weakly, 'I'm not sure that I'm used to –'

'Nonsense!' she cried. 'You know how fond he is of you, he'll be as good as gold.' Clearly there was to be no option. I bent down and hauled the creature into my arms. The weight was stupendous.

With rasping breath I started to stagger upwards. It didn't work of course: the burden was far too cumbersome and the steps vertiginous. I panted and tottered.

76

'Over your shoulder, Francis. Put him over your shoulder!'

I struggled to do her bidding and managed to shift the weight into a more accommodating position. This would have been tolerable had my left ear not now been subjected to prolonged and snuffling slobbers. The heavy breathing from both dog and carrier was enough to raise the rafters, but by dint of superhuman effort we achieved the top and collapsed jointly upon the floor. In comparison, and given the proportions of girth and age, Mrs Tubbly Pole's ascent was remarkably nimble. She had obviously got into her stride, and from my recumbent posture I regarded her with pained envy.

'There you are, you see, not so difficult after all!' she announced. I nodded faintly, still too winded to utter, and watched as once again she embarked upon her reconnaissance. My one relief was that the wretched paintings were safely out of the way. That at least was a mercy and I congratulated myself on the success of their transfer. Gunga Din was now out for the count and the air was rent by his stentorian snores.

I continued to watch as she prowled about. Suddenly she turned, and with a broad grin said, 'I say, Francis, this would make an ideal hidey-hole, just right for the corpse. This belfry must have quite a few tales to tell. I feel it in my bones! I bet they used to shove the R.C. priests up here, not to mention the paintings.'

Sweat poured upon me. '*Paintings*, corpse – what on earth do you mean!' I gasped.

'During the Reformation – all the paintings and silver in the church when it was under threat from Thom. Cromwell and Co. Surely as a vicar you know all about that!'

'Ah yes . . . *those* paintings! Er – yes, naturally.'

'Don't know what other paintings there could be, and as to the corpse – well, the one in my novel, of course. I told you I was thinking of moving it from the woods to the belfry, and now that I've seen the place I'm absolutely certain. Admittedly a major change in setting but the underlying situation will remain the same. You'll see!'

Yes, I thought ruefully, the underlying situation would always remain the same . . .

'Mind you,' she continued breezily, 'I shall still need to hear as much as possible about the original murder in that Foxford Wood close to you. It'll help to establish the mind-set of the assassin (pretty grisly by all accounts!) and I'm sure you can help me there.'

I said nothing and stared glumly at the snoring dog. My back was hurting and I seemed to be sitting on a sack of some lumpy material; it felt like bits of concrete, and not wanting to add to the discomfort I stood up unsteadily. My toe became enmeshed in one of its corners and I nearly tripped. I couldn't recall seeing the thing previously, and was about to investigate when a wave of weariness descended, sapping both energy and interest. Surely there were nicer things to do than mooch about in that freezing belfry pandering to the whims of some half-crazed writer! Irritably I pushed the sack to one side and returned my attention to the latter.

She was stomping up and down apparently in her ele-ment; but then glancing in my direction said in a solicitous tone, 'I say, Francis, you don't look too good – a bit peaky. Too much sermonizing, I shouldn't wonder. What you need is a good nightcap!' What I need, I thought, is a bit of peace and quiet . . .

However, it was not to be, for as the three of us renego-tiated the rickety stairway Mrs Tubbly Pole's walking stick got entangled in my trouser leg. The ensuing complications brought confusion to all and we arrived at the lower floor more promptly than foreseen.

The other two lumbered to their feet. I was unable to do so, my leg having gone through the defective floorboard reproachfully reported by Mavis Briggs. Grist to her bloody mill, I raged.

14

The Vicar's Version

It took me several days to recover from the ordeal in the belfry; and things were not helped by the fact that, my leg being particularly sore, I was reduced to hobbling around with one of my father's old walking sticks. Clearly some emollient treat was due. So pleading urgent business in Guildford, I cancelled my appearance at the Vestry Circle's annual luncheon (an excruciatingly dreary affair) and took myself off to the cinema and cream buns in the Angel.

Driving home sated with the buns and still chuckling over Peter Lorre's performance in *The Maltese Falcon*, I very nearly ran over Mavis Briggs, whose earlier unctuous concern about the leg business had been sickening in the extreme. My mind was still wrapped in the delightful skulduggery of the film, and when she stepped off the pavement looking resolutely in the opposite direction from the oncoming traffic, I very nearly caught her a smacker. This wouldn't have mattered so much had she not been accompanied by Edith Hopgarden (presumably the pair were currently in truce mode), so when I stopped and wound down the window to apologize I was met with a blast of pained expostulation. This, of course, came from Edith; Mavis just stood there wearing her usual look of simpering martyrdom.

She said I had been much missed at the Vestry Circle's gathering and trusted I had spent a nice day in Guildford. For one embarrassing moment I thought she guessed what I had been doing, but then recalled that this was Mavis speaking, not Edith, and thus the remark was free from innuendo. Smiling benignly, I replied that it had been a most productive afternoon. Edith said pointedly that, judging from my speed, I was clearly in a great hurry to get home and that they wouldn't delay me. Occasionally one is granted such small mercies.

Later, feeling generous after my stolen hours, I decided to attack the requirements of the parish magazine. This is a task that can be diverting but is often onerous. Together with Colonel Dawlish, I am its co-editor, and in addition to my own monthly address one of my responsibilities is to vet the letters submitted by parishioners. These can range from the woolly and worthy, via the smugly righteous, to the downright actionable. These last are by far the most interesting but invariably their grammar is defective, so in addition to excising some of the more scurrilous passages there is also the chore of smoothing the syntax.

I was fully immersed in this when there was a sudden screech from the doorbell. What with that and Bouncer's howl of excitement I nearly had a seizure. But before I could collect myself there was another loud clarion by which time the dog was in full tongue. Shouting at him to be quiet, I grimly flung open the front door. It was the bishop.

What shocked me was not so much his presence as his apparel. Clinker was wearing plus-fours, scarlet socks, and a tweed ratting-cap of such vulgar check that 'mine eyes dazzled'. His small feet (surprising for a large man) were encased in the nattiest pair of co-respondent's shoes I have ever seen. The clerical collar was retained: presumably as a passing nod to episcopal sobriety. In every other way he was utterly transformed. As I gazed I caught sight of the Daimler's tail-end gliding into the distance, and with sinking heart realized we were in for a lengthy session.

'Ah, Oughterard,' he breezed, 'hoped I might catch you. Been rather busy – *golfing* you know, my new hobby. Otherwise would have telephoned ahead, but just couldn't tear myself away from that new clubhouse they've opened a couple of miles from you. A fine course they've got there, very fine indeed!' (Busy my hat! Thought he might catch me unawares, that was all.)

Still stunned by the sporting attire, I led him into the sitting room. And this time, not having a concoction of White Ladies to hand, firmly offered a cup of tea. Standing over the kettle in the kitchen, I racked my brain for some sort of defence of the wedding débâcle. None was forthcoming and I returned gloomily to the sitting room with the tea tray. I wondered if he remembered the finer details of his previous visit. To be once more in the context of such spectacular inebriation might have been embarrassing; but he showed no signs of discomfort and, firmly settled on the sofa, sipped his tea with an expression bordering on pleasure. I cleared my throat, awaiting the attack.

Surveying the paperwork strewn across the dining table, he nodded approvingly. 'Glad to see you're hard at it, Oughterard. Always did feel that Molehill was in a safe pair of hands.' Liar, I thought, recalling our last encounter. He's playing for time – just gearing up for the kill.

However, he went prosing on about the usefulness of parish magazines, their place in the community, the vital job of the editor and the general value of workaday endeavour. He sounded so enthusiastic that I began to wonder whether he wasn't preparing to strip me of my sacerdotal duties in favour of some pen-pushing role. It would, after all, be in keeping with his plan of six months previously – to palm me off as chaplain to some dismal home for pensioned clergy. The episode of the White Ladies had scotched that one all right, but he might just try something similar. I was brooding on that possibility when I was startled by a loud snort of laughter.

'I say, Oughterard, that wedding of yours was a bit of a fiasco, wasn't it! A few more like that and you'll have the wrath of Canterbury upon us! It doesn't take much to stir His Grace!' And flashing his scarlet socks he launched into a series of spluttering guffaws. I gazed nonplussed, wondering whether it had been less the Golf Club's sward that had engaged his time, than its bar. However, not wishing to dampen proceedings I joined in the merriment.

Eventually he subsided, and leaning forward said, 'Now seriously, Oughterard, among other things there's something rather important I wish to discuss with you – well, alert you to really. If it works out as I hope, *you* will be partly affected.' Here we go, I thought. What's it to be – banishment to the Cairngorms as I had once feared, or the imposition of some meddling curate? Whatever the case, it would doubtless bring tribulation and make my quest for peace an even wilder pipe dream.

Then, with the numerous possibilities flashing before my eyes, I reminded myself that I did have one very real advantage: the Cocktail Card. Clinker's fear that it still might be played could – as before – provide a useful lever in changing whatever he had in mind. Admittedly, at the moment he appeared to have no obvious recollection of once being sprawled out tight as a tick on my carpet; nor indeed of his remarkable imitation of a cancan dancer, and the ignominious exit beached comatose on the back seat of the Daimler. But I guessed it would take only a few well-placed hints to rekindle the horror.

Braced by those thoughts, I decided to divert him from the purpose of his visit for as long as possible, trusting that in the meantime unsettling memories might assert themselves. To this end I wondered whether I should rouse Bouncer (the previous summer the dog having played a key role in the bishop's downfall), but thought better of it. Confronting Clinker with his erstwhile dancing partner might not so much unsettle as enrage, a risk I could ill afford. The best ploy, surely, would be Gladys: invariably a subject of chastening effect, and one which would at least allow me a satisfying *schadenfreude*.

Thus busily pouring more tea, I enquired politely, 'And how is Mrs Clinker these days? A grass widow, I fear!' I sat back confidently, expecting the usual scowl. To my surprise he beamed.

'Out of the country, Oughterard. *Out* of the country!' He thrust his feet forward, admiring the two-tone shoes, and sighed happily.

I asked if she was on holiday. '*Some* might call it that,' he replied. 'She's visiting her sister in Belgium. Seems to give her a boost. Can't think why! Belgium's bad enough, the sister's worse.' I wondered whether the latter was also worse than Gladys. Unlikely . . . but then it's amazing what people are capable of.

Unsurprisingly, he seemed disinclined to pursue the topic of the two siblings and we turned to other matters, specifically his golfing handicap, his swing, his niblick, and the officiousness of caddies. None of this I understood, but in the interests of time gained and bad news postponed, I sat with a smile of absorbed fascination.

The clock ticked by and I kept a hopeful ear cocked for the sound of the retrieving Daimler. The sound eventually came, but not before he had dropped his bombshell.

'. . . Now, Oughterard, talking of the necessity of a steady arm and a keen eye brings me to the matter of the diocesan appointments. As you know, with the imminent retirement of Archdeacon Blenkinsop we have a vacancy in the dio-cese, and, as I think you also know, there are two strong candidates.' I nodded vaguely. 'But,' he added with a gleam of satisfaction, 'I have another up my sleeve which I've been keeping rather quiet about. However, the time is now ripe for me to divulge my man . . .' He paused expect-antly, awaiting my response.

'Oh yes?' I said.

'Yes, you know him pretty well, I think. In fact quite a chum of yours if I'm not mistaken!'

'Really?' I said, by now intrigued. As far as I was aware I didn't have any chums, as he put it; tolerable colleagues perhaps, and one or two pleasant acquaintances, but not *chums*. I waited for the revelation. It came.

'Rummage!' he boomed.

Once during the war I had been on the periphery of a shell blast, and even now in my dreams I occasionally still feel that dreadful thump on my thorax, the sickening sense of weightlessness and sheer physical disbelief. In like manner I received the news of the bishop's choice.

All along I had assumed Clinker was nursing some dark proposal connected with myself: a transfer, a demotion. But an absurdity of this kind had never entered my head! That Basil Rummage of all people should be in the running for the post of archdeacon was a gaffe of monumental lunacy. Only Clinker could have thought that one up! I gazed incredulously.

'Yes, thought you'd be pleased,' he said. 'I remember how close you two were at St Bede's. If I can get him the job it'll be quite a turn-up for the books! You'd find him a most useful adviser to have around. Very ingenious is Rummage.'

Other than the mistaken memory of our friendship at St Bede's Theological College, there was an element of truth in this. Rummage had ingenuity all right – of the narrow variety, focused exclusively on himself and his own ends. In every other respect he was an oaf. Nicholas Ingaza had once referred to him as a self-serving poltroon. It was an apt description. Nicholas too was self-serving, but at least he had style and 'a talent to amuse'. Rummage had neither.

I brooded on the last time I had seen him – at the vicarage six months previously, as locum when I was 'holidaying' in Brighton after my ghastly event. It had been a terrible period, and not helped by the appalling shambles in which I found the house when I eventually returned in the wake of that dreadful episode. More than anything else I had been in need of calm and order. What I had found was the fallout from his sojourn: a shattered gatepost, a blitzkrieg of litter, empty cans, beer bottles, and the whole-sale consumption of my favourite malt whisky – carefully secreted where none but the most dedicated plunderer would have looked.

As Clinker continued, singing the plunderer's praises and gauging his chances in the clerical stakes, I thought bitterly of the way that Rummage's ability to wreak havoc on other people's houses was matched only by his skill in pulling strings on his own behalf. And so here he was, fast en route to becoming a Venerable – and my immediate overseer! No doubt given a few more years he would be swanking about in a mitre. The thought was intolerable and I suddenly felt very fatigued.

My visitor was obviously too engrossed in freedom from Gladys and delight in his new plus-fours to notice my gloomy responses, and the moment the car arrived he whisked himself off with a cheery wave and an injunction to 'keep up the good work!'

It was barely eight o'clock, but too tired even for the piano, I took the phone off the hook and sloped up to bed for a consoling aspirin and brandy.

15

The Vicar's Version

The telephone rang and I was dismayed to hear Clinker's voice again. I had thought he was off my back for a while, but apparently not.

'Ah, Francis,' he said (always a good sign when he uses my first name), 'glad to catch you in. There's – uhm – something I'd like to discuss with you. It's moderately urgent so oblige me by being at home on Friday afternoon when I shall be in the area. Now don't forget! It's . . . well, of a personal nature and I shouldn't like to waste my time.' I was a trifle worried about that 'personal nature' – his person or mine? – but assured him I would be there, pleased that this particular ill wind had blown in the excuse to cancel a Vestry meeting with Mavis Briggs and her henchmen. Even Clinker was an improvement on that.

Friday afternoon: and glancing out of the window I saw a battered Riley parked at a rakish angle athwart my gateposts. Evidently the bishop had arrived under his own steam without the assistance of Barnes and the official car. I opened the front door and ushered him in. To my relief he was dressed in normal garb (difficult to have faced the golfing gear a second time!) and seemed in semi-cordial mood.

A few pleasantries were exchanged followed by a silence. Then clearing his throat he said, 'Now, Francis, you're a man of the world – well, in a manner of speaking – and there's a matter on which I would value your opinion.'

Notwithstanding the qualification, I was surprised and flattered by his words, and flashed him what I felt was a worldly smile. It wasn't reciprocated and there followed a further silence. Eventually he leaned forward and said in a conspiratorial tone, 'I think you might know Mrs Carruthers, a lady of your parish but not, I think, an actual churchgoer.'

I didn't know the lady but vaguely remembered her name being mentioned somewhere or other. However, feeling it might speed whatever revelation Clinker was about to make, I nodded confidently.

'Well, you see,' he continued, 'Mrs Carruthers and I are on quite good terms – close really. We have, you might say, certain interests in common . . .' He cleared his throat noisily. I didn't like to ask if those interests included Gladys, feeling sure that they didn't, but continued to smile blandly, wondering how on earth I was going to handle the next few moments.

He paused again, looking distinctly shifty, and then said, 'It's – ah – a slightly delicate situation . . .' I had feared it might be and braced myself for embarrassment. 'You see,' he continued, 'once a week – Wednesdays mostly – we meet in the afternoon.'

'Oh yes,' I said casually, 'that's nice.'

'Yes, it is,' he said, brightening, 'very nice indeed. Mind you, there are not just the two of us, others are involved sometimes as well. Spices it up a bit, if you know what I mean!'

I wasn't sure that I did know and felt myself starting to blush. However, this hardly suited my newly acquired role as 'man of the world' and I tried to think mournful thoughts hoping they might restore my customary pallor.

But as I entertained pictures of suicides and graves he went burbling on, his words making me increasingly uncomfortable.

'Of course a foursome is the ideal, evenly balanced and everyone gets a go. Six can be fun but it gets a bit crowded, and at my time of life I tire too easily. Generally though, it's just Mrs Carruthers and me which is all very cosy but – and don't get me wrong here – it *can* be a little predictable!' By this time he was emboldened enough to give a loud laugh, and tiring of my man of the world persona I fixed him with a stern eye. He seemed not to notice.

'Of course I don't suppose you've ever engaged in that sort of thing – not your line of country at all, I imagine, and I realize it's not to everyone's taste, a bit *esoteric* one might say, which is why the whole thing is a little tricky. Wouldn't do for the press to get hold of it – not for a man in my position!' And he giggled.

'No,' I said faintly, 'it wouldn't. And I don't suppose Gladys, I mean your wife, would be too keen either!'

'Exactly,' he confided. 'That's part of the problem. It's not at all the sort of thing she would understand. Still, a chap's got to have his recreations and it takes all sorts.' He was beginning to evince a certain nonchalance which, in the circumstances, I thought rather brazen. How could I tactfully point out the error of his ways while still appearing both deferential and unruffled?

'Er, what does Mrs Carruthers think?'

'Oh, she doesn't care a hoot – no false pride there. Doesn't mind who knows!'

'Good gracious!' I exclaimed, wondering what sort of hussy would choose to live in Molehill of all places!

'In fact that's the chief problem. She's far from discreet, and despite our friendship, unless she can be persuaded to silence I'm afraid I shall have to forgo our little sessions – which would be a great pity.'

'Well,' I ventured diffidently, 'that might be a blessing in disguise.'

'What do you mean?'

'It might give you a chance to . . . well, to get yourself sorted out.'

'I don't need sorting out,' he replied testily, 'I need your help, Oughterard!'

The tone had become querulous and I noted the reversion to my surname, and shifted uneasily. Perhaps in answer to his appeal I should suggest that he try being a little more sober and vigilant – though I doubted its efficacy, and in any case, in view of my own worrying transgression of the previous year, such an injunction might be a trifle de trop even for my conscience. However, clearly some such spiritual advice was in order, so I asked him had he considered that the person most likely to be harmed by those engagements was himself.

'Of course I have, Oughterard, which is why I want you to approach Mrs Carruthers and get her to keep it under her hat. She won't take it from me, we're too matey. But with an outsider like yourself and not one of our little circle, she might see some sense.'

I regarded him in dazed wonder. Surely he wasn't expecting his subordinate to play the part of a pander in his lewd activities! I was incensed. Not of their 'little circle' – I should hope not indeed! Had Clinker taken leave of his senses?

Before I could gather my wits he had stood up, looked wistfully at the glasses on the sideboard and said, 'Don't suppose you've any more of those cocktails, White Ladies, have you, Oughterard?'

'No,' I snapped. (Blowed if I was going to allow my hard-bought drink near that complacent libertine!) He seemed surprised at the asperity of my tone but said mildly that he would settle for a cup of tea if I didn't mind. I did mind, but complied with his request, thinking grimly that a spike of bromide wouldn't have gone amiss!

As I handed him the cup he returned to the subject of Mrs Carruthers and 'the circle'.

'Sounds absurd, I know, but I've become quite obsessed with the whole thing. Keep waking in the night and devising new methods and positions and wondering how different partners will make out. Makes me quite restless and Gladys gets furious. Ridiculous, isn't it, to get excited about such a mere pursuit!'

I maintained a po-face but said pointedly that I was rather surprised that he should deem it so mere a pursuit and that traditionally the Church had always been rather strict on that sort of thing, regarding such practices – especially with the numbers he had mentioned – with a less than tolerant eye. A reference to Sodom and Gomorrah sprang to my lips, but I felt that might be excessive and cause contention. Having to teach moral commonplaces to my superior, even to one such as Clinker, was difficult enough as it was. But clearly the man was going through some sort of crisis and might be grateful for a bit of straight talk. He didn't appear particularly grateful, in fact stared at me as if I was some sort of congenital idiot.

'What *are* you babbling about, Oughterard? Don't know what part of the scriptures you've been reading – unless you haven't been listening at all! I suppose that's it. I've noticed before – your attention span is singularly short, always has been.' He sighed in exasperation, and somewhere from the distant past there echoed my father's equally irritable tone.

'I simply ask for a little help in drawing a veil over my rather puerile indulgence in tiddlywinks and you preach me some prissy sermon on Church precepts. Really, it's enough to try the patience of a saint!'

And you're certainly no saint, I thought. 'Tiddlywinks'! Is that what he called it! ... And then I stared at him aghast.

'I'm, I'm sorry, sir – did you say *tiddlywinks*?'

'Yes, Oughterard, that is exactly what I said. For goodness sake concentrate, will you! Now, I'll give you Mrs Carruthers' address and you must go round and tactfully explain to her that it won't do my reputation a jot of good if it gets out that the diocesan bishop wastes his Wednesday afternoons on hands and knees playing childish games which should have been dropped when he was in short pants. I shall be a laughing stock! It besmirches the dignity of the Church. It besmirches *my* dignity, Oughterard, so kindly do something about it – and quickly!'

When he eventually left I retired to bed feeling that in such matters oblivion was the only medicine.

16

The Vicar's Version

The gaffe itself was bad enough, but now I was faced with the chore of finding Mrs Carruthers and persuading her to keep quiet about the bishop's absurd antics. Would there be no end to these impositions? Apparently not.

The address he had given me was within walking distance so with luck the matter need not take up too much time. I debated whether I should telephone first – it would be tiresome if she were out – but thought better of it. Prior warning might lead to evasive action: in such matters surprise was the essence.

I set out reluctantly but with firm stride and soon found the house. As I had rather imagined, it was a detached residence of mock Tudor design (beloved of Molehill) and with the usual mix of privet and forsythia lining the front drive. But what distinguished it from any other house in the vicinity was the area immediately in front of the gabled porch . . .

I stopped in my tracks, gaping in horrified amazement. Arranged in precise and nightmarish circles was an array of stone garden gnomes whose scale and garish variety defied belief. In every shape and posture, they jostled brazenly: winsome, coy, grotesque. I stared transfixed. At least Clinker had the decency to keep *his* vices under wraps!

I edged around the creatures and gained what I thought would be the sanctuary of the porch; but even here there were more. Armed with rakes and fishing rods, sitting cross-legged, standing on tiptoe, perched on toadstools, they simpered and beckoned, inviting the hapless visitor to join their merry throng. It was a relief when the door was finally opened and I could make my escape inside.

Fortunately the interior was normal – decidedly bland in fact, and I concluded that Mrs Carruthers kept the gnomes as some sort of outlet for artistic perversion. She was a small woman probably in her early fifties, plump and grey-ing. Nondescript really, except for gigantic hoop earrings, a scarlet mouth and trousers to match. In between the two, and neutralizing the effect, she wore a grubby gardening jacket, and since she was holding a trowel had clearly been engaged in some sort of horticultural activity in the back garden – which made me wonder if perhaps more of *them* were there as well.

I introduced myself and she showed an affable interest. But it was when I mentioned Clinker that she really took off. 'Oh, he's a one, he is!' she cried delightedly. 'Quite merciless, you know.' And she laughed with a high and raucous pitch. 'Things always get better when he comes along!' I was surprised, never having observed that par-ticular effect before.

I smiled. 'In what way better?'

'Oh, he's such a love – throws his heart and soul into it, really gets us all going. And very bold too – some of those moves, my, my!' And she laughed again, another jangling shriek to set the mammoth ear hoops dancing.

'What kind of moves?' I asked suspiciously. 'I thought tiddlywinks was quite a simple game, or at least it used to be.'

'Not now, it's not. At least not for us afici . . . afici, oh, *you* know the word!' And rather boldly, I thought, she gave me a prod in the ribs. 'They hold championships these days. And do you know what?'

I said that I didn't.

'Horace is going to represent our circle, and *I* think we're in with a big chance. He's ever so good, you know!'

'Good gracious!' I exclaimed. 'Didn't know he harboured such talent.'

'Oh yes, dear, he's very talented for a bishop. The circle wouldn't be the same without him. We're very proud of our Mr Clinker.'

I have to admit to being fascinated by these revelations (and fortunately they held none of the discomfort of my earlier misapprehension); but since my reason for being there was essentially to silence the lady, I thought this was the moment to broach the matter. 'I'm sure you are proud of him, Mrs Carruthers,' ('Call me Annie, dear!') 'but the problem is that his superiors in the Church might be less impressed – even taking a dim view of his hobby. They can be rather stuffy, you know . . .'

'Didn't think he had any superiors,' she said, 'never gives that impression anyway!' (That rang true all right!)

'Well, there are just one or two of them and they can cut up rough sometimes, so perhaps for *his* sake the less said the better. In any case, sometimes these things are more fun kept private, makes them special and exclusive, a sort of heightened pleasure you might say!' And I smiled confidingly.

It clearly appealed to her sense of drama for she emitted another gunshot laugh, and exclaimed, 'Yes, see what you mean – a sort of conspiracy, I suppose, like a secret cabal!' The paste hoops tinkled with a trill of excitement.

'*Exactly*, a secret cabal.'

There was a slight pause as she absorbed the idea. She evidently liked it, for the next moment she nodded her head vigorously and declared, 'That's it then. From now on mum's the word. His secret's safe with me!'

'And with the others?' I asked.

'Oh yes, they won't let him down. They're *very* fond of him!' Curiouser and curiouser.

A thought struck her. 'Here, I don't suppose you'd like to join our circle, would you? You'd be a match for old Horace, you would!'

I liked the prospect of being a match for Clinker, but not in those particular circumstances, and politely declined the offer. 'I think you would find that one vicar in your midst was quite enough! Besides, I'd hate to cramp his style.'

'Oh no,' she said gaily, 'we couldn't have that, could we! But tell you what – it's half past eleven, let's settle for a nice cup of cocoa!' I recoiled. Personally I was dying for a gin and a gasper, and to be offered such a sickly beverage from one clad in scarlet and diamanté gave me a shock. But on reflection it made sense. Anybody who could house such a monstrous circus of garden ornaments would surely drink nothing else! I wondered how Clinker survived without his White Ladies.

Making excuses and with mission accomplished, I took my leave – but not before putting my finger to the side of my nose as I had seen them do in the films, and whispering, 'Remember, *walls have ears!*' This was greeted with further squawks of parrot-like gaiety, and, deftly circumventing a lurking gnome, I retreated hastily down the drive.

17

The Dog's Diary

I've been doing a bit of thinking lately. I like to do that now and again as it's good practice. Generally I do it in the crypt, but today I thought I'd try the belfry for a change, and do you know – it works just as well up there as it does down below! The only thing is, I was pretty fed up to find my bone bag had been interfered with. After that spot of bother with F.O.'s silly pictures I'd gone to no end of trouble to get those bones in their proper order, but when I went to check them this morning they were all muddled up again and the sack wasn't in the same place either. It had taken me ages to straighten them all out. Maurice said that he had seen F.O. and the Tubbly woman going up there – *and* Gunga Din. If I learn that it was old Fatso snuffling about with them I'll give him a right going over!

Anyway, back to my thinking. There's something a bit rum about those pictures – I don't just mean the scene in that big one with all those daft clouds and fake bones, but the reason for them being there at all. (Or, of course, *not* being there now.) When F.O. first lugged them up I didn't think much about it. After all, he does a lot of funny things which don't make sense, so I thought that putting the pictures in the belfry and not on his wall – like most human beings seem to do – was just another of those.

But then he was dead set on taking them down to that

other house where we had the nice holiday. And the funny thing is, *she* didn't hang them on her wall either. Kept the wrappings on and shoved them up to a spare room, just like F.O. did. And then there was that man who brought them to the vicarage in the first place. He's someone else who can't have wanted them on his wall – otherwise why would he have bothered to bring them to F.O.? It's as if they are all playing that party game which I learnt from my other master Bowler, Pass the Parcel. It's all very queer and I shall have to do some more thinking.

Perhaps Maurice has got some ideas. On the other hand, perhaps he hasn't. Of course, he's very clever and all that, but it's a cat's cleverness. They think differently from us dogs. Still, I'll have a word with him, he's bound to have something to *say* if nothing else.

O'Shaughnessy came round today and he says he's dis-covered a new playground, and the funny thing is it was F.O. who led him to it! O'Shaughnessy happened to be in his front garden doing a bit of digging under the apple tree, when he suddenly saw the vicar's head passing along the top of the hedge. So being a bit bored with the digging and wanting to stretch his legs, he thought he'd follow him and see where he was off to. He said he was careful to keep well back in case F.O. saw him and told his mistress he was on the loose again (needn't have worried, the vicar never sees a thing); and after a while they came to one of those big houses behind the High Street. F.O. traipsed up the drive and O'Shaughnessy sneaked in behind him. Well, that's what *he* says – but I've never seen that setter sneak anywhere: legs too long and feet too big!

Anyway, he says it's not a bad garden for playing Hunt the Cat in – lots of bushes and hidey-holes – and that the best thing is the masses of funny-looking stone things near the front door, masses of them! I told him I couldn't see what was so good about that. So he said, 'Ah sure, aren't they just the loveliest t'ing for a spot of leg-cocking, bejasus!'

I could see his point then, but wouldn't have thought of it on my own. He's very quick-witted, is O'Shaughnessy. He is going to take me there in a couple of days when his mistress is safely at the hairdresser's. She spends hours there so he won't be missed, and we are going to have a competition to see how many of those things we can spray in the shortest time. I'm pretty good at that sort of thing – what you might call a champion pee-er. So I think O'Shaughnessy may have met his match there ... Shan't warn him of course. No fleas on Bouncer!

18

The Cat's Memoir

Despite visitations from F.O.'s superior – an inane person-age by name of Clinker – the vicarage had been going through one of its rare periods of calm and I had enjoyed the unaccustomed luxury. But all good things come to an end, and living with the vicar they tend to end sooner rather than later. Mrs Tubbly Pole and the idiot bulldog had been held at bay for a time, but I surmised that that particular benison could not last and, as so often, I was proved right.

They appeared together one evening just as I was settling down to my pre-prandial saucer of milk, and in the ensuing mêlée the bowl was upset and my nerves put on edge. Mine were not the only ones to suffer, as I noticed that F.O. had started one of his twitching bouts and for a brief moment I felt a measure of sympathy. However, it doesn't do to indulge humans too much, they take advantage; so I was careful not to show undue concern. Luckily the three of them soon set off in the direction of the belfry tower leaving me to the remnants of my evening's rest.

An hour later he returned – mercifully alone – but in a parlous condition of pique and self-pity. Somehow he had contrived to gash his leg (he has always been clumsy) and spent the next half-hour lurching and cursing in what I can only describe as a most unseemly way. Anybody else would have had bandages to hand, neatly coiled in a first-aid box and set aside for just such an emergency. Not of course the vicar. Much energy was expended in blundering around the house pulling out drawers and staring into cupboards in the vain hope that some medical supplies would emerge. Naturally none did, and eventually he settled for a large tea-towel and a brandy. It was all very trying.

The next morning was worse, as by that time the leg had stiffened up and he had taken to hobbling around with a walking stick and emitting loud groans of histrionic agony. I observed to Bouncer that I thought our master was hardly one to win the prize for stoical fortitude, only to be asked what prize was I talking about and who was Fortescue? It is sometimes trying for a cat of my calibre to be placed in the midst of such feebleness and ignorance.

The dog has been in high spirits lately, engrossed in some harebrained venture involving O'Shaughnessy. The latter has discovered the garden belonging to that Carruthers woman, plus her array of nauseous gnomes. Naturally, I have been familiar with the place for some time, making it my business to be acquainted with all gardens in the neighbourhood; and strolling in hers is not uncongenial – always providing, of course, one avoids the porch area. However, I do not always reveal my haunts to Bouncer. As in most things, one needs to preserve a modicum of distance and privacy. Alas, thanks to O'Shaughnessy those conditions can no longer be found in the Carruthers domain. But fortunately there are other patches in Molehill affording contemplative seclusion, and in which, without a gnome in sight, one is assured safe refuge from the gross.

From what I can gather, the two of them have devised a game which entails a contest using the gnomes as lamp-posts: a puerile exercise, but mildly diverting nonetheless.

Indeed, I have told Bouncer that should he succeed in out-spraying the setter I will stand sentry for him when next he is foraging for ham bones in Mavis Briggs's pantry. Now and again it is good to show the dog what graciousness is all about.

He is very excited at the prospect of the game and talks endlessly of 'my peeing prowess' and has embarked on a training regime in the graveyard. Latterly our visits there have not coincided so one has been spared the spectacle, but I gather it involves a lot of racing about from grave to grave and much squirting from different heights and angles. He tells me that during one of these sessions he encountered F.O. – not I think on the same mission – and that the vicar seemed very impressed by his performance. I rather doubt this as our master is not known for his powers of observation. And besides, from what *I* have observed, he seems to be heavily occupied with some matter quite other than Bouncer and his bladder. What it is I don't know, but rather suspect it may relate to those tedious pictures he was getting so obsessed about. I fear there may be further ructions in store . . . In rash moments, which are fortunately few, the thought strikes me that life in the household of my late mistress was marginally less fraught than in the vicarage!

19

The Vicar's Version

It was, I suppose, ludicrous to imagine that the matter of Nicholas's booty could be dealt with in so simple a way. That I could offload it on Primrose with never a thought for consequence was, to quote my father, 'an inanity of the first water'. But panic and Mrs Tubbly Pole were a formidable force and had induced an action which in normal circumstances would have been seen for the absurdity it was. At the time, however, it had seemed the obvious solution, and for several weeks afterwards I was able to pursue my parish duties unencumbered by fear of complication, let alone exposure. My father's voice intoning 'cloud-cuckoo-land' again assails my memory.

It was Monday morning, and after the rigours of Sunday I was enjoying a leisurely breakfast, when I received the telegram. This was an event which even in those days was an increasing rarity, and as I took it from the boy I guessed it could only be from Primrose.

In her youth my sister had eschewed both telephone and writing pad in favour of this particular form of communication. Its gnomic brevity and unlooked-for arrival seemed to fit in with her natural bias to secrecy and flair for the dramatic. During her days at the Courtauld the advent of the little yellow envelopes with their curt demands for money or provisions, or announcing her imminent arrival with escort in tow – invariably unsuitable – had been a source of continuing harassment to my parents. In later life, though more amenable to the conventional mode of telephone and writing paper, she would still occasionally resort to the theatrical. Thus it was with a certain wariness that I slit open the envelope and unfolded its missive. It read as follows: ALL IS UNCOVERED STOP ARE YOU MAD QUESTION MARK TELEPHONING IMMEDIATELY STOP YOUR SISTER STOP

I leaped from the table, and pausing only to discard my egg-stained napkin, rushed from the house. Maurice was in the hall, and in my flight I must have trodden on his tail as there was an outraged howl of fury. But the cat's pain was nothing compared to mine should I be forced to listen to Primrose's voice demanding explanation for the Spendler monstrosities! Distance from the telephone was essential: time to think imperative.

I made my way to the graveyard, where in the lee of a convenient tomb I desperately lit cigarettes and crunched humbugs. The combination of peppermint and nicotine had the desired effect and after a while I was able to assemble some degree of coherent thought.

Obviously Primrose's curiosity (which had seemed so quiescent when I delivered the pictures) had got the better of her, and without any advance warning she had entered the attic and quite calculatedly opened them up. I was peeved to think of this flagrant infringement of privacy, but reflected that Primrose had always been cavalier in her treatment of my possessions, recalling in particular the incident of my kitbag during the war.

Home on leave once, I had casually dumped it in the hall, only to find it two hours later brazenly ransacked for chocolate, nylons, Lucky Strikes, or anything else my sister could lay her predatory hands upon. What had really rankled was the fact that Mother was convinced that the resulting mess of debris and discarded underclothes was something of my doing! Needless to say, by then Primrose had swept herself off for the evening to a dance at the local Officers' Mess and I was left to carry the can . . .

Puffing and crunching, I leant against the tombstone brooding on the petty injustices of family life. But the memory was soon eclipsed by the current more urgent dilemma: how to keep Primrose at bay or at least quiet, and above all what precisely to do with the wretched paintings.

Returning them to Nicholas was not an option. In no respect could I risk provoking his displeasure. One good turn deserves another, and the turn he had done me by colluding in my story to the police was a crucial factor in my continuing safety. Should he feel short-changed in that tacit contract of mutual help things could get exceedingly nasty. I reflected wryly that were I a character in one of Mrs Tubbly Pole's novels I would doubtless set off smartly for Brighton and cut his throat. However, despite my unfortunate experience with Elizabeth Fotherington, I am of a squeamish disposition and one dispatch in a lifetime is more than enough. So what to do?

As I smoked and brooded I could see Bouncer in the distance. He was trundling around the graves in an abstracted sort of way, and then suddenly seemed to be galvanized into brisk activity, bounding from headstone to headstone in a flurry of urgent speed. I watched, surprised by this sudden change of tempo, but was even more curious to note that a tremendous amount of urinating seemed to be going on and that his left back leg barely touched the ground. Had he developed a sudden kidney infection? A gallstone perhaps? I hoped not as it would mean all the chore and drama of a visit to the vet. He had seemed perfectly all right earlier on, and in any case why the frantic pace? Racing helter-skelter from one stone to another he looked in the peak of health!

I gazed absorbed by these antics and reflected vaguely that there was something about the dog which had never really added up. His sudden and dishevelled appearance in the middle of my sitting room two weeks after his master had absconded with the bank's funds had itself been peculiar. Where had he come from? How had he got into the house? Why hadn't the cat protested? And in any case, why choose me? It was a mystery which I had never fathomed. Even more of a mystery, and considerably more unsettling, had been the matter of those appalling bones in the music stool ... and then of course the sinister incident of the cigarette lighter (which even now can haunt my dreams).* Was that too connected with him? I didn't know and hardly liked to think.

Eventually he stopped, saw me, and came trotting over. He was wagging his tail and baring his teeth in that lop-sided leer that passes for a grin. He looked pleased with himself, though quite why was not clear. However, a congratulatory pat seemed in order, and he settled down beside me, breathing heavily. After a moment and with a sort of torpid grunt he dropped off to sleep – worn out presumably by the urinary exertions. I returned my thoughts to Primrose and the paintings.

Other than taking the telephone off the hook there was no escaping her, and even that would only be a temporary respite. Sooner or later, and doubtless sooner, heated confrontation would occur. How on earth should I play it? I stared at the grass and listened disconsolately to Bouncer's snores.

After a while the obvious struck me: the injured inno-cent. That was it. Deny all knowledge, express indignation that I should be so duped, should be the victim of such a dastardly imposition. (Some truth there after all!) Would she believe me? Probably not. Primrose is of a sceptical nature – especially for some reason where I am concerned. But there was no alternative and I should have to brazen it out.

Of course, she was bound to demand what sort of friend it was who had had the gall to involve me in that way (let

* See *A Load of Old Bones*

alone the nerve to intercept the pictures in the first place), but there I could maintain a stoutly loyal silence. Hadn't some writer once said that given the choice between betraying his friend or his country he would choose the latter? Well, substitute 'art world' for 'country' and it still might persuade. With those thoughts in mind I prodded Bouncer and returned to the vicarage braced for the barrage.

Eight o'clock and the barrage commenced. I had made the necessary preparation by consuming two double whiskies and was thus moderately armed to withstand the first salvo. It came hurtling down the line with the force of a torpedo, and to one less fortified might have proved fatal. But gallantly I stood my ground, gripped the receiver, and fixing Maurice with unflinching eye said, 'Frankly, Primrose, what you are saying is utter nonsense!'

The words had a ring of familiarity and I realized that down the years I had heard many a similar thing from Primrose herself. Whether she recognized her own words I do not know, but it seemed to do the trick as there was a sudden and surprising silence. With no time to waste I launched into my defence, assuring her that I had never unwrapped the pictures and knew nothing of their significance, was at a loss to know why my friend had taken such liberties, and that of course I had had no intention of using her attic as anything but the most fleeting repository etc., etc.

Despite the whisky I had some difficulty in sustaining the bravado, and as I went on I could hear my tone trailing off into its usual diffidence. For some reason this had a defusing effect and her voice took on a more conciliatory note.

'Well, it's all very well your saying that, Francis, but what on earth is one going to do? I mean, those paintings are rubbish, we all know that – at least anyone with a ha'porth of sense does – but they *are* famous and for some ridiculous reason absurdly valuable. You *must* get this so-called friend to take them back.'

'I don't think he's in the country at the moment,' I murmured, 'and I've no idea when he'll be home, and in the meantime I can hardly shop him!'

'Why not?'

'Er – well, you know, old friends and all that . . .'

'Old friends my foot! He has used you, Francis, in the most flagrant way and you're under no obligation to shield blackguards!' This time it was my mother's voice I could hear.

'He's not really a blackguard, at least not entirely – quite nice sometimes – but anyway, you know Pa always said we should be loyal to our pals.'

'Yes, but Daddy didn't always talk a lot of sense; and besides, in this case he's a funny kind of pal. Still, you being a parson and all that – I suppose you think differently from most normal people. Really Francis, we'll have to think of something!'

Wonderful! I had an ally. That 'we' was a sure triumph! Even merited a third Scotch. But I suddenly started to feel a little tired and unsteady, and pleading a headache asked Primrose if we could continue the conversation in the morning. She concurred, saying that in the meantime she would give thought to the matter and devise a strategy. Sometimes, I mused, having an older sister – even one as bossy as Primrose – could be an advantage.

20

The Vicar's Version

Primrose's idea of a 'strategy' turned out to be nothing more than the proposal that she should return the pictures to me forthwith. As a means to getting me off the hook with Ingaza, Interpol, the press, and the Church authorities, this struck me as being less than imaginative. I pointed out reproachfully that during our earlier telephone conversation she had appeared to show a constructive interest in her brother's plight. To which she responded that it was not so much my plight as her own which was of immediate concern.

I said coldly that I thought she was being a trifle selfish, and that she had certainly intimated a greater co-operation the previous evening.

'Perhaps. But there's been a development since then,' she replied darkly.

'What sort of development?'

'Haven't you read your *Times* this morning?'

'No,' I answered irritably. 'I have a busy parish to run and unlike those of more *artistic* pursuits do not have the time to read the papers until much later in the day.'

There was a snort of laughter, and then down the line came a thin sing-songy voice, 'High horse! High horse!' A good thirty-five years fell away and we were back in the playroom again.

'It's all very well for you –' I started.

'No, Francis. It is not all very well for me. I suggest you *do* look at the paper, busy or not!'

I told her I didn't have it to hand and would she please explain what she meant.

'If you check the arts page you'll see an item on your Spendlers. Apparently the latest view among those who are supposed to know about such things is that the paintings never left the country at all, and that far from being in America or wherever, they are being harboured on the south coast. There's some dealer with a foreign name who keeps insisting they're bound to be abroad, but the police and some of the specialists are convinced they're being fenced down here. In fact – and this is the really worrying thing – even Lewes is mentioned. Things are far too close for comfort!'

It was a tiresome coincidence admittedly (and I could well imagine Nicholas still trying to divert attention overseas), but I felt that Primrose was being unduly apprehensive. After all, the police had no grounds for turning up on her doorstep out of the blue.

'Don't be so dense, Francis. I have some small reputation in Sussex art circles and often give interviews, talks etc. You know how quickly the police put two and two together and make six. They tar all artists with the same brush and are convinced that we operate a sort of freemasonry and are in cahoots with the underworld. They're bound to come sniffing round asking questions, "following lines of enquiry" or whatever they say they do. I can't afford the risk. There's no question about it: you'll have to fetch them back!'

Having recently become acquainted with police methods via my interrogators March and Samson, I saw what she meant, but nevertheless was exasperated by the dramatizing paranoia and felt she was being unnecessarily harsh.

'Oh, come on, Prim,' I pleaded, 'they won't come near you! And nobody would ever think of raiding *your* attic.'

'Or yours!' she snapped.

I knew I was losing the fight but had one desperate card up my sleeve: bribery. Primrose is not short of a penny – largely through the ruthless marketing of her sheep and church scenes – but she has always had an interest in hard cash and this was where it might just work to my advantage.

'Tell you what,' I said, 'why don't I buy four of your pictures?' – adding generously, 'At the proper going rate of course. They'd be ideal for auctioning at our Spring Bazaar!'

'Six.'

'*Six!*'

'Absolutely. And I would want forty-nine per cent commission on each sale.'

I sighed. 'That's a bit steep, isn't it?'

'Not half as steep as expecting your poor sister to hide your ill-gotten gains.'

I was about to protest that they were hardly *my* gains, but thought better of it. It would only stir further curiosity re the lender.

'All right then,' I agreed reluctantly, 'a bargain.'

That settled, she became quite bright and animated, making suggestions as to which ones would be the most suitable, and asked if I would like to go down to Sussex to make a selection.

'No,' I said wearily. 'Just send the bloody things . . .'

A victory but a tediously pyrrhic one. Tough on my pocket, further clutter in the vicarage, but above all no real solution to the underlying problem: how to dispose of the wretched Spendlers once and for all! Goodness only knew how long Nicholas intended leaving them in my 'safe hands'. And as for Primrose, despite our bargain there was no guarantee that she wouldn't change her mind – or ask for more money. People could be so unreliable!

I lit a cigarette and turned to the *Times* arts page. Yes, the article was there all right, prominently displayed in the first column. It was even accompanied by a photograph of the larger of the two paintings, the so-called *Dead Reckoning*. In black and white the thing looked less gruesome than when I had encountered it in the belfry but, if anything, more dismal. There was the usual gush about metaphysical angst and interior plasticities, and much was made of the artist's brooding sensibility. I bet he was brooding – gnashing his dentures over the loss of a nice little money-spinner! Still, I reflected wryly, it was bound to be insured; and in any case, with all the publicity he was probably raking it in.

Primrose had been right about the speculation regarding their whereabouts. Apart from the lone voice of Nicholas still stubbornly insisting they were abroad, the general consensus was that they were indeed somewhere in the locality of the south coast. It wasn't clear how that assumption was arrived at, but presumably there must have been a tip-off when they were first stolen. Nicholas, one step ahead of the field as usual, had been quick to think of sober Molehill (none of that Brighton raffishness up here!), and it occurred to me that by now I was doubtless featuring in his list of 'useful' contacts. That list had been helpful during my own troubles the previous summer, but little had I thought that one day I should be among its members.

I wandered into the sitting room, sat down at the piano and morosely embarked on the Dead March from *Saul*. This is one of Bouncer's favourites, and sure enough, I had only gone a few bars into the piece when there was a draught from the hallway and I saw his woolly head appear round the door. He was carrying his rubber ring which he deposited at my feet and then sat down solemnly beside the music stool. In his way he is a companionable animal, and for a brief while pianist and listener became lost in the peace of their own harmonies.

Maurice put an end to that; or rather he *and* Mrs Tubbly Pole. Just as I had reached one of the quieter passages I heard a familiar noise – Maurice's wail of affronted rage. But it seemed to be accompanied by another sound, a sort of throaty, scolding obbligato, and I realized that some human intrusion was imminent. There was a crash from the porch and another howl of indignation from the cat. Going into the hall I encountered Mrs Tubbly Pole already halfway through the front door. That was a surprise in itself, but even more of a shock was the fact that she was clutching Maurice to her bosom. Since his arrival at the vicarage nobody apart from myself had ever had the temerity to pick him up, and judging from his expression the shock was not confined to me.

'Ah, Francis,' she boomed, 'I was just passing and saw your dear old moggy loitering in the porch. He obviously wanted to get in, so thought I'd give him a helping hand – though can't say he seems to appreciate it much!'

'Very kind of you,' I said, hastily wresting the cat from her grasp and thrusting him into the kitchen, 'but actually he often hangs about in the porch. It's sunny there and he likes chasing the flies, and when he's had enough he uses the pet flap at the back door.'

'Oh well, it's the thought that counts as they say ... Anyway, now that I'm here you may as well get the low-down on my latest plot. I've invented a marvellous twist to the main theme. You'll be thrilled when you hear it!'

I couldn't recall many thrills in my life and very much doubted whether Maud Tubbly Pole was going to add to them. However, I smiled benignly and tried to look interested.

'You remember my telling you I was going to transpose the corpse from the wood to the belfry?' I nodded wanly.

112

'Well, that's not the only way the original scenario is going to change!' (What on earth could she or anyone else know about that original ghastly scenario!)

'Really? What do you have in mind?'

'The stolen Spendler paintings! I'm going to put them in the belfry along with the body, the ideal place! Don't you think that tying up the two cases in one novel is quite masterly? Plenty of topical appeal *and* ingenuity!' She grinned from ear to ear, almost executing a war dance of triumph, while I stared dumbstruck . . .

It seemed the right moment to invite her to sit down: my own legs were feeling distinctly weak and some sort of physical support was a matter of urgency. We repaired to the sitting room where – rather ungallantly, I recall – I was the first to slump down on the sofa. Fortunately, such was her delight in the feat of her own invention that she appeared not to notice this, or indeed what must have been my look of quivering horror.

But then, realizing she wasn't getting quite the appreciative response expected, she exclaimed, 'You do *know* which pictures I am talking about, don't you?'

'Er – yes, I think so,' I replied vaguely.

'Of course you do! The case has been in the papers for weeks. Quite a little mystery. Though I must say I think the fuss is excessive – they look a dreary pair from the photographs, not at all my cup of tea. Still, linking them with the Fotherington mystery will sell my novel all right. You mark my words!' I did, and shuddered.

'And talking of tea,' she continued, 'what about a glass of something?'

In trance-like state I arose dutifully, fetched the bottle and cast around for a lemon. Settled once more on the sofa, I said the first thing that came into my head. 'Where's Gunga Din? He'll miss his evening tipple.'

'Oh, don't worry about him,' she replied airily. 'We were at a bridge party earlier on and he overdid things rather – bit of a greedy boy sometimes! I've left him at home to sleep it off.' I felt a pang of envy, wishing that I could be doing the same, and preferably far away.

'Anyway, my dear Francis, at the moment we've got better things to do than talk about Gunga Din. I need to pick your brains . . .'

Dear God! I thought.

21

The Vicar's Version

Having my brains picked by Mrs Tubbly Pole was, as I had feared, a grisly business – not least because she was still hell-bent on my accompanying her to Foxford Wood. She said she wanted to have a 'good rootle around' and to 'feel the emanations', and that though she was not now going to have the body found there, a close encounter with the original murder scene would help stimulate the imaginative process. Naturally I ducked and weaved all I could, listing a whole series of pressing duties which would, alas, prevent my being her escort. Indeed, I was quite impressed by the busy schedule I had managed to fabricate in so short a space. But not so Mrs Tubbbly Pole.

'Hmm. That sounds pretty tedious. And all the more reason to take time off and help me in my project. Much more fun! Besides, we could always unleash the monsters.'

'Monsters!' I exclaimed. 'What monsters?'

'The dogs of course: my Gunga and your Bouncer. It will make a nice little outing for them.'

Surely I hadn't staked all just to provide an afternoon's outing for an obese bulldog and a manic mongrel! The woman was impossible!

I cleared my throat and tried other prevarications. To no avail. The scarlet Smythson engagement diary was snapped open, and I was clearly expected to produce something similar. Unearthing a tattered Church calendar, I scanned it with furrowed brow, sighing heavily over the evidently filled dates. She was undeterred.

'After lunch, Sunday afternoon,' she declared briskly. 'You're always free then: the vicar's snoozing hour, if I'm not mistaken. Well, you'll just have to miss it for once; a walk will be much better for you!' And she emitted a back-slapping laugh. I smiled feebly.

The Roman Catholics have a special saint allocated to Hopeless Cases – St Jude, I believe – and I wondered vaguely whether I shouldn't start making overtures in that direction; but on second thoughts felt the challenge a trifle unfair.

The 'outing' settled, she proceeded to regale me with the twists and turns of the projected novel; and despite the delicacy of my own situation I have to admit to being drawn into its convoluted plot. Though unsettling, it was certainly clever the way she had linked the two cases, and in other circumstances I might have been entertained. However, as she continued with her train of outlandish invention, thoughts of those carefully secreted pictures and the too familiar settings of wood, fields, and now belfry, pressed in upon me with a stifling weight. Her fiction was wild yet the relevance uncanny. Despite its ridiculous and lurid inaccuracies, the tale was far too close for comfort! I started to fidget but there was no release.

Slurping her drink and chortling happily, she went on to ask my opinion of the Spendlers: where they might be, how it had been done, how many persons did I think were involved; and then inevitably . . . what was my particular slant on the Fotherington case and that 'unfortunate parishioner of yours'. It was a nightmarish hour, and by the time she had finished my nerves were shot to pieces. One thing was decided though: on no account would I accompany her to Foxford Wood! The 'monsters' would have to forfeit their outing.

* * *

116

The next day Primrose's sheep pictures arrived. A fairish exchange, I supposed – the essential thing being that, technically at any rate, I was no longer 'in possession'. Fortunately they were considerably smaller than the Spendlers, but even so it was tiresome having to find somewhere to store the six of them, and I had no intention of trying the belfry again. Eventually I managed to clear a space in the recess behind the piano, and stacked them against the wall. They were not exactly my favourite articles, being hard on the pocket and intrusive in my home, but I comforted myself with the thought that at least they had a fund-raising use. As such they could certainly cover the costs of the belfry's shattered floorboard, and probably the loose organ seat that Tapsell was always whingeing about. And while on the subject, wasn't it time for an electric fire in the pulpit? All very well dispensing warmth and comfort to the congregation but what about the ice-bound vicar!

As I dwelt on that cheering possibility and debated whether a two-bar model would be excessive, I noticed an envelope on the floor addressed in Primrose's writing. She must have stuck it to part of the packing paper and it had become detached as I was propping the things in the alcove. Perhaps it was to say that she had reconsidered her absurd conditions and was suggesting a reduced commission, or better still, a cut in the fee. Vain thoughts. The note simply confirmed the terms of the deal with a curt request to send my cheque (plus the extra for the delivery charge) at my earliest convenience. I sighed in exasperation. Early or late, it was far from convenient! She would just have to wait. But as I was gauging how long I could delay settlement before incurring further demands, I noticed she had added a scrawled PS:

'Have just re-read that *Times* article about the Spendlers, and the name Ingaza rings a distinct bell. Wasn't that the name of that awful friend of yours at the St Bede's place – the one who all the fuss was about? Seem to remember it being said at the trial that he had "delicate tendencies". Wholly *in*delicate I should say! Brighton's not so far from Molehill, so I just hope you're not consorting with him again. A very suspect character, Francis. Highly dodgy, as Daddy would say!'

I wrote the cheque immediately; thanked her profusely for the paintings, discoursed eloquently on the realism of her sheep, admired the chiaroscuro effects on the church architecture, and made no reference to Nicholas. The last thing I wanted was Primrose pursuing that particular line of enquiry! With cash in hand and ego massaged, she might find the subject of waning interest. I fervently hoped so.

Somehow, dealing with the pictures and settling Primrose's account had imposed quite a strain, and I felt that a quiet potter in the church might put me in a less jaded frame of mind. It was nearing lunchtime and I judged that there would be few people about, so with luck I could enjoy its cloistered calm uninterrupted.

As I had hoped, the building was empty; and with the shafts of the noonday sun dappling the transept and stroking the tombs of the three chain-mailed warriors, it presented a scene of slumbering serenity. The polishers had been at work earlier in the day; and as I strolled towards the Lady Chapel savouring the whiff of the beeswaxed pews, I paused to admire the gleaming candlesticks in the chancel, the freshly scrubbed flagstones, and the angel faces shining out from the frieze on the lectern. It had to be admitted that, tiresome though they often were, Edith Hopgarden and her cohorts of cleaners did a remarkably good job in preserving both the aura and odour of St Botolph's modest sanctity. Perhaps the next issue of the newsletter should include a note of commendation ...

I settled in one of the pews and tried to work out how I could best phrase the compliments without further encouraging Edith's firm conviction that she was indispensable – which of course she was. And then, unwrapping a peppermint from my pocket, I began to think of other things, of this and that . . . and then of *that*. I flinched, shut my eyes, and pondered the final lines of the Herrick poem which I had selected for Elizabeth's Memorial Anthem:

> I write of Hell; I sing (and ever shall)
> Of Heaven, and hope to have it after all.

All very well for Herrick, I reflected. His confidence was touching, but our situations were hardly analogous. I continued to sit with my eyes closed . . .

Suddenly there was an almighty crash, followed by an anguished shriek. The sounds came from the organ loft. I leaped up, startled out of my wits and angry at the unwanted intrusion. Dead silence. Scowling upwards I could see nothing, and nothing stirred. And then, barely discernible, there was the faintest sound of furtive whisperings, followed by a pause and the creaking of a floorboard. Some damn-fool choirboys larking about? It was too bad! Anyway, what were they doing at that time of day? Surely it wasn't half-term yet. I cleared my throat irritably, ready to make stern enquiry. However, before I could say anything, a head appeared gingerly over the loft railing. It was Tapsell's.

Given the location, I suppose the organist's presence was unremarkable, but sensing he was not alone I groaned inwardly. Surely to God they were not at it *again*, and not here of all places! It had been embarrassing enough in the wood a few months earlier. More really, for then I had had the difficulty of explaining my own presence, whereas now no such explanation was required. Still, it was a bit much!

Red-faced, Tapsell craned over the rail and in accusing tones cried, 'Look here, now see what's happened – this seat's completely had it! I've been telling you about it for weeks. Should have been seen to ages ago!' There was a scuffling behind him which I took to be Edith adjusting her hat or whatever else needed attention.

I gave a wintry smile and observed acidly that perhaps his organ practice was becoming a trifle too enthusiastic of late and that those old seats couldn't always withstand the wilder flights of artistic passion. He glared down and started to bluster something, but I turned away and affected to tidy the hymn books. And then, with a casual wave of my hand, I strolled towards the south porch and out into the sunshine.

As I went I reflected that at least it solved the problem of how to write the tribute in the parish newsletter: there wouldn't be any. Edith would just have to settle for her own smug laurels!

22

The Cat's Memoir

'He's in a right buggers' muddle!' the dog announced.

'When isn't he?' I murmured, sipping my milk.

'Well, he hasn't been too bad for a while, Maurice, but you should see him now – doing his nut, he is! I'm jolly sure it's to do with that Tubbly person; she's been at him again. My bones tell me.'

'Your bones tell you too much, Bouncer!' I replied curtly, feeling rather sleepy and not wishing to be drawn into one of the dog's dramas.

'Oh no,' he protested, 'bones are a very good measure of what's in the wind. They tell you a lot of things, and I've got certain views about what's going on. For instance . . .' Not wishing to be subjected to Bouncer's *obiter dicta* I hastily closed my eyes and pretended to drop off to sleep. It didn't work of course, and the next moment I could feel his hot breath rasping down my ear and a cold nose on the back of my neck.

'Wake *up*, Maurice! I've been doing some of my special thinking and I've got something to say.'

'Speak,' I sighed.

'Well, you see, it's like this . . .' and his tone became earnest and confidential. 'Something or somebody – probably Tubbly – is stewing him up again over that corpse business in the woods. *Also* he's in a blue funk about those

121

old pictures: they're on his nerves. For some reason they could put him in the cart.'

'Perhaps, but he got rid of those on his sister. They shouldn't pose a problem now. And as to the corpse of my unlamented mistress – well, that's all over and done with. *We* saw to that.' I noticed a belligerent look come into his eye, and added hastily, 'Thanks to you largely.'

Mollified, he continued. 'Yes, but I've got a nasty feeling it may be brewing up again. And what with that and now this rum picture business, it's all getting on his fins.'

'Things often get on his fins,' I said, 'but he seems to survive.'

'Yes, but will *we*? That's the question. S'pose he goes funny like my old master Bowler, and does a bunk to South America or some such. Where does that leave us?'

I considered. 'Well, I suppose it might –'

'Leaves us in the cat litter. That's what!'

I stared at him coldly. 'I think you might moderate your turn of phrase.'

'Turn of phrase be damned!' he barked. 'What about our skins!'

He had a point but I didn't want to look too concerned. Instead I observed coolly, 'I am sure all will be well, Bouncer. No sense in crossing mole traps before we meet them. Believe me, a steady head is essential in such matters. As my great uncle used to say: "Panic is the bane of self-preservation."'

'*I* am not panicking but F.O. is. And we all know what happened to your great uncle!'

As it happened, my Great Uncle Marmaduke had been shot while bravely plundering a hen-run, but I did not think it Bouncer's place to mention the fact. And taking exception to his presumption I went into one of my better sulks. This had the desired effect: got rid of the dog and gave me satisfaction and time to think.

* * *

122

Emerging from the sulk and having thought, I summoned Bouncer. He came bounding up, wagging his tail as if he hadn't a care in the world. So much for his earlier fears! Then I noticed that his chops were looking more than usually grisly, and realized that F.O. must have given him a fresh marrow bone. Food plays a key part in shaping the dog's frame of mind.

'With regard to your earlier comments,' I began, 'I do recall a conversation I happened to overhear between our master and the Tubbly Pole. It concerned a walk in Foxford Wood which she seemed keen to take him on.'

'Was he keen?' asked Bouncer.

'Distinctly reluctant, I would say.'

'That's probably it then. Just like me when I've been a bit thoughtless on the carpet: he's going to get his nose rubbed in it and doesn't like the idea. Can't face looking at the same patch.'

I nodded. 'Yes, my thoughts exactly. So to calm his nerves and bring peace to the household we must ensure that he never goes on that walk. There are two means of distraction: either we can contrive that something untoward befall Gunga Din which will fluster Mrs Tubbly and thus –'

'You mean like me savaging his bum again!' guffawed Bouncer.

'Or,' I continued patiently, '*you* affecting an illness you do not have. It's called malingering.'

'Don't care what it's called,' he growled, 'I'm not doing it – it'll mean a visit to the vet.'

'You don't mind that really,' I said. 'It's just the thought. Once you're there you generally go to sleep, or so you tell me. Besides,' I purred, 'think of the attention you're likely to get – all that petting and cosseting, and doubtless extra dollops of Muncho. Why, it will be food for old bones!'

He chewed his paw and pondered. And then gave a snort. 'Something to tell O'Shaughnessy, I suppose! He's a bit down since I beat him in the peeing game but this might cheer him up. He likes a good joke – especially if I put on a really nice show with masses of moaning and groaning and eating grass and looking mournful. You know the sort of thing!'

I knew it only too well, but was glad that the dog was entering into the spirit of the thing. With luck, Bouncer's malady would provide just the right pretext to enable F.O. to fob off the Tubbly.

Dismissing him with a winning smile, I curled up for the night well satisfied with my fertile ruse. Distantly, as I began to doze, I could hear the faint tones of Great Uncle Marmaduke miaowing his approbation . . .

23

The Vicar's Version

Sunday was fast looming and I still hadn't devised a way of getting out of the walk. Such was Mrs Tubbly Pole's tenacity that, short of an Act of God or breaking my leg, there seemed little to thwart her plans. I strummed disconsolately on the piano but it yielded no inspiration, and I dropped the lid irritably and lit a cigarette.

Bouncer was sprawled in the far corner and it was strange he hadn't set up a hullabaloo. I had used more force on the lid than intended, even startling myself. But the dog lay torpid and apparently undisturbed. I continued to grapple vainly with implausible excuses, and then as it was close to supper time shelved the matter: Bouncer tends to get agitated if he doesn't hear the sawing of the tin-opener.

I went into the kitchen expecting him to follow, but it was only when I was halfway through prising the lid off the Muncho that I noticed he wasn't there. I called his name but there was no response; and then there came a loud canine groan from the sitting room followed by a half-hearted howl. Was Maurice being bloody again? Leaving the Muncho, I hastened from the room ready to set the cat by its ears. But there was no sign of it – only Bouncer on his own, lolling about on the floor with pathetic look and rolling eye. He seemed distinctly seedy.

I tried coaxing him up and into the kitchen, but he lay firmly anchored to the carpet whimpering feebly. Perhaps thrusting some food right under his nose might perk him up. Not a success. After a few tentative mouthfuls he spat it out over my shoes, rolled over and went into what appeared to be some sort of coma.

This was high drama and I telephoned the vet immediately. Fortunately the surgery was just finishing and Robinson agreed to stop off on his way home. It was only about a ten-minute wait but it seemed an age; and in the meantime, having draped the dog in a blanket, I watched anxiously while he twitched and snuffled, apparently oblivious of everything. Maurice appeared, and wandering over to his ailing companion stared curiously, gave him a thoughtful butt with his head, and wandered out again.

By the time Robinson arrived, Bouncer's tongue was lolling out of his mouth and he looked alarmingly corpse-like.

'Good Lord!' exclaimed the vet cheerfully. 'What's wrong with him, then?'

'How should I know!' I answered irritably. 'Thought that was your brief.'

Though it was mildly reassuring to know that others could be as befogged in their calling as oneself, this did not seem a particularly useful start to proceedings. I looked on gloomily as he set about poking and prodding and doing the usual things with stethoscope and probe. The dog lay with an expression that I can only describe as stricken.

Hearing the door creak faintly, I noticed Maurice glide in once more. He hovered some yards away watching Bouncer intently, and then apparently losing interest proceeded to engage in one of his elaborate grooming sessions. He was purring – which in the circumstances struck me as tasteless. I always thought animals were supposed to share some sort of intuitive empathy. Trust the cat to buck the norm.

126

Finally Robinson knelt back on his heels, and scratching his head said in a puzzled voice, 'Can't make it out really: there don't seem to be any obvious symptoms – nose is cold, heart's all right, no lumps or tender spots on his tummy, temperature's okay. If he were human I'd say he was swinging the lead!'

'There must be something wrong,' I expostulated. 'Can't you give him anything ... pills, medicine?

'Well, I *can*,' he replied doubtfully, 'though don't suppose it'll do much good. Tell you what though, we'll try him with a sedative, that should keep him quiet.'

'But he *is* quiet!' I protested.

'Well, he'll be even quieter then, won't he.' And following that helpful observation he produced a syringe, and with a deft movement stuck it into Bouncer's haunch. The dog emitted an anguished roar.

'Lungs are in good nick anyway,' said Robinson. 'I'm off now – got a nice spot of liver and bacon for supper. Keep him warm, give him water, and any problems get on the blower. Cheerio for now!' So saying, he picked up his case, eased Maurice out of the way with the toe of his shoe, and departed into the night.

I stared down at the now loudly snoring Bouncer, wishing that I could treat my parishioners with the same cavalier bonhomie as the vet did his patients. Oddly enough, the latter invariably thrived; whereas I could never be entirely sure about my own particular flock.

The next day was Saturday, and to my relief the dog seemed more his normal self: still lethargic but certainly back on his food. Indeed, if anything he seemed more avid than usual, presumably the result of the previous day's fast. But there was still a great deal of sprawling about going on and the tail remained resolutely unwagged – an omission which in Bouncer is a sure sign of something amiss. I kept a watchful eye on him (as did Maurice, who barely left the kitchen and kept circling the dog's basket in a really rather irritating way).

Concern for the invalid had temporarily eclipsed my worry about Sunday and what Mrs Tubbly Pole was merrily calling our 'jaunt' to Foxford Wood. I still hadn't worked out an exit strategy ... And then, as I sat at the kitchen table putting the finishing touches to the next day's sermon, the obvious pretext struck me: Bouncer's malady! Clearly no one with a pet in such a perilous condition could possibly leave it all afternoon to fend for itself in an empty house. And besides, wouldn't I be far too agitated to do full justice to her fascinating sleuthing project, not knowing quite what I might find on my return home? Surely as a fellow animal lover etc., etc. ...

I sat there smoking, embroidering the fabric and pumping up the drama. (Not that the drama needed much pumping. After all, the dog had appeared only too moribund the night before.) Glancing at the victim again, I was glad to see that he was beginning to look considerably more human. But that was a detail, and getting up I marched to the telephone.

It is amazing how a few minutes of telecommunication can change one's mood so radically, inducing abject misery or wildest relief. In this case it was mercifully the latter. Maud Tubbly Pole could not have been more attentive to Bouncer's plight, advising innumerable remedies and nostrums and sending him Gunga Din's fondest wishes. Indeed, such was her solicitude that I began to feel mildly guilty about chickening out. But such scruples were short-lived, and with brisk step I went into the sitting room, sat at the piano and embarked on a loud and lavish rendering of 'Me and My Gal'. In the distance I could just detect a howl of protest from Maurice.

Sunday afternoon was bliss: service and sermon over, fire stoked, phone off the hook, a fresh packet of humbugs, crossword amenable – and *no* Tubbly Pole! What could be nicer? Even Maurice seemed in benign mood, playing ingeniously with a cotton reel while Bouncer dozed on the hearthrug. It was at moments like that when I really enjoyed being in Molehill . . . and indeed in the Church.

Of course, God's mercies are tantalizingly brief but they are very pleasant while they last. And with only the occasional parish hiccup to deal with, that particular benison lasted a good few days, after which I was sufficiently rested to face the trials inevitably in store. The first and major trial was Primrose. She had lost one of the Spendlers.

24

The Vicar's Version

'You've done what!' I cried. 'What do you mean, *lost* it?'

'Well, not exactly lost, sort of sent elsewhere ... by mistake, naturally,' she added coolly.

'Some mistake! It's a monumental cock-up! How did you do it – and which one anyway?'

'The smaller one, the one with the beach and the horse-faced youth. Most people would be only too glad to see the back of him – although,' and she giggled, 'come to think of it, with a vast behind like that, I'm not so sure!'

'Vast arse or not, this is no laughing matter. My reputation's at stake!'

'What, as vicar or fence?'

'Both – I mean neither ... Oh, for pity's sake, Primrose, be serious and kindly explain!'

She told me that she had been getting increasingly worried about having the two pictures on her premises and had decided that the safest means of concealment was disguise, i.e. to take them from their frames and slip the canvases into the backs of two of her own paintings. The larger was the problem as she didn't have a picture of comparable size but at least she could deal with the smaller one, and selecting one of the less appealing sheep scenes she shoved it into the back of that.

'Well, that's all right,' I said, 'quite a sensible idea. So what went wrong?'

She explained that her studio was becoming hopelessly cluttered and so she had removed a large number of the sketches and paintings to the attic. With a tight schedule to complete, she had been in a hurry and hadn't bothered to sort or even stack them properly, intending to do it later.

Sensing what might be coming next, I said acidly, 'So in the meantime that priceless Spendler was stuck there overlaid and cheek by jowl with all the sheep rubbish! And now I suppose you're going to tell me that in the general shambles you've shipped it off to some unknown client or gallery!'

'Gosh, Francis, just now and again you're pretty sharp! But actually you haven't got it *quite* right –'

'Why not?' I snapped.

'Well, you see, the client – or purchaser rather – is not unknown.'

'Oh? Who?'

There was a pause, and then she said quietly, 'I think you may know someone by the name of Gladys Clinker . . .'

The receiver dropped from my hand and I sat down heavily on the cat whose screech of horror seemed entirely commensurate with the occasion. Then taking a deep breath and groping on the desk for an Anadin, I asked her as calmly as I was able how she had come to encounter the bishop's wife.

'This large woman appeared one day in the Lewes gift shop where I flog some of my stuff. She was with a couple of others and they all had loud voices, though hers was the loudest,' (Gladys all right!) 'and after a bit of *oohing* and *aahing* over the pots and gew-gaws, she asked if by any chance I would sell her three or four of my things at a discount. Said something about wanting to surprise her husband, and that as she was attending picture-framing classes thought they might also come in handy for practising on. Wasn't too keen on that last part – a bit cheeky,

131

I thought! But four pictures in one go, even with a discount, is quite a haul, so naturally I sold them to her.'

'Naturally,' I said wearily.

'It was only when I got home that I realized the hidden Spendler was among them; and after checking the name and address on the invoice, recognized she must be the wife of that bishop you're always cursing. Small world, isn't it!'

Ignoring the last observation, I told her that her negligence had placed me in an appalling position and I felt deeply wounded by one I had supposed an ally. An apology was surely forthcoming.

'Apology be damned! I've gone to considerable lengths for you and it's been distinctly troublesome. After all, *I* never wanted the things here in the first place. And frankly, Francis dear, if you ever again refer to my sheep as being rubbish I shall lose the other Spendler as well!' I sighed. She would too.

It was a facer all right, and I sat down soberly, trying to concoct some plan of action, even taking up pencil and notepad in the hope that by committing ideas to paper they might look vaguely feasible. This could have been helpful had there been any ideas to commit. As it was, I sat there blankly, chewing the pencil and once more cursing Nicholas. Ten minutes later the telephone rang again. Perhaps it was Primrose in more penitent frame of mind.

It was Primrose all right, but far from penitent and exceedingly angry.

'Do you realize,' she commenced icily, 'the danger this has put *me* in? If that frightful woman starts hacking around with those frames the Spendler will be exposed and *I* shall be required to provide an explanation! Should that occur I shall have no hesitation in explaining that it had been passed to me by my brother, the vicar of Molehill.'

'Ah,' I said.

'Is that all you've got to say?'

'Er . . . for the moment, yes.'

'Well, let me put a few words into your mouth,' she seethed. 'How about, "Yes, Primrose, I will do my level best to prise the painting out of that woman's hands before it is too late. And failing that, should you be hauled before the High Court I will solemnly swear to take the rap for everything and tell the world that Primrose Oughterard is a woman of unimpeachable probity."'

'Yes, yes, yes . . .' I said, tired of the drama and rather badly wanting a restorative. There came a further shell blast from the other end and then the line went dead. I took the receiver off the hook.

It was not one of my better nights, and the following morning was hardly helped by an unexpected visit from the rector of St Hilda's of the adjoining parish. I don't dislike Theodore Pick and he has done me a few good turns in the past, not least by lending me his curate, Barry, when I was forced to make that fateful trip to Sussex with the paintings. However, there is something about Pick which dampens the spirits and weakens the sinews. He is perfectly civil, and it is difficult to understand why he should have this effect, but I know that I am not the only one who experiences a distinct lowering of temperature in his presence. Indeed, I recall Rummage at some conference observing that 'old Theo' was the last person from whom you could expect a good *pick*-me-up! I am always loath to agree with Basil Rummage about anything, but in this particular case I think he was right.

Anyway, Pick appeared just as I was finishing my last slice of toast. He was still in his cassock from early service, and with his beaky nose and furrowed brow had the air of a careworn raven.

'Hope you can get rid of these,' he announced dolefully, thrusting a bunch of leaflets into my hands, 'flyers for our Spring Fête. It's some centenary or other and we've got to put on a good show. Need all the numbers we can get – *and* helpers,' he added pointedly.

I gave a wan smile. 'You'd like me to come along, would you? Help with the teas or something?'

'Exactly!' he replied. 'That would be most useful, Francis. Thought I could rely on you to put a shoulder to the wheel!' (As if I hadn't got enough wheels of my own to shoulder!) 'The problem is finding something new to offer – one gets so tired of the Mothers' Union hammering their tambourines all over the place and Major Pegley doing his impressions of an Indian snake charmer . . . Don't suppose you've got any ideas, have you?'

I told him my mind was like kapok that morning but I would alert him should inspiration strike. He sighed heavily. 'Oh well, I suppose we shall get through it, we generally do. At least the bishop is coming which is something, though I fear *Mrs* will be accompanying him – as usual. Think she said she'd be bringing a picture for the White Elephant stall. Much help that'll be!'

The word 'picture' struck a Pavlovian chill of fear, but I nodded sympathetically and enquired casually what sort of picture and did it have any sheep in it.

'*I* don't know. Why on earth should it have sheep? Anyway, does it matter? It's all junk and never raises more than a pittance! . . . Matter of fact, I think she said something about finding it stuck behind another canvas – it's some beach scene or other – but she's always spouting garbage, I never listen to the woman. One thing's for certain, it's not going to help my fête get off the ground!' And producing more leaflets from the folds of his cassock and dropping them on the table, he took his leave and flapped mournfully down the path.

After he had gone I lit a cigarette and brooded. The news was dire. Thanks to Gladys's framing zeal, the Spendler's fate was problematic to say the least. Given its artistic awfulness this wouldn't have mattered a jot, despite the high price. But if Nicholas Ingaza were to forfeit a nice fat pay-off on account of my negligence, it would not just be the picture's fate that hung in the balance! Recalling our days at St Bede's, I remembered how firmly he had embraced the principle of *quid pro quo* and how those less scrupulous in their adherence to the code had suffered accordingly. Were he now to feel my *quid* had short-changed his *quo* I suspected that things could get more than bumpy! The spectre of the forest glade with its in-criminating binoculars danced before my eyes,* and I shuddered.

Besides, quite apart from the Nicholas angle, supposing the thing were recognized anyway? The excitement would be intense, questions asked, trails pursued. The Clinkers would be interviewed, Primrose traced ... the vicar of Molehill arrested. I sat sick with fear as the awesome pos-sibilities crowded into my mind. If they started investigat-ing my part in the picture theft, what *else* might they not uncover! Despite the room's warmth, I felt cold and my hands clammy with fear. Limbs numbed, imagination horribly active, I sat staring at the mantelpiece and the photograph of my father, whose large cigar and com-placent expression did little to assuage the mounting panic. I turned my gaze to the dozing dog; and calming a little, reflected that at least I knew where the thing was, who had it and where it was currently destined. Knowledge is power. How to exercise it? Letting an hour elapse to allow him time to reach home, I dialled the number of the Reverend Theodore Pick.

'I say, Pick,' I began, beaming down the telephone, 'I've been thinking about your fête and would be more than happy to man the White Elephant stall, I rather enjoy that sort of thing – if nobody else has offered of course.'

* See *A Load of Old Bones*

135

'Who on earth would offer?' he intoned grimly. 'Surprised you don't want the tombola, people seem to like it for some reason. Still, far be it from me to question a gift horse . . . Thanks, Oughterard, you're on!' I was about to replace the receiver when he added, 'I tell you what would be really good, if you could organize a coachload from Molehill to help swell the numbers. I don't trust my lot. It's a Saturday and they'd as soon be at the cinema or the races as support their parish fête. Bound to be a poor turn-out. Probably rain anyway.'

Always the optimist, Pick. 'Of course,' I cried gaily. 'No problem at all. Molehill will be there, you can count on us!'

I would pledge him anything if it meant I could secure that White Elephant stall and pip the other beggars to the post!

25

The Dog's Diary

Well, I can tell you, I was JOLLY GOOD, and thanks to me F.O. didn't have to go with Tubbly and be forced to loiter around the murder patch. We could see he was working himself into a lather, and that's the last thing that's needed. If he cracks we've all had it! It suits us here and if anything was to happen to our master, things could get pretty hairy! In any case, the vicar's kind and we like him. At least *I* do, though you never really know what the cat likes except for the sound of his own voice. (You'd never guess the number of instructions he kept giving me when I was dying in my basket. Made snoozing a nightmare!)

As a matter of fact, Maurice has been very civil lately. Probably impressed by my MALING thing or whatever he calls it. I know it was his idea but it was me who *did* it – just like with the cigarette lighter in the wood last year. Goes to show, I'm quite a useful dog to have around. Maurice said he overheard F.O. telling Tubbly about me being ill and why he couldn't go with her on the walk. He was perched right by the telephone and could hear her saying that Gunga Din sent me his love. I always knew bulldogs had a soppy side to them!

Anyway, this last week has been pretty good: F.O. on form and playing endlessly on that nice piano, Maurice busy with his mice (there's a new lot arrived and they haven't got the hang of him yet), and me getting extra Bonios on account of my AGUE. All in all, everyone's had a nice easy time of it, but I don't suppose it'll last – it never does. He had a phone call from that sister of his today and went as white as the cat's left paw. Something's brewing, I feel it in my bones . . .

The bones were right: he's on the pills again and crunching humbugs like some berserk rabbit with fangs. Even Maurice has noticed. That nice Mr Savage came to tune the piano this evening and I thought that might help, as his visits generally have a calming effect and put the vicar in a good mood; but it didn't work, or at least not for long.

It's bound to be something to do with those boring pictures again. Ever since that flash type from Brighton brought them here there's been trouble. It's a great pity that when Maurice and me first found them in the belfry we didn't do a nice little demolition job. With his claws and my teeth we could have buggered them up in no time and they'd be gone for ever! (O'Shaughnessy could have lent a paw as well, he'd have enjoyed that.) Still, as Maurice is given to saying, it's no use mewing over spilt milk. We'll just have to keep an eye on things, try to be *good*, and do what we can . . .

You know, after all this thinking I'm beginning to feel pretty peckish so perhaps I'll raid the pantry. In his present state he'll never notice a thing!

He did notice and now I've got a tanned backside.

26

The Vicar's Version

The next fortnight was a time of great tension and I could think of little else except the wretched painting. It was typical of Fate's law that the picture chosen by Gladys as victim for her framing practice had been the one concealing the Spendler. But why had she not recognized the thing? After all, I reflected, the case had received wide publicity with photographs appearing on the arts pages of at least two of the broadsheets. It was curious . . . Or was it? For surely my own interest had been sparked only by force of circumstance. Had I been less intimately involved I should probably have given the matter scant attention. Perhaps, like thousands of others, the Clinkers were not remotely interested in contemporary art (Gladys in particular, I suspected, being far more absorbed in reading the obituary columns and the Court Circular than dwelling on matters cultural). Yes, quite clearly they had simply overlooked the newspaper reports and had no idea of the value of their find: hence the White Elephant stall. I just prayed no one would enlighten them in the meantime!

The main thing was that I had got charge of the stall. Items were generally delivered prior to the event, and thus if all went well I could intercept the donation before the need to display it. Bolstered by that thought, my mind turned to drumming up trade and organizing a charabanc.

Local interest proved more keen than I had expected, and rallying forty people for the coach required little effort. In this respect Edith Hopgarden was unusually helpful, distributing the bulk of Pick's flyers and even designing posters coyly decorated with beribboned Easter eggs and prancing fairies (or angels – the distinction being unclear). When I congratulated Edith on her artistic endeavours she sniffed loudly and said that the embellishments were not of her doing but had been appended unsanctioned by Mavis Briggs who was beginning to fancy herself as a latter-day Leonardo. I might have guessed.

Three days before the event I had a phone call from Pick asking if there might be a spare seat in the coach on its way back to Molehill. Barry, the curate, was due for some leave starting the following Monday, and Pick had suggested he should begin it a couple of days early as soon as the fête was over. 'He lives up in Scunthorpe or Wigan – or somewhere,' he said vaguely, 'and there's an evening train from Guildford going in that direction. Failing that he'll have to wait till after the weekend as the Sunday service is hopeless. You could drop him off at the station. The sooner he gets away the better. No need for the poor fellow to hang about more than he has to.'

What Pick meant was that the sooner the curate was off his hands, the sooner he could enjoy his absence. Barry Smith's probationary stint at St Hilda's had not been an unqualified success (something of which he himself seemed happily unaware). On arrival he had been quiet, diffident and ineffectual: six months later he was still ineffectual but had grown unnervingly loud and eager. The boy's cheerfulness was endearing but it was a cheer unproductive of anything remotely useful. I was glad that he belonged to St Hilda's and not St Botolph's.

As I had surmised, the arrangement for the White Elephant stall was that items should be delivered in advance and stored in Pick's garage. On the day itself I was required to drive over a good hour before the opening to select the merchandise and set up my wares. This suited me very well for it meant that with a combination of nonchalance and sleight of hand I could appropriate the painting and surreptitiously transport it to my car without anyone being the wiser. It seemed straightforward enough and I felt relieved that the matter was at last settled. The piano began to beckon and I spent a pleasant hour reminiscing with Ellington and Cole Porter.

The Saturday was sunny but cold, and I was glad that St Hilda's fête committee had had the foresight to lay on a tent for the teas and some of the stalls. The hoopla and the tambourine players had the misfortune of being allocated a particularly draughty corner of the rectory field; but by arriving early I was able to secure a place well within the portals of the marquee.

I went to investigate Pick's garage. He had been right: there was an awful lot of junk to be accounted for and it would be quite difficult setting things up to give an illusion of enticement. Garish plastic flowers, rusting tea trays, a blue knitted giraffe with mangled ear, and an object that looked uncomfortably like some ancient truss, were some of the items which would have challenged the ingenuity of the most practised window-dresser. How on earth could such things attract attention, let alone coins! I scanned the rubbish for Gladys's picture, and seeing a large parcel wrapped in brown paper eagerly tore off its covers. What was revealed was not the anaemic youth on his sodden beach, but a mildewed tapestry of faded blooms, its frame bent and glass splintered. I was aghast. Surely even Gladys wouldn't have had the nerve to present something quite so useless! It couldn't possibly be her offering. But in which case, where on earth was it? My renewed scrabblings produced nothing. The painting simply wasn't there.

I surveyed the collection in furious disappointment, cursing Gladys for her treachery. Why promise the

141

wretched thing if she had no intention of giving it? It was too bad! In the distance I could hear the strains of the Scout band and then the fractured garglings of the loudspeaker: Pick doing his warm-up act. Gloomily I gathered up the bits and pieces and started to tote them over to the marquee and arrange them on the table. It was a rather meagre display and I felt embarrassed being associated with such a sorry collection. In fact I said as much to the stallholder next to me, an angular lady with wild hair and friendly face.

'Oh, don't worry!' she said. 'It's always like this to begin with. It's amazing how quickly the spaces fill up once they start bringing their bits in. What you've got there is only the beginning, there'll be far more junk to come!'

'But I thought the idea was for things to be delivered in advance.'

'Oh, that's the *idea*, but the system always breaks down. People never take any notice of what they're told, they just bring the stuff and dump it on you. You wait!' So conceivably there was hope yet.

Gradually people started trickling into the marquee and I assumed an expression of benign encouragement. It didn't work terribly well, but the boredom was palliated by playing the game of 'Spot the Bishop'. In fact the bishop was conspicuously absent, and as time wore on I grew more and more agitated.

Almost an hour had passed and still no sign of Clinker, let alone Gladys. And then I saw Pick approaching wearing one of his habitually harassed expressions.

'My Lord Bishop is late,' he announced acidly. 'Just telephoned. Claims he's had a puncture. More likely too busy sleeping off his lunch!' ('Or practising tiddlywinks,' I nearly said.) 'Still, it all seems to be going perfectly well without him – plenty of punters, so can't complain, I suppose . . .' and he loped off to rummage in the Lucky Bran Tub. I sighed. Confound the man. Surely he could have got Gladys to change the wheel!

A few minutes later Edith Hopgarden minced by, stopped, and cast a disdainful eye over my wares.

'I see they've given you the wooden spoon, then,' she observed with satisfaction.

'Oh, it's rather jolly,' I replied enthusiastically. 'It's fascinating guessing what people are going to buy, you know!'

'Is it?'

'Yes, it is. How's Mavis? Don't think I've seen her this afternoon.'

It was a topic she could not resist. 'Oh, she's bound to turn up! Been to one of those Art Appreciation classes in Godalming – so of course we shall all have to hear about *that*.'

'Goodness!' I exclaimed. 'Is this a new venture? I didn't know Mavis was so keen on art.'

'It is and she isn't,' Edith replied tartly.

'Oh – so why . . .?'

'Because she likes to give the impression.'

'Ah well, we all have our foibles . . .' I observed vaguely.

With a final withering look at the contents of my stall, she departed in the direction of the cake display. Needless to say no purchase had been made.

A further twenty minutes elapsed and still no sign of the Clinkers. If they didn't come soon the whole thing would be over – and what then, for God's sake! My mood grew progressively darker and it was not helped by the curate sauntering over grinning foolishly.

'Hey, that's a right load of cobblers you've got there, Francis. Not much mileage in that lot!'

I was about to retort that he could call me sir and get me a cup of tea – when out of the corner of my eye I suddenly glimpsed Gladys. She was talking volubly to anyone fool enough to listen; but other than the usual rucksack of a handbag, held nothing in her hands. Hope took another battering. Still, where there was Gladys there must also be Clinker.

I scanned the crowd. And then, out of the blue, saw him standing only a few yards away ... clutching a large square packet! Frantically hustling Barry out of the way, I adopted an air of ingratiating welcome.

'Good afternoon, Oughterard,' he boomed genially. 'Glad you're doing your bit. It's what I always like to see, parishes getting together. Spreads the load, you know. What one might call ECU-MEN-ICAL!' He chuckled.

I laughed dutifully and eyed the package. 'Is that something for the stall, sir?'

'This? Oh yes, yes ... nearly forgot. My wife sent it. Some frightful picture she dredged up. She's been doing a spot of picture framing and found this at the back of another one. Presumably the last owner had had enough of it – though I'd have thought the bin a better place! Anyway you're welcome to it, just right for your stall.' He took off the wrappers and handed it over.

I was about to place it unobtrusively against the side of the table when suddenly a familiar voice exclaimed, 'Oh my, what a striking picture! How deeply *significant*!'

Only Mavis Briggs could make an observation like that. We stared at her. 'Yes,' she continued, 'such interesting *tones*: the dark shore, the dark sea, the dark sky, the dark moon, the dark-haired young man – though I hope he's not too chilly!' And she tittered coyly. 'Then of course there's the composition – waves, rocks ... and er, pebbles,' she added vaguely. 'And, and – such *depths*!'

'Depths?' echoed Clinker blankly. 'And I suppose they're dark too!'

She smiled pensively. 'Oh yes, deeply dark ...'

Clearly the Art Appreciation classes were not adding much to Mavis's wits and I wished she would clear off. The afternoon was drawing to a close, and with mission accomplished I was eager to shut up shop and make my getaway. However, it was not to be.

'Well, if you think so much of it you'd better buy it,' said Clinker challengingly. 'Nothing's more than one-and-sixpence on this stall, and since it's the end of the day I'm sure the vicar will let you have it for a bob. Though come to think of it, I doubt if there'll be any customers for this sort of *artistry*, so you can take it with my compliments.' I shot him a furious look but he saw nothing. 'Not my sort of thing at all, glad to get rid of it, dear lady. My wife found it and . . .'

Mavis became even more animated, picked up the Spendler, and clasping it to her thin bosom exclaimed breathlessly, 'Oh, *Your Grace*, what a wonderful gift, a truly wonderful gift. My lucky day, my lucky find!' And bowing her head, she curtsied theatrically and precariously. Even Clinker had the grace to look embarrassed by his sudden elevation, and indeed so surprised by her obeisance that for one moment I thought he was going to curtsy back.

'It will have pride of place in my little cottage and fit in so well with the stampeding elephants. Are you sure you have no use for it – I mean, what about your good wife? Surely a *sensitive* picture like this is bound to delight!'

Clinker stared bleakly at the sensitive picture, contemplating the lugubrious youth with his emaciated shanks and outsize posterior, the raging seas, the desolate beach . . . 'No,' he said firmly, 'she has no use for it.'

'Well, it must be worth something,' Mavis bleated. 'And I'm sure the Church can always do with a little extra!' And so saying, she began to scrabble in her bag, eventually locating a purse from which, after further frenzied gropings, she produced a coin and thrust it into the bishop's hand. And then, clutching the picture firmly, she capered off into the thinning crowd, pink-faced and babbling.

'*Why* does she think it's sensitive?' exclaimed Clinker, staring down in wonder at the half-crown in his palm. 'And what did she mean about the elephants?'

'I have no idea, sir,' I murmured, leaden-hearted. 'You know how the ladies have their whims.'

'I do indeed!' he replied, staring balefully at the figure of Gladys in the far distance. He moved off, and I looked around wildly for Mavis thinking she might be cajoled into yielding up her prize. But she was already far ahead, gripping her trophy and tottering purposefully towards the waiting charabanc.

'Dear God, don't let her show it around!' I implored. And then looking at her companions clambering on to the bus, I decided it wouldn't really matter if she did. Festooned with thermoses and cake-stall produce, they were clearly far too engrossed in the teatime ritual to bother with the dreary daubings of Herr Spendler. In any case, as Nicholas Ingaza might have remarked, 'Couldn't tell a Spendler from a spent knitting needle!' And why indeed should they?

Nevertheless, she could not keep it – that was for certain. Nicholas would hardly be content with the return of only half his plunder. Something had to be done, and done quickly!

Thankful that I had waived my right to a lift in the coach, I left the overseeing of the return journey in the incapable hands of Barry, and sought the sanctuary of the Singer. Here I meditated – or rather, cudgelled my brains for some means of wresting the picture from its new owner. Nothing emerged, and enveloped in gloom I let in the clutch and started for home. Halfway there I overtook the coach, and through its window saw the curate standing at the front waving his arms as one possessed: presumably conducting a sing-song. I shuddered and pressed on grimly.

All in all, an abortive day. And now once more I was faced with the impossible task of retrieving the picture! Slumped on the sofa and chewing an aspirin, I stared morosely at Maurice. He returned my stare with a look of searing

146

indifference and then proceeded to groom his nether parts. No help there. From the hall came the faint sounds of the dog tackling his bone. After the previous year's fracas with the music stool, bones were supposed to be off-limits in the sitting room (a rule, needless to say, consistently flouted). He had a perfectly good basket in the kitchen for such activity but seemed to take a perverse pleasure in grappling with the things as near to the forbidden area as possible, i.e. just on the other side of the door. However, despite its guttural overtone, the noise had a certain rhythm which was oddly soporific, and worn out by the day's exertions I gradually dozed off.

I awoke to the shrilling of the telephone. To my surprise it was Savage, the piano tuner. I say 'surprise', because although I liked Savage and our random meetings had always been amicable (indeed, he had helped me out on a couple of rather crucial occasions some months earlier), we were not so close as to be on telephoning terms. He must have felt the same sense of novelty for his tone sounded guarded and apologetic.

'Ah,' he began, 'the wife's been getting on at me to give you a call. She's made some more of her fairy cakes – went a bit mad this time and the place is full of 'em. All over the shop, they are! She seems to think you could do with a batch. Don't suppose you could – could you?'

The first time I had encountered Mrs Savage's fairy cakes was the occasion when Bishop Clinker, a little worse for wear, had just concluded an exhibition of the finer points of the cancan by collapsing on my sitting-room floor. Savage, bearing gifts of cakes, had arrived just in time to help heave the episcopal burden from the carpet and assist in its semi-revival. It had been a stressful experience, but when all was over, those sugary cakes had brought much comfort to jangled nerves. Perhaps this time too their silver balls and cochineal icing would induce a similar calm (or better still, inspire solution to the current difficulty).

Thus I told Savage I would be most glad to help him out, and suggested he came round in an hour's time. He sounded rather relieved and I wondered whether Mrs S. was having another of her 'turns'. I never quite understood what these actually comprised, but judging from Savage's cheery allusions presumably nothing unduly dire. Was frenzied activity in the baking department one of their symptoms perhaps ...? I pondered this briefly but was soon re-immersed in thoughts of my own problem: how to tackle Mavis Briggs and her 'lucky find'.

Indeed, so absorbed was I by this question that I had quite forgotten to pour a drink or even light a cigarette. Both omissions were remedied with the arrival of Savage.

He came in clutching his white stick and a large cardboard box which he was insistent I should open immediately and sample the contents. I wasn't quite sure whether fairy cakes would go with whisky, but wanting the latter rather badly I was prepared to try the com-bination. As was Savage.

We sat quietly, sipping and munching. The mixture was not unpleasant.

'Nice bit of Scotch,' he observed.

'Jolly nice cakes!' I exclaimed.

He beamed. 'Yes. Taste good, look good. She's pretty slick at that kind of thing.'

'How do you know how they look?' I asked curiously. 'I mean, you can't see much, can you?'

'Oh, that doesn't matter,' he replied blithely. 'After all, I *used* to see. Besides, she describes them so often I know them like the back of my hand!' And he chuckled indul-gently. I recalled that Savage had indeed once seen – until 1944 on the Normandy beaches, when, to quote his own words, 'A landmine well nigh blew me to buggery.' Unlike his companions he had – again to quote his own words – 'got off lightly', losing neither his life nor his manhood ... merely his sight. My own war had been prosaic, tiring, occasionally frightening, but never heroic. We were different, Savage and myself, and I respected him accordingly.

'So,' he said, settling further into his chair and finding the crisps, 'what have you been up to, Rev? Not seen much of you recently. Piano all right, is it?' I assured him it was fine thanks to his ministrations, but I was still struggling hopelessly with the 'Goldberg' pieces.

'Oh well,' he laughed, 'they'll see you out, make no mistake! I keep telling you to try the drums instead. Gene Krupa. Now there's a marvel. Cor! If I could play like that I shouldn't have to spend my time footling around with Molehill's pianos!' And he grinned blissfully, obviously seeing himself in some louche dive revving up the timpani Krupa-wise.

I smiled sympathetically, knowing what it was to have unrealized dreams, and thought irritably of Nicholas Ingaza and his genius for messing them up. But it was not drums I hankered for, merely a little peace and quiet. And, between them, Nicholas and Mavis Briggs had made sure that I wasn't getting either! I gazed at the two remaining fairy cakes, ruminating dolefully on the contrariness of things, as Savage continued to discourse on drumming and neighbourhood gossip, for both of which he had an unfailing ear.

'. . . Anyway she's hell bent on Bexhill,' I heard him saying, 'but I told her Las Vegas was more her style!' And he roared with laughter.

'Sorry – I missed that . . . who did you say?'

'Mavis – Mavis Briggs. She's off on holiday next week. Keen as mustard to go to Bexhill for some reason. Can't think why, even the wife thinks it's dreary!'

I took another sip of whisky and then a bite of my cake, and examining its magenta icing said casually, 'Well, that will be nice for her. How long is she going for? A week, I suppose – Monday to Monday or something like that . . . ?'

'Wednesday, I think. Something about the coach being cheaper mid-week.'

149

'What about the house? Does somebody look after it for her?'

'Matter of fact I asked her that. But you know Mavis! She twittered a bit and then said that people were far too nice to think of breaking into *her* house and that she was blessed with a trusting nature, unlike some people she could mention – meaning me, I suppose!' He grinned broadly and added, 'Mavis's idea of household security is to hide the spare key under the front mat! Told the wife so only last week. When Mrs S. asked if that wasn't a bit dangerous, she said it suited her there because it was easy to remember. I ask you!'

We laughed indulgently, drank some more whisky, and spent what was left of the evening putting the world and Molehill to rights.

The clock struck ten. 'Ah well,' said Savage, getting up to go, 'time I was off. Any later and the missus will be starting her baking again – can't have that, not just yet anyway!' I opened the front door for him, and still chuckling he tapped his way down the path and into the night.

Returning to the sitting room I poured a final drink, dimmed the lights, and thought about Mavis being hell bent for Bexhill. And wondered . . .

27

The Vicar's Version

Exactly as threatened in his postcard from Le Touquet, Nicholas soon alerted me to his imminent intention of taking back the smaller Spendler and replacing it with an unspecified other. He was to arrive in two days' time. Thanks to Savage's revelation about Mavis's intended holiday I had been able to make certain rudimentary plans re the picture's retrieval. Nevertheless, I cannot say that the prospect of his visit filled me with rapturous delight.

He arrived in what my father would doubtless have called 'some damned Frog job', i.e. a black and sprawling Citroën Traction Avant circa 1945, which had the air of something one might have encountered winding its way up the tortuous bends between Berchtesgaden and Hitler's Kehlsteinhaus. I thought irritably that it was typical of Ingaza's perversity to prowl about in some sinister foreign car. Why he couldn't run a decent Rover or Hillman like anyone else the Lord only knew!

However, such irritation was swiftly eclipsed by acute anxiety: for reaching into the back seat he proceeded to extricate not simply another closely wrapped canvas, but one whose dimensions outstripped the two Spendlers put together! I watched bleakly as he manoeuvred it up the front path, and with heavy heart opened the porch door.

'Well, old mate,' he breezed, 'nice to see you on your own holy ground again. Suits you better than the Old Schooner – more in keeping, you might say!' And he grinned around quizzically at the tired linoleum and worn stair carpet adorned by a couple of Bouncer's chewed Bonios. I said nothing, but indicated he should prop his burden against the banister, and took him into the sitting room where, dreading the news I had to impart, I poured him a particularly lavish gin. Two thirty in the afternoon was not exactly the normal drinking hour, but that was immaterial. What mattered was trying to soften the wrath which, after my confession, would surely come.

It came. Unsoftened. 'What the hell do you mean, you haven't got it!' he rasped. 'Where is it, in God's name?'

My garbled and largely fabricated explanation was cut short by a graphic diatribe in which the phrases 'twisting bastard', 'witless nincompoop' and 'frigging fruitcake' seemed to feature quite forcefully. Other terms were also used. Eventually he subsided, and sleeking his hair with practised poise asked me in tones of silky menace how I proposed to retrieve his property. Not wishing to risk further ire by querying the accuracy of the possessive adjective, I told him it was all perfectly in hand and that we would go that very afternoon to Mavis's empty house, remove the object from the wall and return to the vicarage for a celebratory cup of tea and cream bun.

He stared at me in cold silence, and then went to the sideboard and helped himself liberally to more of my gin. None was offered to me. He sipped it steadily while I nursed the cat, which for some reason had made one of its rare forays on to my lap.

Then suddenly, and to my considerable relief, he started to laugh – one of those protracted nasal titters that in our student days at St Bede's had so irritated the authorities. 'Well, Francis,' he said, 'you may be dull but at least no one could accuse you of being predictable! How you cope with this job or it with you I just don't know. Bloody shambles, I should think!' And the titter turned into a splutter of mirth.

I was glad that his mood had changed (albeit at the expense of my gin) but a trifle peeved by the aspersions cast on my pastoral competence. Apart from that disastrous wedding and the occasional near drowning of a baptismal infant, St Botolph's services conformed to the strictest protocol, maintaining standards of professionalism quite alien to one such as Nicholas! However, in the circumstances it seemed imprudent to dispute the matter, and instead I suggested amiably that if he had finished his drink it was time we paid a visit to Mavis Briggs – or rather her deserted house.

Having managed earlier in the week to inspect Mavis's grossly inadequate security measures (and checked with Edith Hopgarden the exact date of her departure), I was able to stroll along the road with Nicholas confident in the knowledge that the coast was clear and access assured. We would slip in and out in a trice, lift the picture, and toting it casually in a large shopping bag bought specially for the purpose, return swiftly and unremarked to the vicarage. It wouldn't take a moment.

The only thing clouding my mind was the thought of that outsize object (presumably of similar ilk to the Spendlers) blocking up my hallway. Give Ingaza an inch and he would invariably take several miles! The situation was no better now than when he had first deposited the awful things with me two months ago. To be rid of the dreary seascape with its over-endowed and horse-faced youth was relief indeed, but to have a replacement foisted upon me – and one of so mammoth a size – was intolerable. And this time I couldn't even shunt it off on to Primrose. Not that that had done any good – quite the opposite in fact. Elizabeth Fotherington, I mused, certainly knew how to direct her Nemesis!

With Nemesis in mind I suddenly clutched Nicholas and hauled him into the hedge. My other persecutor, Maud Tubbly Pole, followed by her drooling bulldog, had appeared around the bend and was lumbering straight in our direction.

'Christ, Francis,' gasped Nicholas, 'what *are* you doing! Not here, dear boy, it wouldn't be seemly!'

'Shut up and keep still!' I hissed between clenched teeth.

'Whatever for?'

'Just shut up,' I repeated, dragging him further into the thicket and its nettles.

'Bloody hell, Francis –' he started to protest. But I silenced him with a sharp elbow to the ribs as dog and mistress drew level . . . and then went wheezing past.

'Phew, that was near!' I gasped, releasing Nicholas and picking up the fallen carrier bag.

'It wasn't near – it was effing mad! Just look at my suit, all covered in burrs, and I've got a scalding nettle sting on my cheek. It's a bit bloody much! What were you *doing*?'

In view of the trouble he and his pictures had put me to I have to admit to experiencing a whiff of satisfaction as I regarded the burr-strewn suit and reddening skin. However, Christian charity prevailed and I apologized for the inconvenience, explaining that I had been trying to side-step a parishioner.

For some reason, that seemed to silence him. And then he said musingly, 'Of course, I always knew you were quietly barking. I remember when –'

'Barking I may be,' I replied with asperity, 'but at least I've never been rampant in a Turkish bath!'

And thus, wrangling and carping, we continued our way to Mavis Briggs's cottage. Once there things were remarkably easy. The blinds were drawn and the key still lay obligingly under the mat. However, it proved redundant for surprisingly the door was unlocked. Poor Mavis, she really hadn't a clue! And just for a moment I had a pang of guilt and hoped she was enjoying the Bexhill air.

We stepped smartly into the small hallway, its silence lacerated by the ticking of the cuckoo clock, took our bearings and edged towards what I vaguely remembered to be the drawing room. I say 'vaguely' as I had only once before been in Mavis's house – a dismal occasion held ostensibly to welcome the new vicar (me), but in reality an excuse for its owner to indulge in some of her execrable and interminable recitations. The memory was indelibly incised upon my mind, and even as I crossed the threshold a terrible weight of gloom came upon me. We scanned the walls, but apart from random flying ducks and geese, plus of course the stampeding elephants, there was no sign of the Spendler.

'You see,' whispered Nicholas querulously, 'it's not bloody here!'

'Have faith,' I answered, 'it's not the only place. I think the dining room is next door. We'll try that.' We moved back into the hall, passed the kitchen, and entered the dining room. It was rather dark, and apart from a table and sideboard there was little to see. I went over to the window and swished back the curtains. The afternoon sun flooded in. And there, displayed over the serving hatch, hung the Spendler in all its grim glory. I winced and Nicholas emitted a sound of rapturous relief.

'That's the fucker!' he exclaimed.

'Would you mind ...' I started to protest, and then stopped abruptly. From above there was the unmistakable sound of movement. Footsteps could be heard stomping across the ceiling. A door creaked, and as we froze there came the quavering voice of Mavis Briggs!

'Hello ... hello. Is there someone there? Do you want something?'

Caught in that dreadful instant of fear and unreality, we stared at each other like paralysed rats in a trap, while Mavis repeated her question. 'Excuse me, is anyone there? Can I help you? Who is it?' The timid tones, though faint, seemed to echo around the house like the voice of doom.

Taking a deep breath I cleared my throat resolutely, and marching into the hall said, 'It's all right, Mavis. It's only me, the vicar. Just passing – thought I'd check to see that everything was in order. Can't be too careful, you know!' The words sounded falsely hearty, as indeed they were, and my confidence was hardly helped by a sneeze and strangulated curse from Nicholas hovering in the dining room. I shut the door firmly and went to the foot of the stairs. At the top stood Mavis whey-faced and draped in what looked like a shroud. I recoiled, but then realized it was her nightgown.

'I – er, thought you were in Bexhill,' I began, 'otherwise wouldn't dream of disturbing . . .'

'Well, I *was* going,' she said still quavering, 'but you see, I was struck down at the last moment by a very nasty cold' (and she coughed delicately to make the point) 'and I didn't think I could do justice to the seaside. My friend down there agreed with me. Indeed she was most insistent I should not come.'

'Quite right,' I replied, trusting the friend was making the most of the reprieve. 'There's nothing worse than being on holiday and not feeling a hundred per cent.'

'And then of course there's my arm,' she continued plaintively. 'It's not mended yet, you know – I still have spasms.' And like some mesmerized ghost she flapped it vaguely in the air. 'So what with that and this cold I decided . . .'

At that moment there was what you might call a spasm from the dining room and something that sounded hor-ribly like splintering glass. Desperately I searched for some explanation or pre-emptive tactic – for surely Mavis could not have failed to hear. What the *hell* was he up to!

In fact, Mavis now seemed oblivious of all disturbance for she was clearly intent on apprising me of her various aches and ailments, and appeared deaf to any racket of Ingaza's making.

'. . . and so you see,' she continued, 'although aspirin *can* be useful I really prefer Friars Balsam and a nice cup of Horlicks. It works wonders for most things – but not unfortunately for *spasms* . . . Do you ever suffer from those, Vicar?' (Yes, I thought bitterly, all the time.) 'I notice that your leg is still causing problems, but of course in *my* case . . .' And thus she droned and droned.

Out of the corner of my eye I sensed a shadow at the hall window, and shooting a furtive glance saw Nicholas. He must have forced the garden door in the dining room (hence the tinkling glass), and was now holding aloft the Spendler, while simultaneously pulling faces and making frantic movements with his elbow. I think he wanted the shopping bag.

At that moment Mavis broke off her ramblings and enquired graciously if I would like a cup of tea. 'I fear my poor throat can't cope with anything at the moment but I'm sure *you* would like one, Vicar. I'll be down in a jiffy – just let me slip on a dressing gown. Oh, and while I think of it, you must see my *fascinating* acquisition in the dining room. The dear bishop will be so glad to know that it's come to a good home. Now you'll be sure to tell him, won't you?'

'No!' I shouted. She looked startled.

'Why ever not?'

'Because I don't like it!'

'Oh,' she said, sounding pained, 'I think it's very nice – very nice indeed. Still, they tell me it's all a matter of taste . . .'

'Not to my taste, it isn't – at least not at this time of day. Only in the morning!'

She looked even more moronically baffled than usual. 'Well, Vicar, I can't see what the time of day has to do with it, and in any case surely it wouldn't hurt to tell him.'

'Tell who?'

'Why, Bishop Clinker of course!'

'Not Clinker, *tea*!' I expostulated. 'I don't like it. Do NOT come down!'

'Oh, but I must!' she insisted. 'You may not like tea but at least you'll love the picture!' And so saying she shuffled back along the landing to fetch the dressing gown. I shot to the front door and found Nicholas skulking in the porch with the picture propped up against a decorative urn just outside.

'For Christ's sake give me the bag!' he cried. 'I can't carry it like this, far too risky. Where's the old bat now?'

'About to come downstairs and raise the roof. Bugger the bag, just get *going*!' I tried to propel him out of the way but it was too late. Mavis was descending the stairs, shroud on shroud.

Framed in the doorway as we were, even she could not fail to see the pair of us. 'Oh dear – so you're going. But who is . . .?'

'This is Archdeacon Benchley,' I answered firmly, closing the door and ushering Nicholas forward.

28

The Cat's Memoir

'And then what happened?' asked Bouncer as we crouched beneath our favourite yew tree.

'Well, by then F.O. had shut the front door and it was quite difficult to ascertain the exact procedures . . .'

'You mean you don't know,' the dog said.

I told him that I most certainly did know and that if he had the courtesy to listen I would apprise him of events. He sighed, scratched his ear and said, 'All right then, go on.' I went on.

'The instant the door was closed and my view impeded, I whisked round to the side of the house and positioned myself on the window ledge overlooking the hallway. The window was slightly ajar and so, Bouncer, I could see and hear *everything.*'

'So what happened?'

'The Ingaza man stood there white and twitching while F.O. discoursed on the length of their friendship, claiming that his companion was a visiting archdeacon from Brighton called Benchley who had a passion for geraniums.'

'What's geraniums got to do with it?' asked Bouncer.

'Kindly don't interrupt, I am coming to that. Mavis Briggs – the apparition on the stairs – has a penchant for geraniums –'

'Has what?'

I sighed. 'She *likes* them. Has them trailing in pots all round the house and garden – a little like the Carruthers woman, only with that one it's gnomes. Personally, I find them rather tasteless – too obvious. Now the occasional bergamot and drifts of *Nepeta mussinii* would be a different matter altogether, but unfortunately –'

'Oh, do go *on*, Maurice!' the dog growled.

I sighed, and continued my narrative. 'Well, as she likes geraniums and takes great pains to cultivate them, I suppose F.O. thought she might be disarmed by the archdeacon's interest and thus be diverted from wondering what two parsons were doing in her house in the middle of the afternoon stealing her painting.'

'And was she?'

'In a manner of speaking, yes.'

'What do you mean "in a manner of speaking"?'

'Oh, really, Bouncer,' I hissed impatiently, 'there are times when you are singularly obtuse!'

'And you,' he replied, suddenly lurching to his feet and fixing me with a belligerent stare, 'you are . . .' He hesitated, panting loudly and shifting from paw to paw. 'You are – PRO . . . LICKS!!'

I recoiled, momentarily stunned by both content and delivery. And then swiftly recovering my wits, put two and two together. He had been in truculent mood all afternoon, something to do with O'Shaughnessy beating him in the weekly race around the graveyard, so obviously the ill temper was due to injured pride. But *prolix* was more difficult to explain. Where had he got it from? And then of course I remembered: he had been in the crypt again – quite a long sojourn, only two days ago. It's all that dog Latin on the tombs and plaques, it has a curious effect on his canine psyche and he comes out with the most extraordinary terms which you would never think he could know! Of course, he doesn't know them really; just snaps them up and spits them out, but occasionally they can be

160

uncannily apposite. Not in this case, naturally. After all, no one could accuse yours truly of being prolix!

Anyway, feeling in benign mood I chose to overlook the dog's outburst, and after a casual ablution continued with my account.

'In the circumstances,' I opined, 'the vicar dealt with the matter tolerably well and had that Briggs woman eating out of his hand – though of course she is not exactly renowned for her acumen. The friend was less convincing; and standing there with Brylcreemed hair, flashing signet ring and spivvy suit, anyone less like an archdeacon it would be hard to imagine. F.O. forced him to examine the geraniums and make appropriate remarks but he looked distinctly sick and one felt not really entering into the spirit of the thing.'

'But it worked, did it?' pressed Bouncer anxiously. 'They got out all right?'

'Oh yes, they got out – and with the picture.'

'So everything's OK, is it?'

'Well, yes and no.'

'MAURICE!'

I continued hastily. 'You see, just as they got into the lane there was a great cascade of shrieks from the house.'

Bouncer guffawed. 'Old girl discovered the theft, had she?'

'Yes, and that really set them running – puffing and blinding all along the Guildford road and back to the vicarage. I thought that the Benchley/Ingaza man was going to expire. An absurd spectacle, only humans can behave like that!'

'Or vicars,' said Bouncer.

29

The Vicar's Version

Crises provoke excessive reactions, and conferring the status of archdeacon upon Nicholas Ingaza was clearly an error of judgement. At the time it had been useful, inducing in Mavis a state of such fawning deference that we had been able to make our getaway with relative ease – despite the return to the vicarage being necessarily energetic. It was the repercussions that were embarrassing. Incensed by the robbery, Mavis had taken it into her head to telephone Clinker lamenting the loss of his gift, but applauding myself and the archdeacon – without whose presence, she declared, dire and intimate results might have ensued! I learnt this from Clinker himself who the following day had contacted me in some annoyance.

'Look here, Oughterard, that woman who accosted me about the picture I brought to Pick's bazaar – I've just had her on the blower telling me she's been burgled, and apparently rescued from a fate worse than death by you and some archdeacon called Benchley. I can't imagine you rescuing anybody, whatever the circumstances ... but who's this chap Benchley? What's his diocese? Certainly not mine! She seemed to think he was an expert on geraniums – I don't know anyone of that kind. Where does he come from? She said something about Brighton, but

that's nonsense. I'd look him up but can't find my confounded Crockford – Gladys dusting the books again!'

'Ah . . .' I ventured.

'What?'

'Yes, it's always annoying when one's books are disturbed.'

'That's hardly the point, Oughterard! *Who* is Benchley?'

'Oh,' I laughed, 'she's got it wrong! Benchley has been
staying in Brighton but *comes* from Australia – the Outback
actually, special work among the aborigines . . .'

'I see,' said Clinker drily. 'Helping them to grow their
geraniums, I suppose.'

'Er ...'

'Anyway, I've quite enough on my plate without being
rung up by witless females from your parish thinking
they've been on the point of rape. Kindly see that it doesn't
happen again. Wednesday is my busy day, I've got a full
programme this afternoon and I am running late as it is.'

'I am sure Mrs Carruthers won't mind . . .' I began, but
he had already rung off.

There were of course other embarrassments: Nicholas
and the police. The former was in even poorer physical
condition than myself, and when we arrived back at the
vicarage it was some time before he could recover and,
unfortunately, speak. When he did so, it was to provide a
colourful and imaginative account of my parentage embellished by quizzical references to my sanity. Once that was
over, I suggested he try one of the cream buns specially
reserved for our return; but he didn't seem to think much
of that so I dropped the idea.

However, at least the crisis produced one good thing: I
would not now have to suffer the penance of harbouring
yet another of his 'belongings'. Mavis's Spendler was not
the only picture to be deposited in his car: for after more
heaving, the large item in the hall was also returned to the

Citroën's back seat. Apparently, I was not to be entrusted with further consignments from the art world! Theoretically, this should have been my cue to suggest that he also relieve me of the remaining one stored in the belfry – except, of course, that by now it wasn't in the belfry but with Primrose. It did not seem quite the right moment to reveal this fact . . . indeed, I was fearful that the same idea might occur to Nicholas, but mercifully he was too preoccupied with the matters in hand and nothing was said.

Getting rid of both visitor and merchandise was one thing: but there was surely still the inevitable problem of a police interview. I sighed morosely and scowled at Bouncer who promptly wagged his tail. Another brush with the law to be endured and parried!

The following day my spirits might have been soothed by the prospect of Choral Evensong – had I not been met in the church porch by Mavis, clearly recovered from her ague and eager to rake over the robbery. The clerical presence had, she felt sure, affected the conscience of the intruder and deterred him from making further inroads. Indeed, were it not for myself and the nice archdeacon *anything* might have happened! Recalling Clinker's words, it struck me that her evident excitement was perhaps based on the hope that the burglar's motive was less the theft of her picture than her honour. I was about to observe that surely nobody in their right mind would consider the latter, when Edith Hopgarden appeared and the two got into a heated huddle over the distribution of hymn books.

Evensong over, I was again waylaid by Mavis bursting to relate her experiences with the police officers.

'. . . and that Mr March, *so* sensible and comforting. He assured me he would get my painting back in next to no time!' (Was Ingaza aware of that? I wondered.)

Having previously encountered March engaged on the

164

Fotherington case, I was unsurprised that the detective inspector had so far failed to link Mavis's picture with the Spendler work. He was not somebody who struck me as being especially clued up on artistic matters, or indeed on anything of a cultural bias – unless one counted the prize dahlias. But I just hoped that this time his investigations would not be aided by the weedy Samson, a sallow, sharp-nosed type whose presence some months previously I had found more than irksome. Surely by now he would have got promotion and gone elsewhere.

Naturally, no such luck. So once more, looking rather like a sinister parody of Abbott and Costello and clad in matching raincoats, they appeared together on my door-step: the one narrow and pinched, the other stout and grizzled. And, as before, I faced them in a state of genial terror.

After the preliminary pleasantries (from March, not Samson) they got down to brass tacks.

'Lucky for the lady that you were actually there at the time of the intrusion,' March commenced, 'you and the, er, other clerical gentleman.'

'Well, ye-es,' I replied hesitantly. 'But of course one isn't entirely sure if we *were* there, I mean . . .'

'Are you saying you don't *know* whether you were at her house or not?' cut in Samson with his usual acidity. I recalled how like a suspicious whippet he had seemed that first time around; and confronting him now, almost a year later, I felt the resemblance even more marked. He quivered in his corner as I patiently explained my position.

'I was about to say that although we were indeed there, it is quite possible that the robbery took place long before our arrival.'

'*She* doesn't think so.'

'Perhaps the lady is mistaken,' I suggested gently. 'After all, we didn't hear anything.'

'No? And what might you have expected to hear?'

The words 'breaking glass' sprang to my lips but I bit them back, realizing that although Mavis had mentioned the shattered garden door it wouldn't do to sound too knowledgeable. Instead I said the first thing that came into my head: 'Bumps, I should imagine.' He wrote something in his notebook ('bumps'?), and I was about to continue but was interrupted by March clearing his throat loudly.

'You see, Mr Oughterard, Miss Briggs says she had occasion to go down into the dining room just before you and the other gentleman arrived – said something about looking for a chest poultice in the sideboard. Funny the places people like to keep things.' And he grinned. His colleague did not. 'Apparently the picture was on the wall then all right, in fact she kept going on about how nice she thought it had looked.'

'So it's obvious the theft took place while you were both there,' snapped the Whippet.

'So it would seem . . . how extraordinary!' I exclaimed. 'That means the burglar must have already been in the dining room when we arrived, skulking there and –'

'*I* think there were two of them,' interjected Samson. I didn't like the sound of that but assumed an air of fascinated curiosity.

'Really? Whatever makes you think that? They must have been jolly quiet!'

'Yes. *Jolly*.' He had always been impertinent.

'Ah, Samson and his hunches!' March laughed. 'Often they're wrong – but mind you, more often they're right! Isn't that so, Sidney?' The latter sat in silence examining his nicotined fingers. 'Anyway, Reverend, what about this other gentleman, the, uhm, archdeacon. Are you sure he didn't see or hear anything?'

'He didn't mention it,' I said, 'besides, he's rather deaf.'

'And blind?' asked the Whippet.

I ignored that, as did March, who went on to ask if I had Benchley's contact details. This was what I had been fearing, but hoped they would be fobbed off with my reply that the archdeacon had embarked on an indefinite walk-ing tour of the Austrian Alps prior to returning to Australia, and was thus currently without fixed abode.

To my relief March seemed to accept this, saying he had always enjoyed Kitzbühel himself though had never really taken to all that snow and skiing business. To my even greater relief he added vaguely, 'Oh well, when all's said and done, it's only a picture she found in a jumble sale or some such, small value, no great loss ... Might turn up eventually, I suppose. It's what they often do when they realize their mistake – chuck the things in the nearest ditch or front garden and then scarper. Someone will come across it, I daresay.' (Given the earlier assurances to Mavis, his attitude struck me as a mite cavalier, though it was not a point I was keen to raise.) He nodded to Samson and they got up to leave.

'Nice to see you again, sir,' said March, belting his rain-coat across his paunch. And then, pausing, he added, 'Singing your praises she was, that Miss Briggs. Seems to think you being there had prevented an *assault* – if you get my meaning!' And he leered gently.

I smiled in return. But as I showed them out Samson suddenly turned, and said in an expressionless voice, 'I expect you miss that other lady, don't you, sir? That Mrs Fotherington. A pity about all of that ...'

'Yes,' I said faintly, the smile evaporating, 'a great pity.'

30

The Cat's Memoir

'He didn't like that,' observed Bouncer. 'Didn't like it at all.'

'Didn't like what?' I asked.

'What the rozzer said.'

I sighed irritably. 'I take it you are referring to one of the investigating police officers here earlier – though which one and what he said, I have no idea! Kindly clarify.'

He took another chew at his Bonio and then said slowly, 'The scraggy one, the one that looks like something the cat's brought in.'

It was clearly meant to annoy, and not wishing to give him the satisfaction of seeing me riled, I replied smoothly, 'Ah yes, Samson.'

'Yes,' he answered, sounding disappointed, 'that one. Just when he was leaving: the bit about old Fotherington. It was as if he was trying to make a point – letting the vicar know that *he* knew!'

'Well, he doesn't know – there's absolutely no proof.'

'Ah,' Bouncer replied darkly, 'you don't have to have proof to *know* something.'

'Those of us who are rational do!' I exclaimed.

He continued worrying his Bonio, and then peering at me through the drooping fronds said, 'You know, Maurice, you may have nine lives but what you could really do with is a sixth sense like us dogs. You would find it helpful.'

'I was not aware that I needed help!' I replied crossly. It was really getting too much, and I concluded that he had either been down in the crypt again or consorting with O'Shaughnessy. The latter's influence is not of the best.

'Keep your fur on, I was just saying that –'

'You are saying too much, Bouncer. Enough is enough!' And to stress the point I arched my back and flattened my ears. I liked to think that he looked suitably chastened but it is not always easy to tell what goes on behind that shaggy pelmet.

He burped, and continued. 'Anyway, he was pretty upset even *before* the cops came – just after that Ingaza man left. Sat there drumming his fingers and crunching those humbugs. I tried to cheer him up – wagging my tail and that sort of thing – but it didn't seem to help.'

'Not surprised,' I observed mildly, 'probably drove him mad.'

There was a sudden deafening explosion of canine mirth. 'I say, Maurice,' he spluttered amidst rasping yelps, 'you mean like I drive you mad!'

'Precisely.'

At that point there came a crashing of chords from the sitting room: F.O. drowning his sorrows in the piano. It only needed the church bells to burst forth their din, and pandemonium would be complete. I got up hastily, slipped through the cat flap and commenced my evening prowl.

On my return the house was mercifully quiet, with Bouncer asleep and F.O. chewing his pencil over the cross-word. With dog and man thus engaged I was able to enjoy my milk undisturbed and reflect on the current situation. The dog, I conceded, was right: although there might be a temporary respite from the Brighton type, the police visitation had clearly unsettled our master; or at any rate, the scraggy one's parting comment had. Yet, as I had noted to Bouncer, their earlier investigations had yielded no evidence to link the vicar with the Fotherington murder (thanks largely to our manoeuvres with the cigarette lighter), and with that dead tramp providing a convenient scapegoat, the fuss had subsided. But from the outset there had been mutual dislike between F.O. and Samson, and it could well be that the latter was intent on stirring up trouble – probably seeing F.O. as a stepping stone to promotion. It was doubtful whether there was anything concrete to go on, but it was a worrying possibility nevertheless.

I finished my milk and then mewed in exasperation. Typical of F.O. to get embroiled with that Ingaza person and his unsavoury paintings! If that hadn't happened our life here would have been proceeding in relative calm: the murder buried like Bouncer's bones, and the two of us left safe in clover. Kind though our vicar was, he could also be painfully obtuse! But still, what else could you expect from a human . . .

I spent an unsettled night, and was less than pleased to be woken in the early morning by Bouncer scrabbling at my tail. The dog was clearly in sociable mood and, undeterred by my twitching claw, eager to talk. I listened with closed eyes and half an ear.

He rambled on for a while, and then announced excitedly, 'I'm going to see the rabbits again!'

'What rabbits?'

'You know, Boris and Karloff – at that place F.O. took us to.'

'How do you know?'

'He was on the phone last night talking to the Prim person.'

'His sister.'

'Yes, that's right. I heard them arranging it. He's going down for the day to fetch back that other picture and he's taking ME with him – though he didn't mention you, Maurice.'

170

'Well, that's a *great* pity,' I murmured sleepily. 'How on earth shall I survive the day without you two crashing about?'

'Oh, that'll be all right – I'll get O'Shaughnessy to come and keep you company.'

'What!' I hissed, suddenly awake.

'O'Shaughnessy, I'll ask him to spare a few hours. He's got quite a soft spot for you, Maurice. Why, only the other day I heard him telling Gunga Din that you were a fine fellow of a cat, so you were, "bejasus"!'

'Nice to know the creature has *some* discernment,' I observed. 'What did Gunga Din say?'

'He didn't. Just looked glazed.'

'Well, what can you expect – obviously hung over as usual!' And then requiring some light diversion, and after telling the dog that on no account was he to issue any invitations to O'Shaughnessy, I sauntered into the garden to set myself among the pigeons.

The rest of the day proved quite eventful – harrying recalcitrant hedgehogs in the graveyard, squaring up to an intrusive Siamese, and laying waste the Veaseys' prize primulas. (Most deservedly, considering the disgraceful way they had treated me over the matter of their goldfish the previous summer!) Thus when I returned to the house I was all ready for some quiet repose.

No such luck. Bouncer was still in garrulous mood (excitement presumably at the prospect of seeing the chinchillas again), and seemed intent on regaling me about some parish visitor that F.O. had been entertaining.

'Anyway,' the dog said, 'he was talking about that geezer with a lady's name – Dolly Vera, the new Irish batsman. He said he had a great future if only they could get him over to England . . . some problem or other.'

I stared at him. 'What *are* you talking about?'

'Well, I don't suppose you know much about cricket, Maurice, not being a lover of ball games, but some of us are up in these things.'

'*Excuse* me,' I said, 'I know a great deal. Certainly enough to know that he happens to be South African, and his name is not Dolly, it is –'

'Yes it is!' he growled.

'Nonsense. And in any case you are getting confused. The other one, the Irish gentleman, is a distinguished statesman – although opinions are sharply divided as to whether –'

'Yes, yes, but he plays *cricket*, doesn't he?'

'I doubt it. Hurling more likely.'

'Hurling what?'

'Hurling sticks at stupid dogs!' I screeched.

It had been a tiring day and we retreated to our respective sanctuaries: me behind the sofa and he to his crypt.

31

The Vicar's Version

I had been holding my own fairly well until Samson's remark about Elizabeth Fotherington. But his parting shot had left me quite weak at the knees, and it was with a prayer of thanks and a glass of brandy that I watched their ambling departure down the garden path. What on earth had he *meant*? Nothing or everything? I stared into Bouncer's solemn eyes and then sat down on the sofa to meditate.

For the first twenty minutes meditation yielded nothing except unsettling past images of Elizabeth and the sounds of barking roebucks and snapping twigs. And then I think I must have drifted off, for soon those sounds were replaced by others: *her* still so familiar mincing voice overlaid with blasts from Maud Tubbly Pole. It was a disturbing mixture, and I awoke uneasily to a dark but thankfully silent room.

Whatever the earlier matter might bode, I still had to deal with the present problem: disposal of the larger picture, *Dead Reckoning*. Once Nicholas had recovered from his pique, sooner or later he would want it back. And judging from his recent comments about my custodial capacity it would probably be sooner. There was nothing for it: a further trip to Primrose to retrieve the wretched thing – assuming of course that, like the first, she hadn't slipped it behind another of her own works and dispatched it God knew where! I switched on the light, picked up the receiver, and announced my intention.

Primrose sounded more than receptive to the idea but was clearly sorry that it was to be only a day visit. Evidently the garden was ready for another seeing to. I told her that I would have to bring Bouncer.

'Well, that creature's all right,' she said. 'It's the other one that's such a pain!' For once I felt defensive of Maurice and asked her what she meant.

'It's got very funny eyes, that cat. Does nothing but stare. And when it's not staring it's snooping.'

'Well, he prowls about, I suppose . . . but you know cats, they do that sort of thing.'

'Not like that,' she replied. 'Last time it was here I caught it putting the evil eye on Boris and Karloff. They didn't like it at all – quivering wrecks, they were!'

'He was probably curious. Only looking, you know.'

'Exactly. And very peculiar looks he has!'

Primrose gets these bees in her bonnet so I didn't pursue the matter. The main thing was to get my hands on the painting and bring it back safely ready for Ingaza's mercenary grasp.

Two days later Bouncer and I set off once more for Sussex, arriving at Primrose's in time for lunch. The dog hung about for a while waiting for titbits from the table, and then scooted off into the garden looking purposeful. Primrose, pleased with the prospect of ridding herself of the picture, seemed in an unusually mellow mood and had produced a decanter of more than tolerable burgundy.

'Remains of Pa's cellar,' she announced. 'He always enjoyed a good Beaune. In fact, come to think of it, wine was the one thing he really *did* know about!'

'And model railways,' I was going to add, but thought better of it. She would only bring up the dreadful incident of my blunder with the Hornby train, from which I suspect my father never fully recovered. It had certainly been a perennial topic of his conversation for years afterwards. Instead I said, 'Yes, but he generally gave a fair impression of knowledge.'

'Only to the gullible,' she replied.

We brooded in silence on our late and partially lamented parent, and then raised our glasses in dutiful salutation.

'Well, this is all right, anyway!' Primrose exclaimed, and with unwonted generosity refilled my glass almost to the brim. She then asked about the smaller Spendler and seemed quite unabashed when I told her that thanks to herself and Mrs Clinker it had been consigned to the White Elephant stall of Pick's fête.

'What a hoot! You mean to say that valuable piece of daubing is now gracing the walls of some shed or semi in Horsham. How droll!'

'It was not a hoot,' I retorted irritably, 'and neither is it droll. The whole thing put me to considerable trouble, but fortunately it has since been retrieved and restored to its owner . . . Well, to its custodian at any rate.'

'Your friend presumably – the one who stole it in the first place.'

'Yes – no. I mean, I don't think he exactly stole it, just acquired it temporarily, and then he needed a spare place to –'

'Yes, you've explained all that before. It's a load of hooey, as well you know. He's obviously up to his ears in skulduggery and has dragged you into it. And you're the very last person equipped for that kind of thing, everyone knows that!' And she laughed accusingly. I smiled wanly, wishing the skulduggery involved only the paintings.

After some more wine and a pleasurably pungent Camembert, she suggested it was time for me to bring the picture downstairs. 'And once that's done I know you'd like to say hello to Boris and Karloff!' I had no particular hankerings in that direction but, feeling indebted for the good lunch, indicated I could think of nothing nicer. She offered to give me a hand carrying the thing down, but by now I felt fairly practised in manhandling stolen goods and said I could manage.

It was still in its wrappings, but I noticed that the sello-taped bindings which had taken me so long to attach had been ripped apart and replaced by string. 'Can't think why you had to interfere with them in the first place!' I exclaimed irritably.

'Well, naturally I was going to take a look. What else did you expect? Still, don't know about *interfering* with them – it's not as if I were a scoutmaster in the *News of the World*!' And she began to giggle. Whether her mirth was the result of the wine or relief at offloading the thing back on to me, I wasn't sure. But whatever it was, the giggling gathered momentum until she spluttered, 'I say, Francis, they really are awful, far worse than the photographs. The first one with the dreadful youth was bad enough, but this bone-strewn thing is simply frightful!' And she collapsed on the stairs in peals of laughter. Being, as you might say, in the thick of things, I hadn't exactly appreciated the comedy of the matter; but watching Primrose hooting her head off I too started to laugh, and for a few moments it was as if we were back at home again savouring one of Mother's many absurdities.

Bouncer appeared from the garden, stared at both of us, and then slowly wagging his tail added something of his own cacophony. Thus the visit ended on a surprising note of noise and merriment. The gruesome Spendler was once more stowed in the Singer, and, mercifully spared the charms of Boris and Karloff, I departed for Molehill.

The prospect of yet again having to lug the picture up to the belfry was not a happy one – especially as Mrs T.P. had made that crack about it being the ideal place to conceal a painting. So I delivered it to the alternative cache: the church crypt. Descent into Avernus was marginally easier than negotiating the perilous ladder to Elysium. But it was an awkward business all the same, and made the more so by Bouncer showing an officious concern in the matter. His snuffling attentions almost had me falling headlong down the steps, and it was with relief that I at last gained the comfort of the sitting room and the solace of a smoke with a good John Buchan.

This, however, was only temporary solace, for later that evening I was scheduled to attend the St Botolph's Ladies' League AGM: an event not known for its wit and gaiety, and this time interminably protracted by bleating interruptions from Mavis Briggs as she struggled to record the minutes. I made a mental note to suggest that perhaps in future she might like Edith Hopgarden to relieve her of that chore. I suspected she wouldn't like it at all. And my vision of the two ladies battle-locked over who was the better fitted for the task helped to ease a little of the tedium.

Eventually the meeting wound up and we trooped into the night. Declining the offer of cocoa from Miss Dalrymple and some of the more socially minded of the group, I started to make my way home. And then just as I rounded the corner of the parish hall, I heard what can only be described as a loud 'Psst!', followed by thudding footsteps. My elbow was suddenly caught in the steely grip of a well-sprung gin-trap. It was Mrs Tubbly Pole.

'Good gracious!' I gasped. 'I didn't expect to see you here!'

'No,' she chuckled, 'but *I* expected to see *you*. They told me this was where you'd be, so I've been lying in wait!'

I suppose it was the tone of triumph and the words 'lying in wait' which touched a nerve and induced a sudden and appalling déjà vu. And for a mad panicking moment I was back in the wood, confronted by that dreadful beaming apparition . . . Surely not Maud Tubbly Pole as well! Oh dear God, not *another* unhinged predator!

The horror must have shown, for she said, 'Goodness, Francis, you've gone quite white – I didn't mean to startle you. You're obviously not used to being accosted by ladies

177

from the shadows!' And she emitted a long and braying cachinnation. That steadied things all right: I was quite safe with Mrs T.P.! ('And she with him!' the cynical might add.)

Taking my arm firmly, she propelled me along the pavement, and then said in throaty *sotto voce*, 'My dear, I've discovered something quite extraordinary, and you are the first to know!'

'Really? What's that?'

She clutched me more tightly. 'One of the missing Spendlers has actually been in *this* locality, and is perhaps still here! What do you think of that!' She almost danced, while I froze.

'Whatever gives you such an idea?' I gasped.

'Well, you know the woman who looks like an emaciated hamster and always seems to have a cold and was burgled recently – Mavis somebody.'

'Briggs,' I said tensely.

'Yes, that's the name. Well, there was only one item taken, and it just happened to be a painting and –'

'But Mavis wouldn't have had a Spendler!' I laughed.

'Oh, but she did!' she cried. 'I am convinced of it.' By this time we had reached the vicarage gate, and as we paused she said, 'I must get back to poor old Gunga, he gets fractious if Mummy's out too long – but there's still time for a quick nightcap and then I can tell you more! What do you say?' I said nothing, but dutifully opened the gate and ushered her up the path.

I was tired and the whisky low. But I was also desperate to know what she had to say about Mavis's picture. 'Er, what makes you think that painting was a Spendler? It was only a bit of White Elephant junk . . . I was there when she picked it up, nothing of any interest.' I tried to sound as casual as my nerves would allow.

'I happened to be behind her in the queue at the post office. She was talking to a friend about the robbery, though I don't think the friend heard a word – looked

bored out of her mind – but *I* heard, and it got me thinking. She was describing the picture: a dark seascape, all
swirling clouds and waves and a naked youth in the foreground – seemed embarrassed about that part and kept
giggling – so don't you *see*, Francis!'

Trying to sound as unmoved as possible, I muttered
vaguely, 'Not really – afraid I'm not up in these things.'

'But it's obviously *On the Brink*!'

'On the blink?'

She looked impatient and took a large gulp from her
glass. '*On the Brink* – that's the *title* of one of the stolen
paintings. And from what the newspapers said at the time
it sounds exactly like it.'

I smiled indulgently. 'But surely there must be hundreds
of pictures of beaches and bathers, they're churned out all
the time.'

'But not with male nudes, I shouldn't have thought.'

'Oh yes,' I said firmly. 'Quite a fashion back in the early
twenties, almost a cult, you know, especially in Germany;
but it caught on here too.'

She looked surprised (as was I by my powers of invention). 'Thought you said you weren't up in that sort of
thing – you seem very knowledgeable on the subject!'

I had obviously overplayed my hand, but replied
smoothly that for some odd reason it was the one thing
that I remembered from school art classes. 'It's simply a
coincidence, you know. And besides, all the experts are
agreed that those pictures are halfway across the world by
now – they'd never have been kept here, far too dangerous!' And I laughed loudly. She looked so deflated that I
almost felt a pang of guilt.

'What a bore. I was going to offer my services to the
police and see what they thought of my theory, but if you
think –'

'I do think,' I said quickly. 'You know what the police are
like, no sensitivity. They would give you short shrift and

make you look a fool – and that you are certainly not, Mrs Tubbly Pole! And can't you just see the press headlines if they got hold of it? Newspapers can be so crude ... Just imagine: "Famous lady detective writer fails to sift fact from fiction." Wouldn't do that renowned literary reputation much good, would it?' I flashed a warm smile and poured her the remnants of the whisky. It seemed to do the trick.

'Yes,' she sighed, 'you are probably right. Just jumping to exciting conclusions. It's the novelist's imagination – runs away with me sometimes. I do love a bit of drama! Don't *you*, Francis?'

'Rather overrated,' I replied drily.

'Oh, come now! Everyone needs a little spice in their life – even you, dear friend. Your life is far too staid. You should have become a big-game hunter instead of a clergyman, *much* more fun!' And she gurgled merrily. Given my present situation, I couldn't help feeling that the role of big-game hunter might have been infinitely soothing.

She continued to speculate about the robbery. And in the hope of leading her away from the subject, I asked how the novel was coming along and whether she had managed to find a title for it.

'I most certainly have!' she cried. 'So far there have been four murders, two suicides and a manslaughter, so I have called it *No Dearth of Death*. Pretty neat, eh? Of course, it *has* moved some way beyond the original case, i.e. your corpse in the bluebells,' (how I wished she would stop using that possessive!) 'but I couldn't stop at just one, could I? Far too tame! But it's got all the Molehill features, not to mention the church and that marvellous belfry. You'll love it!' I thought bitterly that Mrs T.P.'s conception of 'tame' differed widely from my own; and then asked her warily whether, in view of its ecclesiastical setting, the murder plot contained any parsons.

'Oh yes, dozens,' she replied gaily. As I had feared. But at least, I supposed, there was safety in numbers ...

Eventually she got up to go, exclaiming that it was long past the 'little man's' bedtime and there were bound to be ructions if she stayed any more. For once I felt grateful to Gunga Din, and made a mental note to give him a drop more gin when next he called.

32

The Dog's Diary

I don't think much of those rabbits. They haven't got anything of what Maurice keeps calling SAVVY FUR. In fact, in normal dog lingo I'd call them jolly rude! I mean to say, when F.O. took me down to his sister's I naturally went to call on them. Don't suppose they get many visitors and I thought they would be pleased to see me. Not a bit of it! They twitched and glared and rolled those popping pink eyes; and then just as I was going to speak, the really giant one turned round and thrust its fluffy backside right up against the wire of its hutch. In my face, if you please! I tell you, I would have given it a socking big bite if I could but the meshes were too small – otherwise he'd have felt it all right!

The other one, Boris, was no better. Sat there crunching its stupid carrot, and then had the cat's neck to ask me if I hadn't got something better to do with my time. I told him I had HEAPS of better things, but being a well-brought-up dog was just being polite and paying my respects. He told me where to put my respects and said that if I didn't take my snout away from his wire he would spit in my eye. Well, I didn't fancy a shot of chewed carrot hurtling my way, so I backed off. But they needn't think they've seen the last of me. Oh no! I'll ask Maurice what to do. When he's not preening himself he's got a fiendish mind and is bound to think of something.

Anyway, it was fun being down there for a change. She's got a nice garden, bigger than the vicar's, with some good bone-burying areas and plenty of trees for sniffing and spraying. (You have to keep your leg in practice, you know, otherwise it seizes up.) So apart from those pink-eyed loons, I had a very nice time. I think F.O. enjoyed himself too. When I went back to the house they had finished their lunch and for some reason were roaring with laughter. That doesn't often happen with the vicar, so I took the opportunity and joined in. There wasn't half a racket! Probably just as well that Maurice didn't come, he'd have complained non-stop!

The journey back was good fun and we hurtled along like cats out of hell, with F.O. singing some hymn about a cross-eyed bear called Gladly. Don't know who *he* is, but the tune's all right and I joined in myself a couple of times – though that seemed to make the vicar wince, so I stopped and went to sleep.

Anyway, all was well until we got back to Molehill. And then, blow me, if he doesn't take the picture out of the car and start to haul it down the steps to my crypt! Usually I wouldn't care a bit, but the belfry isn't the only place I keep my bones: there's a special heap of them in the crypt, just in the corner behind the door where it's darkest and the mice don't go. One or two spare toys are stashed there as well – useful emergency stores for when I get bored with Maurice. It would be just like F.O. to shove his picture there and mess up my whole system like he did in the belfry. So I tried my best to head him off, but he was hell-bent on getting it down there and I had to give up in the end. You could hear him blundering about and cursing; but afterwards I saw he had put the parcel at the far end, so with luck things should be all right . . . though it doesn't do to bank on it – not here at the vicarage, it doesn't!

183

He came back late last night, some church meeting I suppose, but he wasn't alone: got the Tubbly person with him and they sat jawing for ages – leastwise she did. He didn't say much at all, just sat there with that dazed expression he often has. Still, getting the picture back here again seems to have calmed him down, and I think he's sleeping better – less crashing about in the middle of the night searching for fags and aspirin. Who knows, perhaps we are in for a smooth run. And if he gets in a good mood he's likely to give me a bath again. I should like that, but the cat won't!

33

The Cat's Memoir

I was in the kitchen toying quietly with a dead mouse when Bouncer suddenly announced that he felt a bath coming upon him and hoped that I wouldn't mind. Well, of course I minded! The last occasion had been an affair of epic horror; a dreadful assault on my nerves from which I was barely recovered. The noise had been atrocious: an ear-splitting cacophony of clerical curses, canine shrieks, and the squawking of butchered rubber ducks (the dog fancies himself as a retriever at such times). But it was the bathroom floor and landing which had been especially distasteful – water everywhere (my particular aversion), with filthy towels and shredded cigarettes littered all over the place. Why the vicar finds it necessary to smoke when he baths the dog, I do not know. Calms his nerves presumably, but it does little for mine. Having to pussy-foot my way among sodden butt-ends and pools of wet is not good for a cat of my sensibilities.

I asked Bouncer what made him think the household was due for another such deluge, to which he replied gnomically that he knew what he knew! I suppose he was implying it was his sixth sense at work again. He grossly exaggerates this faculty, although just occasionally *does* exhibit an uncanny prescience of things. So I told him that if he had any more aquatic premonitions would he kindly inform me in advance so that I could escape to the graveyard for the duration. He agreed to this, and than proceeded to tell me about his day down in Sussex.

It was clearly going to be a lengthy saga with the usual theatrical embellishments. So I settled myself comfortably by the boiler, and to pass the time embarked on my ablutions. He took umbrage at this and had the nerve to tell me to sit up straight and pay attention. Naturally I immediately lay down with my eyes tightly shut. However, I did assure him that I was all *ears*, and seeming satisfied with this he commenced his tale.

As Bouncer's tales go it was not without interest – mainly for what it revealed of the vicar's dealings with his sister. They seem to have an oddly collusive relationship – close yet mutually wary, a mixture of guarded affection and irritable impatience. He said that he went into the garden leaving them bickering like billy-o but when he returned they were in fits of laughter! I find this blend of coolness and mirth quite beyond me – but then I am a mere cat and cannot be expected to fathom the mystery of human absurdity. It's bad enough coping with the dog. Talking of which, much of his tale was taken up with descriptions of those crackpot chinchillas. They had obviously got on his whiskers and he grumbled endlessly about their uncouthness. A tinge ironic coming from Bouncer of all creatures! However, I was my reasonable forbearing self, and listened patiently to his complaints.

'. . . so you see, Maurice,' he grumbled, 'I can't let them get away with it – it's not right! I mean to say, why should a decent dog like me put up with insults from those poncey layabouts? You've got to think of something!' He looked sullen and started to shove his rubber ring around.

I was about to tell him to stop rabbiting on, but in his present mood thought that might not go down too well. So instead I suggested that he took his mind off things by chasing Gunga Din. 'After all,' I purred, 'you've not had a go at him for some time – mustn't get out of practice, you know!'

'Oh, I can do that any day,' he said. 'It's those bastard bunnies I've got to get my teeth into!' I pointed out that the chances of his making a repeat visit to the sister's house in the immediate future were fairly slim, and it might be some time before he could settle his score.

'I can wait,' he growled. And he sat back heavily on his haunches with paws splayed and furrowed brow.

I sighed. 'All right, Bouncer, be assured. Should the time ever come, I will devise an appropriate strategy: one to afford you maximum pleasure and them minimum comfort.'

'That's the ticket!' he cried. 'You mean we'll duff 'em up!'

'Well,' I replied cautiously, 'not in so many words, but . . .'

'How many words?' he barked eagerly.

'Enough to do the trick,' I replied, and with a swish of my tail made it clear I had no intention of pursuing the conversation further. He grinned amiably, and dragging his ring squeezed himself through the pet flap into the garden. Off into the crypt, I surmised, doubtless to christen the new acquisition. Peace at last.

There came a loud clearing of throat from the sitting room followed by a thunderous crash of keys. F.O. tuning up . . .

When I returned from my enforced stroll it was to find the vicar sitting at his desk amidst swirls of smoke, writing feverishly. There was an intensity about his look not normally noted in his efforts with the Confirmation lists or his sermons, so I assumed something was in the air. I also observed that in addition to the cigarettes there were a number of his favourite mint humbugs strewn across the blotting paper. The simultaneous consumption of smoke

187

and gobstoppers suggested a task of some moment, and I was curious to find out what.

Adopting a benign expression I sidled over to his chair, twitched playfully at his trouser leg, and gave a winsome mew. The writing stopped and he looked startled. (Admittedly, I don't often make such generous gestures.) Then asking me what I thought I was up to – surprising how cynical even vicars can be – he reached down and settled me on his lap. I purred reassuringly and he continued with his task. By gradually shifting into an upright position I was able to see over the top of the desk and get a fair view of the writing pad.

Now, although I am an animal of some erudition (unlike Bouncer), I have never quite managed to grasp the intricacies of human hieroglyphics – especially those scrawled by F.O. – but at least I can recognize the vicarage stationery when I see it, and so deduced he was writing one of his rare letters. And judging from the bits of screwed-up paper cast among the mints, this had obviously been occupying him for some while. It was tiresome not being able to satisfy my curiosity, and by way of diversion I extended an idle paw to toy with one of the crumpled drafts.

I have observed that F.O.'s fountain pens are invariably defective, and seem to require constant replenishment from the ink which he keeps close at hand. Thus it was that, just as I reached for the discarded paper, my claw happened to catch the top of the bottle causing it to teeter . . . and then fall. Unfortunate.

Ink trickled on to the carpet, my ears, and his trousers; and with an explosive oath he tipped me to the floor. I was nettled, to say the least, and emitted a particularly fearsome screech. That woke the dog, who started to howl, whereupon F.O. made a lunge for the whisky crying, 'Bloody cat, and bloody Rummage!' As he clattered with the ice and decanter I took refuge behind the sofa and brooded.

Rummage, I vaguely recalled, was the name of the raucous type who had stayed at the vicarage the previous year while F.O. was in Brighton recovering from that fatal contretemps with my mistress. At the time the visitor had served a certain purpose, but I had found the uncouth joviality tedious and he was not to my taste – nor, I subsequently learned, to F.O.'s. Yet now, I concluded, it was this very Rummage who was the recipient of the vicar's urgent attentions. Why? There was no obvious answer and I decided to shelve the matter until I had had my evening milk and attended to my poor besmirched ears. First things first.

In the kitchen Bouncer was already bolting his Muncho and at first too engrossed to notice my presence. When he did, he stared for a few moments, and then grinning inanely asked if I had been at the sheep dip. I told him coldly to keep his feeble jokes to himself and that if he had nothing better to say he might like to listen instead. I then proceeded to tell him about the vicar and his letter to Rummage, adding scathingly that perhaps he or his sixth sense could shed some light on the matter.

He pondered, and then said, 'No, we can't. But you don't know that he was writing to Rummage.'

'I have just explained,' I replied patiently. 'When the ink was spilt and you woke howling like a dingo, apart from rudely cursing me he *also* cursed Rummage. The name just came out of the blue. Obviously that was because F.O. was in the middle of writing to him and the wretched man was on his mind!'

There was silence and the dog looked vacant. Then he said slowly, 'Well, if you say so, but it seems to me that –'

'Of course I say so! It is what is known as intelligent deduction. Some of us have that facility!'

189

He started to grin again. 'I say, Maurice, you do look funny with your face all navy blue!' It was too much. A claw to the snout was what was needed, but as I stretched out my paw he suddenly barked, 'Not *to* but *about*!' Just occasionally the dog has a point.

34

The Vicar's Version

Maurice's antics on top of my letter to Archdeacon Blenkinsop had been the last straw, and for the rest of the evening I took refuge in the lamentations of Job – a set of afflictions mildly more bearable than my own. It had been a particularly hectic day. Tapsell had thrown one of his more spectacular tantrums, the Mothers' Union had burst its tea-urn boiler, and at the last minute I had been summoned to stand in for one of Pick's cremations halfway across the county. By the time the four o'clock post arrived I was in no mood for further trials. But trials there were – firstly the letter itself and then Maurice's circus trick with the ink bottle. The latter was messy, the former dynamite.

'I have it on good authority,' Blenkinsop fulminated, 'that the dolt has already anticipated his appointment and had the nerve to order a new cassock. It is insufferable to think of that man being my successor. It reflects badly on me and I take it as a personal slur. And after all I have done to bring dignity to the diocese. The whole thing is monstrous!'

He was, of course, talking about Basil Rummage. Recent events had rather jostled Clinker's curious choice for the archdeaconry out of my mind. When he had first told me that Rummage was up his sleeve as trump card in the appointment stakes, I had been shocked but sceptical.

Clinker is given to hare-brained whims and I had not thought that this particular folly would see the light of day: the Cathedral Chapter would surely never countenance it. But according to Blenkinsop the Chapter was weakening, and the joker in the bishop's pack close to becoming his ace!

Over the years Blenkinsop's vaunted 'dignity' had often been wearisome, but was as nothing compared to the havoc that Basil Rummage would wreak were he to get his hands on a few clerical levers. As if there wasn't enough to contend with already! The awful incident in Foxford Wood had unleashed a train of turbulence from which it seemed impossible to escape. And now on top of everything, Rummage as archdeacon! Isaiah was spot on – there was indeed to be no peace for the wicked.

I brooded dismally on the news, and was even more depressed when it became clear that Blenkinsop was expecting me to do something to forestall the event.

'As the retiring incumbent,' he wrote, 'I of course hold little sway in such matters – at any rate not in any formal sense – but you, Oughterard, are in a different position, and of course will be directly affected by the new appointment. So not only is it in your own interests, it is your duty to the diocese and your brother clergy to organize some sort of ground resistance. Rummage is a most unsuitable candidate, and the bishop has always been wayward. Both need curbing. To this end I have taken the liberty of informing your immediate colleagues – Pick, Dooley, young Rothermere at Alfold – that you will shortly be convening a meeting and urging their support. This thing must be stopped!'

It was reassuring to learn that Blenkinsop shared my aversion to Rummage, but it was irksome to have been pushed into a position of required action. He had always been officious, and presumably this was his last chance of exercising control before retirement. Certainly the last thing I wanted was Rummage trumpeting about – but then neither did I want the chore and responsibility of heading a pressure group of Blenkinsop's devising! Being in thrall to Nicholas and Mrs Tubbly Pole was trouble enough; to have yet another ringmaster would be unendurable.

Lighting a cigarette and opening a fresh packet of humbugs, I began to grapple with penning a reply at once expressive of firm agreement yet somehow retaining a bland evasiveness. It was an arduous task but brought to an abrupt end – though not resolution – by Maurice's dastardly raid on the ink bottle.

Two days later I was still in a stew, having made no headway in my reply to Blenkinsop and certainly done nothing to summon the prescribed meeting. I am not very practised in 'ground resistance', and in any case doubted whether I had the flair to inspire others to the sort of insurrection Blenkinsop had in mind. The issue hung heavily upon me and I spent much of my time escaping at the piano in the musical reveries of Cole Porter. An impractical response but soothing.

Of all people it was Nicholas Ingaza who provided the answer, and to whom, despite his usual tiresomeness, I had reason to be grateful.

After the episode with the picture he had returned to Brighton in a state of pique and had remained mercifully silent. But I knew it could not last as he was bound to start agitating about the remaining Spendler still in my care (although I don't think 'care' was quite how he saw it, 'frigging useless!' having been his last remark to me). However, now safely installed in the crypt, the picture awaited his instructions.

These came over the telephone one evening, when he informed me that he would again be in the Cranleigh area doing some business with one of his 'old contacts' (scheming? hounding? putting the frighteners on?), and he could thus collect the goods on the way home. He sounded in a relatively mellow mood and I was glad that I had had the foresight to fetch the thing back from Primrose.

The next day I lugged the picture out of the crypt (yet again obstructed by Bouncer's antics) and placed it in the hall to await the arrival of its 'owner'. He appeared promptly at six o'clock the following evening, looking quite pleased with himself and evidently ready to enjoy a light supper of liver and baked beans before relieving me of the item and departing for Brighton. I assumed the negotiations with his 'contact' had gone well.

Now that I was about to see the end of the Spendler I felt much more relaxed and could almost take pleasure in Ingaza's presence. On form and uncrossed, he can be an engaging companion, and we spent a pleasant enough hour reminiscing about St Bede's and sipping the Beaujolais which I had bought as an emollient should he have been in less amiable mood.

Somehow the conversation got around to Rummage, about whom he made caustic remarks before adding, 'But you have to hand it to him. I mean, that card-sharping racket of his was a pretty slick business and they never rumbled it, you know.'

'Card-sharping?' I exclaimed.

'Oh yes. And for one as crass as Rummage, very successful,' Nicholas said bitterly. 'Fleeced me out of a nice little lot, I can tell you!'

I wasn't sure which astonished me the more – Rummage's activity at St Bede's or that in the course of it he had succeeded in fleecing Nicholas. I felt a twinge of unaccustomed respect for Rummage but it passed swiftly.

'But before I could even things up,' he went on, 'I was overtaken by events.'

'Thrown out, you mean.'

He blew a smoke ring. 'For a country parson, Francis, you have an amazingly subtle way with words!' There was silence as he appeared to brood, not on my verbal infelicity but on the missed opportunities of bringing Nemesis to Rummage.

After a while I cleared my throat, and said tentatively, 'Well, he's still making trouble all right. So actually, Nicholas, it might not be too late now ... to even things up, I mean.' He raised a quizzical eyebrow, and I proceeded to tell him about Rummage's outlandish aspirations and Clinker's determination to fast-track him into the archdeaconry. 'It's virtually a fait accompli,' I moaned.

'Shouldn't count on it, dear boy. After all, it's surprising how a judiciously placed word here or there can scuttle a chap's chances. I've seen it happen often. Of course, compared to when we were students, I gather the Church is pretty broad-minded these days. But even so, I doubt whether their lordships would be too keen on it being known that one of their archdeacons had been the godfather of a dodgy gaming syndicate!' He grinned slyly.

'No,' I said hesitantly but with vague stirrings of hope. 'No, I don't suppose they would ... Er, do you have any details?'

'I should say so!' And he proceeded to supply them with graphic zest.

'Good gracious!' I exclaimed. 'I had no idea. What an incredible set-up. Who'd have thought it!'

'Well, certainly not you, Francis. Little Johnnie-Head-In-Air, that was you in those days. In fact, come to think of it, not much change there – judging from the cock-up with the pictures!' And he pulled a mocking face. I affected not to notice.

Then helping himself to more wine, he said smoothly, 'Would you like me to do something about it? Might serve both our purposes – you know, tit for tat, *quid pro quo* etc. ...' The term struck echoes from the past, and I thought wryly that lack of change was not confined to me. But I think it was not so much the lost stakes in themselves that annoyed Nicholas, but rather the blow to his pride in being duped by Rummage.

I took another sip of wine and said slowly, 'But how could you possibly drop a word anywhere? I mean, let's face it, Nicholas, you are not exactly *persona grata* with the Church authorities, I rather doubt whether they would . . .'

'Take any notice, you mean? Easy. Ever heard of anonymous letters?'

I recoiled. 'Oh, don't be absurd, that's ridiculous! Besides, who on earth would be persuaded by something as crude as that?'

He grinned. 'Caspard would.'

'Caspard? Who's he?'

He sighed. 'Your memory, Francis! He was in your year at St Bede's, and now if I'm not mistaken – well, according to the *Times* clerical column – quite a powerful influence at Lambeth, one of Fisher's *éminences grises*, so I gather.'

I cast my mind back, trying to recall. And at last the image came. Yes, that was him, always in the front seat of the lecture hall, feverishly writing down every syllable: that boring little twerp Hugo – Hugo Caspard, white of face and slow of wit. Fancy him climbing the heights to Lambeth! Just went to show . . . something or other at any rate.

'But why should Caspard in particular be persuaded by an anonymous letter?' I asked.

'Rummage decapitated his rubber duck.'

'He did *what*!' I cried.

'Yes, garrotted the duck and drank the gin.'

I stared blankly. 'What gin?'

'The gin in the duck of course.'

I began to wonder whether the Beaujolais was more potent than I had thought, or whether Nicholas was in the early stages of dementia. Clearly one of us was having problems. However, I politely asked him to explain.

'You remember that St Bede's was a dry house – still is probably – and alcohol strictly off bounds and the nearest pub three miles away?' I nodded. 'Well, Caspard had a kid's floating duck which had originally contained some scented squirty stuff – swiped it off a small niece, I think – which he replaced with gin. So every time he took a bath (which was pretty often), out would come the duck. Quite sharp really for Caspard. Anyway, Rummage got wind of this, stole the duck, and because the valve was clogged with soap or something, cut its neck with his penknife and demolished the contents. In a hurry, I suppose. Caspard never got over it.'

At first the tale seemed wildly improbable; but remembering Rummage's outrageous plundering of my best malt whisky when staying at the vicarage the previous year, I began to think it was very likely true.

'So you think Caspard might be susceptible, do you?'

'I'd put a tenner on it easily. After all, he wouldn't need to *believe* the gambling business; simply use it as a convenient pretext to query the candidate and scupper the appointment. A lot would be made about "no smoke without fire" and "can't afford the risk" etc. etc. Oh yes, he'd be susceptible all right: a heaven-sent chance to even up the score and get Rummage out for a duck, you might say!'

The prospect was enticing but I felt uneasy. 'It's all very well, Nicholas, but I don't think I really like the anonymous letter bit. It seems rather extreme – and besides, it's not quite cricket, is it? You know, poison pens and all that . . .' And with a pang of humiliation I recalled my father's withering scorn when he had once caught me surreptitiously forcing the lock on Primrose's tuck box.

'Oh, come off it, Francis. Ever the moralist!'

'Well . . .' I began defensively.

'So what do you suggest then?'

'Perhaps we could get someone else to drop a word in Caspard's direction, someone who knows him and whose views, unlike yours, he might listen to.'

'Can't help you there. Rather out of touch with the network, dear boy!'

I took another helping of baked beans, and pondered. 'Blenkinsop,' I said. 'He's often at Lambeth and may well have met Caspard – or he'll make it his business to once I've alerted him to one or two things!'

'You're learning, Francis,' laughed Nicholas. 'Should have been in the Vatican!'

'Certainly not,' I protested. 'Heaven forfend!'

It worked. I convened Blenkinsop's prescribed meeting, explained the situation and told them of the incipient dangers should Rummage be appointed, i.e. labour and mayhem. They were as disinclined as myself to be harried by some manic narcissist, and voted unanimously that Blenkinsop be apprised of what I had learnt of the candidate's past activities.

'Of course,' I said, 'one cannot be sure that one's informant is entirely reliable and there may well be an element of exaggeration, but in the circumstances I think it is something that at least ought to be *aired*.'

There was a snigger from Rothermere. 'Yes, and who better to air it than old man Blenkinsop! Give a dog a bone . . .'

I fixed him with a sober eye. 'The archdeacon has the interests of the diocese at heart, and it is incumbent upon us to assist him in his efforts to secure a calm and worthy successor to his own office. It ill becomes you, Rothermere, to treat this matter as a jest.'

'No blooming jest,' moaned Pick. 'Mark my words, if Basil Rummage gets in we shall have church fêtes foisted upon us for every season of the year!'

'Tell Blenkinsop anything you like,' cried Dooley. 'We must get to the pub, it's nearly closing time!'

Thus I was able to report to the archdeacon that I had done as he wished: organized the meeting and secured the full support of my colleagues in questioning Rummage's fitness for the post. I added that it had come to our notice that rumours were circulating suggesting that the bishop's candidate was not unacquainted with gambling dens – scurrilous tales, of course, but then . . .

Rothermere was right about the bone. Blenkinsop seized it, rushed up to Lambeth and laid it smartly at Caspard's feet. The latter must have thought it was Christmas and moved like lightning, for only a week later I had a telephone call from Blenkinsop informing me that the 'little problem' of his successor had been removed and the normal selection procedures resumed. 'It is reassuring to know,' he said acidly, 'that one's contribution to the diocese will not now be rendered futile by the cavortings of a demented Scaramouche. Caspard's got his wits about him all right, grasped the matter instantly and moved accordingly.'

Huh! I thought. Could never grasp anything at St Bede's – except for the perishing duck of course!

The following week I had to go up to London for one of the conferences so beloved of The Powers That Be. 'Parish Strategy' was this month's theme, and not finding any obvious excuse for staying away, I duly caught the train to Waterloo and made my way over to the conference centre in the Brompton Road. The one real benefit of these meetings is that I have the chance to pop into Harrods and stock up with my favourite brand of peppermint, Jumbo Johnnies. These are a rather superior kind of humbug to which I am particularly partial, but which, as far as I can make out, are obtainable only from Harrods. In this respect the bi-monthly meetings are very useful.

As a matter of fact, I quite like visiting the pet department in Harrods. It is next door to Toys on the third floor. You used to be able to buy kittens there and even puppies, but nowadays it seems confined largely to guinea pigs and hamsters. However, it makes a pleasant little prelude to the gruelling complexities of Church policy. Indeed, so engrossed was I in the antics of a white mouse on its wheel that I nearly forgot the time and arrived at the conference hall breathless and ill-prepared. In my haste I think I had dropped the agenda somewhere near the white mouse's cage, and as there didn't seem to be any spare copies around, I had little idea of the topics under discussion. However, at such times I generally find that a sharpened pencil and an enquiring expression do much to conceal the inner void.

Eventually proceedings came to a close and we repaired to the canteen for tea and cake. There were more people than usual and long queues at the counter. Deciding that it wasn't worth the wait, I was about to leave when I received a hearty thump between the shoulder blades.

'Wotcha, Francis! How's it going?'

Rummage. I hadn't noticed him at the meeting and presumably he must have arrived even later than me and slipped into the back row. For one who had just seen advancement slither from his predatory fingers, he seemed remarkably sanguine, not to say jaunty. I told him that things were going very well, thank you. But then to my annoyance he proceeded to rake over the events of the previous year, i.e. the Foxford Wood affair.

'Funny that old girl getting bumped off like that,' he observed cheerfully. 'Must have caused quite a stir in the parish. You knew her pretty well, didn't you? Always at the church apparently – keen as mustard, they say!'

'She did attend,' I murmured.

'Must have happened just before you popped down to Brighton. Funny to think of her lying there only half a mile away, while there was me sitting in your kitchen keeping the cat company and reading the papers!' (*And* drinking my best malt, I thought bitterly.) 'Anyway, I suppose it's all died down now – though don't think anyone was actually nailed for it, were they? Some nutter probably.'

'It has completely died down,' I said firmly. 'And in any case, it is generally presumed to have been the flashing tramp.'

'Ah, but they don't *know*, do they? replied Rummage darkly.

'No,' I agreed, 'they don't know.'

'Oh well, nice little mystery waiting for some cub reporter to cut his teeth on! "Investigative journalism", I think they call it . . . Anyway, how's the cat?'

I don't normally talk about Maurice. His presence has an insistency requiring no further reference. But for once I was only too glad to turn the conversation in his direction and talked fulsomely of his latest sulks and antics.

Rummage listened for a time, and then said suddenly, 'You know, Francis, some swine ruined my chances over the archdeacon business. I'd had Clinker eating out of my hand, and then just at the last moment it was all off and they turned me down flat. Very fishy. Just goes to show – they're so hidebound they don't know a good man when they see one. Shame really, I was all geared up to give the diocese a real rocket – had some *very* bright ideas up my sleeve, I can tell you!'

I recoiled, but said soothingly, 'Ah well, plenty of time yet – you'll get your chance, I'm sure . . .'

He grinned. 'Not here I won't! I'm off to Swaziland.'

'To where?'

'You know, one of those African outposts. Got an uncle there who's quite big in Church administration, and he says they're crying out for archdeacons and there's a nice little number all lined up for me if I care to take it. It's got the added kudos of being Director of Missionary Studies. Just up my street. With my flair and energy I'll soon put the skids under our coloured friends!' And giving me another hearty slap on the back he sauntered off. I winced and offered up a prayer for Swaziland.

The Spendlers off my hands, Blenkinsop mollified and Rummage's hash settled, I began to feel mildly relaxed. For the next couple of weeks life in Molehill continued at its normal stately pace, and apart from being regularly buttonholed by Mavis Briggs complaining about the loss of her picture, I spent a tranquil time.

This was not to last, for Primrose telephoned announcing her imminent intention of coming to stay for a couple of nights on her way up north to some sheep-etching fest. It sounded a rather dreary affair to me but she seemed to be relishing the prospect, and I set about making the spare bedroom moderately habitable. This took rather a time as it hadn't been used since Rummage's visit nearly a year ago and still bore his traces – discarded socks, rusting razor blades, dust-laden copies of *Sporting Life*, deposits of chewing gum, and under the bed a well-worn vest. Such had been my nightmare preoccupations in the weeks following the Wood Incident that domestic matters had sunk low on the scale of priorities. But now, in slightly better frame of mind, I could attend to the room's cleansing with a degree of zeal.

I was pleased with the result and began vaguely to look forward to Primrose's stay. The first night of this proved congenial; the second less so, for events occurred over which I had no control – although she clearly thought I should.

35

The Cat's Memoir

There was a sudden squall of fur and fury as the dog cannonballed through the doorway.

'They're here!' he bellowed.

'Who's here?' I cried, leaping on to the desk-top.

'THEY are here! Those sodding chinchillas!'

'She hasn't brought those, surely!' I exclaimed. 'You're imagining it. They are on your mind too much.'

'They are not on my mind. They are in THIS HOUSE!' he bawled. Slipping from the desk, I scurried across the room and poked my head round the door and peered into the hall.

The dog was right. The rabbits sat there fatly in their cage, munching complacently as their owner talked volubly and defensively to her brother.

'Well, you always bring your creatures to my house,' I heard her exclaim. 'And these are so much better behaved than yours. They'll be no trouble at all! All they need is a bit of warmth and some lettuce. A few kind words wouldn't come amiss either, but I suppose that is too much to expect!' She threw her hat down decisively on the hall table, an action that seemed to stake a claim for the rabbits' rights. I could see F.O. wilting.

Returning to the study, I found Bouncer in a state of high agitation. Excitement at the creatures' presence coupled with the prospect of 'settling their hash' was making him scuttle about the room in a maddening way, and it took me some time to calm his nerves and restore a modicum of quiet. Eventually, however, he subsided and I promised I would do what I could to help him secure retaliation for their earlier rudeness. I suggested gently that he might prefer to sleep in the crypt that night, but he rejected the idea, saying that it was imperative he kept guard on the house as you 'never knew' with chinchillas. Quite what he expected the chinchillas to do I had no idea – but then, as I have remarked before, the minds of dogs move in mysterious ways.

The next morning he was up at the break of dawn, scrabbling around, sniffing the air and muttering continuously about 'bastard bunnies'. I began to wonder if he was quite right in the head – but then I often wonder that.

Mercifully some of the fuss was defused by the vicar's sister coming downstairs in her nightdgown to make some early morning tea. Ever since she fed him a marrow bone on our visit to Sussex, the dog imagines he has a special relationship with her and is invariably eager to please in the hope of getting another. Thus the moment she entered the kitchen he turned meek and fawning, a spectacle which I found distinctly nauseous. In fact, after she had gone upstairs again I told him exactly that. Needless to say he was quite unabashed and simply grinned, saying something about 'survival tactics'. I reminded him that since he was one of the most privileged dogs in the neighbourhood the matter of his survival was hardly in question. That too cut no ice, and still grinning he squirmed his way through the pet flap and out into the garden. Peace was brief, as ten minutes later he was back again.

'I've been having a good look at them,' he announced.

'Oh yes? So what are they doing?'

'Sleeping.'

'Well, that *is* exciting!' I observed.

'Yes, but you see, Maurice,' he said eagerly, 'while they're like that you can prepare your plans!'

'My plans! What plans?'

'Your plans for settling their hash!'

'Ah yes, *those* plans,' I said hastily, remembering my rash promise. Fortunately I am never wrong-pawed for long, and a ruse quickly presented itself.

'We'll set Goliath on them,' I murmured.

'Goliath!' he yelped. 'You don't mean that squitty little midget with the red bow? Fat lot of good he'll be!'

'That squitty little midget has very sharp teeth and hellish screams. Put him near the rabbits and they'll go berserk. The sound alone should do the trick! Those lop ears are extremely sensitive.' And I winced, remembering the last time I had heard theYorkshire terrier in full cry.

'Think I'd rather have a go myself,' he growled. 'I don't much care for that Goliath, he's a stuck-up little prig. Swaggers around on those titchy pins as if he owned the place. And he looks silly anyway, with that stupid ribbon on his head!'

I told him that sartorial matters were hardly our concern, and that the essential thing was to give maximum disturbance to the chinchillas while exposing ourselves to minimum attention. 'After all, Bouncer, you wouldn't want that Primrose woman to think that you'd had anything to do with her rabbits' discomfort. No chance of marrow bones then! And *I* certainly do not propose getting my paws sullied in the affair.'

'I suppose so,' he agreed grudgingly.

'Look,' I said briskly, 'it's quite simple. You go and chat up Goliath – ask him round to play. He'll be so surprised he'll turn up out of curiosity. Then when you two are busy sniffing and racing around I will saunter over to the rabbits' cage and with a deft flip of my paw release the catch. The rabbits will come thumping out on to the lawn, at which point you give Goliath the slip and go and lie down quietly in your basket. The garden table is thus set for a feast of Yorkshire Batter and Rabbit Pie!'

I was rather pleased by that witty sally and laughed loudly, not something I do very often. But the dog looked puzzled as he often does, and merely said, 'If you say so, Maurice.'

36

The Vicar's Version

Were it not for the rabbits, I am sure Primrose's visit would have been a moderate success. As it was, Boris and Karloff played a major part in ruining the peace that might have prevailed had she been travelling alone. Their appearance in my hall, hutched and munching, took me by surprise and I was irritated that she had not forewarned me of their advent.

At first she was set on their spending the night in the kitchen next to the boiler, but I explained that, being conservative by nature, Bouncer might not take kindly to flop-eared strangers usurping his favourite spot. Eventually she conceded that they would fare best under the apple tree in the back garden. The process of carrying the hutch there, watering and feeding the inmates, and establishing whether they preferred a southerly or westerly outlook, seemed to take an unconscionable time; and when eventually my guest was satisfied, I was in acute need of rest and sustenance myself.

Finally the ritual was complete, and we retired to the kitchen and to supper. The rest of the evening passed pleasantly enough, with Primrose talking animatedly about the injustices of the tax system and how she, as an artist, should be allowed substantial concessions in matters fiscal. I asked whether that might not also apply to vicars, but from what I could make out she didn't seem to think they counted in the scheme of things.

My earlier domestic efforts were rewarded, for Primrose appeared well satisfied with the spare room and actually complimented me on the choice of bed linen. The next morning she announced that she had slept well – something I had failed to do, being kept awake by the dog roaming about below grumbling and scrabbling. He doesn't usually do that and I concluded it must have had something to do with the invasion of foreign pets. However, despite such minor irritations the visit was proving fairly congenial ... It was the afternoon's events that curdled the cream.

Primrose had decided to do a spot of shopping in Guildford before setting off for the north. And after tackling the usual paperwork I had settled down for a brief session with the crossword. I wasn't making much headway, and glancing out of the window saw Bouncer ambling around accompanied by what at first I took to be a large red squirrel. Such creatures are rarely seen in these parts of the country, and I was intrigued. But squirrels, red or grey, are not normally known for sporting scarlet topknots, and I quickly realized that the dog's companion was no squirrel but Goliath, the miniature Yorkshire terrier belonging to Tapsell's aunt. However, as the two dogs seemed to be behaving themselves I lost interest and began to doze off ...

A minute later sleep was shattered by ear-piercing yelps. And leaping from my chair I was horrified to see Primrose's chinchillas bounding about the lawn pursued by the screaming Goliath. Fortunately the study has a french window and I was able to intervene before carnage occurred, but it was a close-run thing. The miscreant scooted off through the hedge and I was left to minister to his victims as best I could.

The smaller one – Boris, I think – lay spread-eagled on the grass clearly in a state of imminent demise. Desperately I started to stroke its ruffled fur and psyche. And then crooning words of comfort and shoving a carrot under the twitching nose, I eased the creature back into the hutch where it sprawled vacantly. So engrossed was I with Boris that I had overlooked his stable mate; and when I turned round, Karloff was nowhere to be seen. I wasn't sure what to do about this and tried a few tentative whistles and sundry coaxing noises which I thought perhaps congenial to rabbits. They obviously weren't, for Karloff remained resolutely out of sight while I spent a good half-hour vainly peering into bushes and scrabbling about in flower-beds and the depths of the potting shed. To no avail: the creature had completely vanished. I trailed back to the house dreading Primrose's return and cursing everything and everybody.

In the kitchen Bouncer lay curled in his basket snoring loudly, and I envied him his innocent ease. Then, just as I was working out how best to mollify Primrose, there was a loud banging on the front door. It was rather early for my sister, and I assumed it was some parishioner too myopic to see the bell. Irritably I flung open the door . . . and came face to face with the Whippet.

Instantly all thoughts of rabbits evaporated and were replaced by images of the summer beech wood with its torn bracken, barking roebuck, and mangled bluebells. With frozen smile, I ushered him in.

Normally March and Samson would appear in tandem and I was surprised to see the latter on his own for once. Somehow Samson without March was more worrying than with, and I could feel a tightening in my chest as I tried to work out the reason for his visit.

'Glad to find you in, sir,' he began nasally. 'Got something important to ask you.' He paused, glanced at me quickly, and then started to scan the room as if choosing his words. I noted the sallow cheeks and darting eyes, and wondered numbly what it was to be – Foxford Wood or the Spendlers. 'Yes,' he continued slowly, 'Mr March sent me. He's got one of his ideas . . .' (When hasn't he! I thought. And my mind raced frantically, trying to predict which aspect of my pathetic subterfuge was about to be explored, exposed.)

'Oh yes?'

'Yes. Wants me to find out whether you'd be prepared to support the Police Benevolent Fund. Says what with you being charitable and all that, you might like to contribute to our fund-raising drive.' And thrusting his thin fingers into his raincoat pocket, he pulled out a biro and crumpled booklet. 'Raffle tickets,' he said. 'Half-a-crown a strip.'

I gazed incredulously. 'Of course . . . er, of course . . . I'll, uhm, take five strips!'

Such was my shock I might easily have suggested ten or twenty, but Samson seemed entirely satisfied with the five and was already intent on laboriously tearing them from their perforations and scribbling down my name. The normally sour expression had relaxed somewhat (satisfaction at an easy touch?), and in a sudden access of gratitude I invited him to sit down and have a cigarette. I had forgotten that he rolled his own, and lit a Craven 'A', while he ferreted around with his tin and Rizla papers. In the process copious threads of tobacco were shed, and while to my inexpert eye the resulting cylinder looked thin and squashed, he began to draw upon it with obvious relish.

Given the social nature of the visit I felt that perhaps a few pleasantries were in order, and was just about to embark on these when I noticed him staring past me with a look of glazed horror.

'God in heaven!' he ejaculated.

I turned, and was confronted by the mountainous white fur and staring pink eyes of the chinchilla. It sat stolidly on the table by the open window, its fat flanks moving rhythmically and nose twitching. For a few seconds I was mesmerized, and then made a lunge to grab it; tripped, missed, and fell on my knees. The rabbit scuttled to the far end of the table, plopped heavily on to the sofa and then on to the floor.

'Quick!' I yelled to Samson. 'He's valuable, head him off!'

Whether it was the reference to money, or whether chasing rabbits was a more stimulating option than selling raffle tickets, I do not know; but the Whippet suddenly bestirred his legs, and in a sort of wild rugby dive flung himself in the direction of Karloff. The latter was quick and, for all its size, nimble. But Samson somehow managed to grab the creature's scruff, and with a yelp of triumph and grinning from ear to ear, scrambled to his feet brandishing the kicking trophy aloft.

It was at that moment that Primrose walked in.

Presented with the sudden spectacle of her brother on all fours, and an unknown man standing with smouldering fag-end in one hand and her rabbit swinging from the other, I suppose it is not surprising that Primrose went mildly berserk. With a cry of fury she launched herself upon Samson, relieved him of Karloff, and with a spare fist knocked him into the armchair.

'Here!' he protested weakly. 'You can't do . . .' His voice trailed off as, clutching the chinchilla in her arms, she towered menacingly above him.

'Oh yes I can!' she snarled. 'I've read about your sort. You're one of those urban poachers who go around stealing people's prize pets and then sell them for vast sums of money. Well, you're not going to get away with it here. I'll have you know my brother's the vicar!'

'Yes,' said Samson wearily, passing his hand over his eyes, 'I know.'

I got up off my knees and cleared my throat. 'Uhm . . . actually, Prim, he's not a poacher, he's a policeman. He was just helping me to . . .' And I proceeded to outline the afternoon's events.

37

The Dog's Diary

Sometimes that cat can be too clever by half! Take last week, for example. Those lop-eared loons really got their come-uppance, but the point is I didn't see any of it! I mean, it was all very well him getting me to invite Goliath over and then opening their cage door, but it's not much cop getting your own back if you're not there to enjoy it! 'Go to your basket,' the cat directed, 'and lie doggo.' Well, I did just that and then missed all the fun!

Maurice says that it's not seeing but *knowing* that matters. He can say that of course – he knows *and* saw! Apparently that little snitch Goliath gave 'em a right run around and I did hear some of the noise, but by then I was doing what Maurice told me to – lying in my basket pretending to be asleep. Mind you, it worked all right. F.O. came traipsing into the kitchen effing and blinding because he had lost Karloff, and I just lay there snoring my head off. He gave me a pat and I heard him say what a good boy I was. Still, I'd much rather have been with Goliath giving those rabbits a seeing to! Oh well, can't have everything, I suppose, and at least I'm in the vicar's good books for a while. Perhaps if I play my biscuits right he'll give me another bone.

I don't think that sister was too pleased with things. Maurice said she didn't half rough up the policeman, and then gave F.O. a right earful. But she smiled at me when she left (though I noticed not at Maurice), so that was all right. Somehow I don't think we'll be seeing those chinchillas again.

He's beginning to calm down now, and I heard him in the bath this morning belting out 'Fight the Good Fight' (generally a good sign); though can't say I've ever seen him fighting for anything much, gets knackered too easily. I like a good scrimmage myself, clears the lungs and tones the muscles. That's why I was fed up missing out on the rabbits. Still, I've got a lot to tell O'Shaughnessy, and perhaps when I get to the main part I'll put myself in the picture a bit more. After all, if I *had* been there I would have been JOLLY GOOD.

I had a nice time in the crypt today and really put the frighteners on those spiders. If you leave them alone for too long they get smug and bossy, so now and again they need to be reminded who's really in charge. I told them – 'Bouncer's Boss down here!' – and they soon got the message. After that I had a good listen to the old ghosts gabbling on. They make a terrible row sometimes, but if they get too noisy I start on my baying practice, and that generally does the trick – they go as silent as the grave!

I did a lot of my special thinking too. I know that the type from Brighton has gone away with the pictures, and the vicar's pleased about that. But *I* think he's counting his bones before they're safely buried. I've got one of those feelings coming on that Maurice is so sniffy about. *I* think the Brighton man is going to come back and mess things up again. Shan't tell the cat just yet as he'll only get tetchy. But mark my words, something's brewing up and it's not the vicar's tea!

38

The Vicar's Version

It is painful to dwell on the mood of Primrose's departure. Suffice it to say that she went, and I survived. For some days afterwards my nerves were not at their best, and it was with particular horror that I once again heard a thundering on the front door. I opened it with knotted fears, convinced that I would see March and Samson, this time presenting not raffle tickets, but handcuffs. It was, in fact, Mrs Tubbly Pole.

Relief turned to dazed wonder as, pushing past me and striking a charadic pose, she announced breathlessly: 'Gunga Din has slain Goliath!'

'What *do* you mean!' I exclaimed.

'What I say! My poor boy has scuppered that little beast, and we must get away from Molehill immediately or I shall be lynched by the owner and Gunga put down. You must help us, Francis! Where's your gin?'

I silently poured her the drink, disturbed less by the news itself than by the part I was evidently required to play in it.

'Er – what on earth induced him to do it? He always seems so docile!' (Euphemism for bovine.)

'That tarty ribbon the little beast always wore. It was a red bow to a bulldog. Gunga hated it. All the owner's fault!' She paced up and down swigging the gin and chewing the lemon abstractedly. 'We must make our escape,' she continued, 'out of season, threading dark-eyed night.'

'What?'

'*King Lear, King Lear*!' she cried impatiently.

'I'm sorry, I don't know what –'

'*Lear* – don't you know your Shakespeare? Really, Francis, for a parson you are totally illiterate!'

'I'm not!' I protested. 'I know a good number of poems. Learnt them at school. For example there's that nice one beginning –'

'For goodness sake, Francis, stop blathering and let me think. It's action we need, not poems!' She frowned and sat down heavily on the sofa. I lit a cigarette and waited.

'Now,' she said in more reflective tones, 'what I shall need is your car. You must drive us up to London tonight. I shall deposit Gunga Din with my niece, Lily, and embark for America the day after.'

'America?' I queried. 'Isn't that a trifle excessive?'

She looked up. 'Ah, didn't I tell you? They want me to do a lecture tour in a month's time – *very* lucrative. Thought I could get my researches here wrapped up and then take off, but this little matter has rather accelerated things. Shall have to leave immediately. Pity, really, as I was just beginning to get the feel of Molehill's murder. And because of your hound's mysterious illness you haven't even had time to show me the crime spot . . . Still, I shall have to go. Can't risk being had up in court and Gunga being impounded. Needs must when the devil drives!'

'I know just what you mean,' I cried eagerly. 'You'll have to go!'

We sat a little longer discussing the logistics of her decampment. It was arranged that I should collect her at half past eight that evening when she would be ready with dog and essential luggage. I apparently would be responsible for boxing up the remaining impedimenta, dispatching

215

it to London and returning the keys to the estate agent. Normally the prospect of such onerous tasks would have filled me with gloom, but in the circumstances I agreed to undertake them with sprightly heart.

As directed, I arrived at Mrs Tubbly Pole's promptly at eight thirty. The house was unlit and, without the glow of the porch lamp, the garden in darkness. I made my way up the front path, tripped over a watering can, and cursed.

'Ssh!' came a loud stage whisper from inside the porch. 'You'll wake the whole neighbourhood!'

'It is awake,' I said, peering into the depths and seeing nothing, 'it's only half past eight.'

'Don't be so literal, Francis,' the voice exclaimed impatiently. 'Here, take the dog.' And the next moment a leaden weight, draped in what seemed an army blanket, was thrust into my arms. It proceeded to lick my face with dedicated vigour. From behind my burden I could now make out the bulky form of its owner, clad also in something resembling an army blanket but darker and more voluminous. Clamped on her head was the Bud Flanagan velour. 'We're wearing our escape gear,' she hissed excitedly. 'Good camouflage, don't you think?' I said nothing, trying vainly to dodge Gunga Din's doting kisses. The slaying of Goliath, it seemed, had done little to chasten the bulldog's inbred mawkishness.

Fortunately she seemed to be carrying only modest baggage, a small suitcase and a holdall – the latter, I suspected, containing the essentials of typewriter and dog food. We processed slowly down the path: she leading the way on a sort of lumbering tiptoe, and me, with my now squirming and loudly panting companion-in-arms, bringing up the rear.

'Keep his *head* covered, Francis!' she hissed, looking over her shoulder. 'It's essential he's not recognized!' I struggled to adjust the blanket but to little effect. As we reached

216

the car, she added, 'Can't think why you didn't leave your collar off.'

'Whatever for?' I whispered. (Mrs T.P.'s conspiratorial stealth was becoming infectious.)

'Disguise, of course. We don't want all and sundry noticing the vicar driving hell for leather out of Molehill at this time in the evening.'

'I have no intention of driving hell for leather,' I protested.

'Well, you can't mess about, you know. It's imperative we make good our escape with maximum speed and minimum observation. Now put Gunga in the back and hurry up!' So saying, she wrenched open the passenger door of the Singer and started to install herself. The Singer was small and low slung, Mrs Tubbly Pole large. The logistics of squeezing much into little proved a challenging task. However, it was finally achieved and she sank back with a sigh of relief. It was at this point that the dog, suddenly tiring of its slobbering attentions, leaped from my arms, and grasping a corner of the blanket in its teeth shot off down the road. 'Shot' perhaps is an overstatement. It lumbered briskly.

'Gunga!' she bellowed out of the car window, all care of secrecy gone. 'Come back, you hound! After him, Francis! After him!'

I began the pursuit, but as he reached the kerb he was joined by a large setter that I had seen on a number of occasions loitering near the vicarage. There followed a spirited skirmish, each dog intent on gaining/retaining the blanket. It was a kind of running battle with a good deal of growls and yelps but not, mercifully, much aggression. Just as the setter wrested it from the bulldog, a diminutive figure appeared round the corner, got caught in the mêlée, and was promptly knocked flat by the victor's war dance of triumph.

I went forward and began to pick up Mavis Briggs.

* * *

217

There is not much difference between Mavis standing and Mavis supine. In neither position does she make much sense. 'Where am I?' she asked fatuously. 'What happened?'

'On the pavement. You were run over by a dog,' I replied shortly, hauling her up.

'Oh dear! How dreadful, how dreadful!' she quavered. 'Do you think I've broken anything?'

'Not for one moment,' I said briskly. 'Now sit on this bit of wall, you'll soon feel better.' And I tried to propel her towards the crumbling masonry. She eyed it doubtfully.

'It looks rather damp, Vicar, and I don't think I'd like to . . . Oh, isn't that your car over there?'

'My car?' I muttered vaguely. 'Er . . . oh, yes it is, actually – but you can't sit in there!'

'Why ever not? After all, I may have broken some bones – people do, you know.'

'Yes, but you haven't and I am afraid the car is full.'

'Full? Full of what?'

I thought of Mrs Tubbly Pole slumped and shrouded in the passenger seat. 'Sacks of coal. Stocking up for the winter, you know!' And I laughed encouragingly. She seemed disinclined to share the mirth. Out of the corner of my eye I could see the errant Gunga scrabbling to get in at the rear door which had been left slightly open. It was now nearly nine o'clock and he must have been missing his evening gin – as presumably was the occupant. I stood squarely in front of Mavis, blotting her vision.

Suddenly, the air was rent with the blaring of a klaxon; a single burst, its provenance unmistakable. I spun round in horror. For God's sake, what was she *doing*!

'But that's your car!' Mavis exclaimed. 'I thought you said it was full of coal. There must be somebody –'

'Oh no, it's the electrics,' I gabbled, 'awful trouble with them recently. Completely up the spout! It keeps doing that for no reason, must get it fixed!' She looked dazed, as well she might.

And then just at that moment I heard the familiar tap-

218

tapping of stick on stone, accompanied by the faint notes of tuneless whistling . . . Savage, returning home from one of his late calls.

'Why, here's Mr Savage,' I cried, 'the piano doctor! Just the chap to keep you company on this wall, Mavis. You can tell him all about your accident and those marauding dogs!' Mavis brightened. Savage did not.

'Here, what's going on?' he said.

'Mavis has had a little upset,' I explained, 'but I'm sure if you stay with her for a moment or two she'll soon be to rights.'

'Why can't you stay?' he asked suspiciously.

'Sorry, in a rush. Got to see a man about a hymn book . . . terribly late!'

Not that he could know, but Mavis had resumed her victim's expression and I felt a pang of guilt as I scuttled away knowing that Savage was in for a long saga.

Regaining the dubious sanctuary of the car, I pressed the starter, crashed the gear, and propelled us forward with a lurch.

'What did you do that for?' I expostulated. 'Woke the whole neighbourhood!'

'I thought you said it was awake already,' she replied sweetly. 'Anyway, I didn't do it, it was Gunga. He wanted to sit on my lap and knocked against the horn. Getting agitated, poor boy.' Not the only one, I thought grimly.

My passenger pulled the Flanagan hat further down over her eyes, turned up the collar of her escape garb, and with a sigh settled into sleep and what she fondly supposed to be anonymity. I gave thanks for very small mercies and pressed on into the night.

I arrived back in Molehill well after midnight, having stopped first at Lily's to deposit Gunga Din, and then on to Mrs Tubbly Pole's flat in Maida Vale. The parting between dog and mistress had been lengthy and lachrymose, but Lily assured me it was always thus and that each rallied the instant the other was out of sight.

'The reconciliations are far worse,' she confided gloomily. 'Total mayhem. I have to lie down for two days afterwards.' Knowing what I did of both parties, and sharing similar sensitivities, I did not think this latter claim exaggerated. Nor had Lily exaggerated her aunt's speed of recovery. As we drove towards Maida Vale, Mrs T. P. was in gloating mood, delighted to have eluded 'my pursuers', and talking volubly about the loot she was going to rake in from her American lecture tour.

Unlike the dog's, my own parting from her was fortunately without drama, but she thanked me effusively for 'assisting the Muse', and threatened to return to Molehill immediately the dust had settled on 'that little beast's demise'. I prayed fervently that the dust be permitted to circulate for a considerable time.

Oddly enough, relieved though I undoubtedly was to be rid of her relentless sleuthing, I drove home in a curious state of deflation. Her presence in Molehill had been disrupting, preposterous; but she had exuded a humour and vitality which, largely lacking these qualities myself, I had found strangely companionable. It is true that I feel safer in monochrome, but a little colour does not come amiss; and I trusted that despite my hopes regarding the dust, one day – some *distant* day – we should meet again.

39

The Vicar's Version

It was the day I had been most dreading: June 17th – the terrible anniversary of the business in the woods. And just like that day, the morning dawned mistily bright, fresh and inviting. But this time I was far from being enticed to wander those sylvan paths with the melodies of birdsong and their memories of beauty, calm . . . and mind-numbing nightmare.

Instead, with curtains drawn and phone off the hook, I stayed glued to my desk, immersed first in the drudgery of parish accounts, and then in the curiously absorbing task of the following day's sermon. I say 'curiously' because although I have always taken the act of composition seriously, it is rare for me to be totally engaged – at least not in any dedicated sense. But that day something was different: I wrote rapidly, compulsively, and with a sense of conviction that normally only displays itself when I tackle the intricacies of the 'Goldberg' Variations or rehearse the insidiously soothing notes of that elegantly well-tempered *Klavier*. Now, however, instead of notes it was the words on the page which engrossed me – gripped my mind – and which made me write with such intensity and confidence.

When it was over I was exhausted; and went to the piano and played . . . not Bach, but Ellington. 'The "A" Train',

'Mood Indigo', 'Love You Madly' – anything in fact that came into my head – all was belted out, unsubtly, but with a zest and verve I hadn't experienced for a long time. The noise was thunderous – to blot out the ghosts? – and Bouncer, whose preference is usually for something more sombre, came snuffling in and sat companionably by the stool. Maurice was absent, but he generally is when things get musical.

The concert over, we retired to the graveyard where we were graciously joined by Maurice, and cat and dog bounded happily among the tombs; while I, lighting a cigarette and turning my back resolutely on the far prospect of Foxford Wood, sat down on the grass and meditated . . .

The following day, the Sunday, I quickly reread my sermon and prepared for church. For some reason I had an urge to take Bouncer – a desire not conspicuously shared by him as he was obviously intent on remaining in his basket with ball and bone. However, I pointed out that he was an idle hound and that if he wanted a good lunch he had better have the grace to come with me, otherwise it would be short commons for the rest of the day. That did it.

We set off briskly and arrived early. I went to kit myself up in the vestry and sent the dog on ahead to the pulpit. Bouncer has a liking for the pulpit, a fact I discovered early on in our relationship when, not sure whether he could be trusted to stay alone in the house, I would take him with me on my parish rounds. Walking up the path to the church one day, I had let him off the lead; and then, distracted by conversation with some worthy parishioner, had completely lost him. Half an hour was spent in aimless whistling and scouring the surrounding area. I was just thinking hopefully that he might have trotted off home, when Edith Hopgarden had emerged from one of the side doors and announced accusingly that the 'hearthrug' which I 'dragged around' was fast asleep in the pulpit and what did I intend doing about it?

Relieved that the animal had been found – and safely in innocuous slumber – I remarked mildly that I was a great believer in letting sleeping dogs lie, adding that I was sure that Bouncer was not the only one who slept in church, and that as long as he didn't snore there seemed no reason to disturb him. She gave me a funny look and marched off. Thus Bouncer had gained entrée to precincts ecclesiastical, and thereafter his occasional presence became an accepted fact. Apart from Edith (and Tapsell her musical paramour) none seemed to object, and services proceeded unaffected.

So that particular Sunday, with Bouncer installed in his customary place, things took their predicted course: ritual was punctiliously observed, my sermon duly delivered, Communion distributed, and the ceremonial brought to a close with the usual parleying in the porch. Except that this time the parleying was far from usual! There is a term which in my younger days used to be applied to the crooner Frank Sinatra: *mobbed*. But in this case it was not bobby-soxers who were doing the mobbing, but mature ladies and gentlemen of the Surrey and Anglican ilk.

Apparently they had approved the sermon: for I was pinioned against the porch wall, hand grasped and wrung, bombarded with questions I didn't really understand, asked earnestly for copies of my 'fascinating' address, showered with spit and invitations, urged to speak at Ladies' Guilds and Golfing Luncheons – and (slightly worryingly) requested to become the Visiting Pastor at the Home for the Afflicted and Intemperate.

Eventually I managed to make my escape, but not before being collared by Miss Dalrymple who, temporarily diverted from her normal pursuit of gum-chewing choir-boys, was clearly in magnanimous mood.

'Nice bit of preaching, Vicar, nice bit of preaching! Not like your predecessor Purvis – we couldn't understand a word he said. All very holy, I'm sure, but totally unintelligible. Your words make sense – that's what's needed! You see, *you* have the common touch.'

I winced at her choice of adjective but reflected ruefully that that was exactly what my father had once said, when as a boy I had thoughtlessly put out my tongue at one of his clients. There had been a fearful row.

'I liked your theme,' she said stoutly, '"Hope and Perplexity" – very fitting for today's society.'

I thanked her warmly but refrained from saying that although the latter was a very familiar condition, I was on less certain terms with the former . . .

'And what's more,' she breezed on, 'you are not an *interferer* – not like that dreadful man who was your locum last year, Rum something. Most officious!'

'No,' I acknowledged silently and gloomily, 'not an interferer, merely a dispatcher.'

And with that sobering thought, I called Bouncer to heel and we made our way home to lunch and sanctuary.

40

The Cat's Memoir

With the pair of them out of the house, it had been a restful morning. And I had been passing it lazily, dozing on the windowsill and occasionally toying with the knitted mouse presented to me by one of F.O.'s brighter parishioners.

The front door slammed loudly, heralding their return. And I heard the vicar's feet thudding up the stairs, followed by the sound of the dog's paws padding across the hall to the kitchen – obviously going to seek out fodder before regaling me with his exploits. I closed my eyes, savouring the final moments of quiet. All too soon the sitting-room door was pushed open and Bouncer wandered in, beard embellished with bits of Muncho, and crunching noisily.

'That was a cracking good sermon!' he announced cheerfully. 'Cracking good, it was.' I stared at him blankly as, biscuit demolished, he proceeded to worry his rubber ring.

'How can you possibly know?' I enquired. 'You wouldn't have understood the long words ... Besides, since when have *you* been a student of moral theology?' And I smiled indulgently.

'I know what I know,' he rejoined tartly. The dog likes that expression and uses it frequently, although it rarely enlightens.

'Really, Bouncer, just because F.O. occasionally lets you sit in the pulpit with him you don't have to pretend that you are *in* on the act!' And I waved my tail impatiently.

He looked up from the ring and said solemnly, 'Ah, but you see, Maurice, it's my sixth –'

'Your Sixth Sense. Yes, yes, we all know about that! But if you ask me, a bit of *common* sense wouldn't come amiss. How can you possibly declare that the vicar preached a good sermon when you do not produce a shred of evidence!'

'Oh, there was plenty of evidence all right,' he replied airily.

'Such as?'

'When he's burbling on I sometimes get a bit fidgety, and so I poke my head round the edge of the pulpit just to see what they are all doing down there in the pews.'

'Oh yes? And what are they doing?'

'Sometimes they are just sitting there like Christmas puddings. And other times they look silly and prim and pious. And now and again they look shifty – just like you do when you've been at the haddock in the pantry. And quite often I see that Hopgarden woman gazing at the organist and powdering her nose, and Colonel Dawlish having a crafty go at the crossword. But today they were all staring at F.O., and they looked, they looked . . . ALIVE!' And the dog started to bound about the room, rolling his eyes and flaunting his tail in what I took to be a copy of human animation.

Once the thespian antics had subsided, I asked gently whether that was his only proof of the sermon's quality.

'Oh no. Other things too.'

'Go on, then.'

'You see, for one thing there was the way they sung the hymn after the sermon was finished. Roared their heads off, they did. Roof nearly collapsed!'

'That doesn't mean anything,' I said indifferently. 'Probably relief that it was all over.'

'It was *not* relief,' he growled. 'It was . . .' There was a long pause while his brow furrowed and his jaws worked silently. This invariably means that he is grappling to deliver some new word or Latin term he has learnt from the tombs in the crypt. I waited patiently.

'EX-UL-TAT-IO!' he exploded. I leaped back, deafened by the blast but just able to execute a neat side-step as the dog raced up and down the room in triumph.

'Very nicely put,' I conceded, 'but is that all?'

He looked thoughtful, and then said, 'You know at the end of the service, when he hangs about in the porch and they all troop past?'

I nodded vaguely.

'Well, this time there was a big snarl-up. They were all flocking round – smiling, shaking his hand and jabbering away nineteen to the dozen. In fact there was such a scrum I thought I'd never get out from under their feet. Quite a bruising experience, you might say! Still, I managed to escape and went and sat quietly on the grass waiting for him to come back from the vestry. They were still muttering to one another as they walked down the path, and I kept hearing things like "good stuff", "makes you think", "he's got something there", "better than the last man". I tell you, Maurice, they all seemed pretty chuffed . . . So you see, he *did* preach a good sermon. And what's more, my bones and sixth sense tell me it won't be the last!'

He sat back on his haunches peering hopefully through the curtain of his fringe. Had I been a human he would have expected me to give him another biscuit or at least a kindly pat. As it was, he had to make do with a prod from my paw.

'Well, Bouncer,' I observed, 'fully focused attention, exultant hymn singing, expressions of thanks and approval – yes, you are quite right: it does indeed seem to suggest that our master delivered a tolerable address!' And I emitted a gracious mew of congratulation, while he beamed and wagged his tail vigorously. Then, without thinking, I foolishly added, 'And your Latin is coming along quite well too.'

I don't normally give lavish praise and immediately regretted the lapse, for it unleashed a maelstrom of such frenzied prancing and barking that I feared F.O. would come floundering down the stairs and set about the pair of us. But he was evidently locked in his afternoon collapse, for nothing stirred and one was thus spared the usual swirl of smoke and oaths. Nevertheless, I spoke sternly to Bouncer and warned him that if he didn't restrain himself he would be in line for a smart clip on the ear from Above.

'No I shan't,' he snorted. 'After that sermon he's out for the count – won't surface till drinks time. Bet you a Bonio!'

'I have no intention of engaging in games of chance – least of all for one of your teeth-shattering biscuits,' I replied, attempting to settle down to snooze. It was of course impossible.

'I say!' he exclaimed.

'What?'

'I wonder how many murderers can preach nice sermons? I mean, sermons that deliver the goods.'

'What goods?'

'Well, the goods that make you feel sort of hopeful and better. You know, like I feel when I hear the bells!'

'Not those confounded church bells again!' I groaned. The dog has a thing about bells. Says they churn him up inside – whatever that is supposed to mean. Fortunately I have never been thus affected. 'I have no idea,' I replied wearily, '. . . does it really matter?'

'P'raps not. But then again p'raps it does!'

I sighed. 'What *are* you talking about?'

'Well, the point is that if F.O. did something bad when he got rid of Fotherington – which I suppose he did, because of all the fuss and the way the cops kept nosing about, and the danger of him being caught and going to prison or being HUNG – then how is he doing good to people in church and making them feel alive and sort of strong?'

'Certainly doesn't make *me* feel strong,' I murmured sleepily. 'In fact there are times when he's in one of his panics that I feel distinctly fragile and debilitated . . .'

'Ah yes,' replied Bouncer affably, 'but then you're only a cat.'

'I *beg* your pardon!'

'Maybe I'll have a word with O'Shaughnessy – see what he thinks.'

'You will do nothing of the kind!' I cried, now thoroughly awake. 'On no account are you to discuss the Fotherington issue with that madcap setter. He may have helped us dispose of the evidence last year but he didn't know the crucial details of the case – and nor shall he! This is something we must keep strictly to ourselves. *Careless talk costs lives.* Just remember that!' And I fixed him with one of my more fearsome glares.

The dog does not often look abashed but he did then, and said meekly, 'You mean if I let the cat out of the bag there won't be any more Bonios and haddock.'

'Precisely, Bouncer. And kindly moderate your metaphors!'

'What?'

'Your metaphors, kindly adjust . . . oh never mind.' I was in no mood to instruct him in the niceties of semantic tact. And gathering my woollen mouse, I hastened from the room to view the sparrows on the terrace.

41

The Vicar's Version

The period following the success of the sermon and my farewell to Mrs T. P. turned out to be unusually soothing and productive: pressing paperwork had been completed, the Young Wives' annual gymnastic display less embarrassing than usual, another hefty chunk contributed to the Spire Fund by an unknown 'well-wisher', and St Botolph's actually featured in the *Church Times* as being an example of 'conservative calm and mellow dignity' – qualities, the writer lamented, which were fast disappearing from the current social scene. This last was an accolade indeed, and to celebrate I put a whacking fiver on the two-thirty and bought myself a half bottle of Glenfiddich. The horse fell at the first fence but the Scotch went down a treat.

Unfortunately it has generally been my experience that periods of pleasure are invariably paid for by events of dire discomfort. And this was no exception. Walking home with Bouncer from Evensong one evening, I saw Mavis Briggs coming towards me with intent expression. I sighed, assuming she was about to deliver another elegy on the theft of her painting. However, she seemed to be in a state of some considerable excitement and had started to gabble several yards in advance of our meeting.

Drawing level, she exclaimed, 'Oh Vicar, you'll never guess, never guess . . . not in a month of Sundays!'

'Really?' I said. 'Guess what?'

'You know my art class?' I nodded, and she continued. 'Well, our tutor is taking our little group up to London . . . to the *Tate* Gallery for a *lecture*!'

'That's very nice, Mavis. I am sure you will enjoy it,' I said indulgently.

'Oh, but I will, I will!' she cried. 'You see, it's to be a *very* special lecture.'

'Oh yes?' I replied abstractedly, debating whether I could goad myself into giving Bouncer a bath when we got home.

'Yes, it's going to be given by that great Austrian artist – Herr Spendlow! And our tutor has actually managed to get us seats. He's only in London for two days. Aren't we lucky!'

I gazed open-mouthed. 'You don't mean *Spendler*, do you, Mavis? He can't possibly be coming! He's far too old, and anyway –'

'Old or not, he *is* coming – it's all in today's papers. And we are *so* privileged!' She beamed rapturously.

I had not had a chance to read *The Times* that day, and felt suddenly very tired. But after a pause to collect my thoughts, I asked cautiously, 'Do you know much about Spendler, Mavis? I mean, have you ever seen photographs of his paintings?'

'No, I haven't. And as a matter of fact, Vicar,' she confided apologetically, 'until our tutor said she had got tickets, I had never even heard of him – but I understand he's very good, and very avant . . . avant . . .'

'Garde,' I completed.

'Yes, that's it, avant-garde. And what's more, he is bound to tell us all about his stolen paintings. Just think,' she giggled, 'he and I might have something in common. Why, we'll have to compare notes!' And she prattled on while my tiredness grew to inner prostration.

However, I cleared my throat and said with as much authority as I could muster, 'He's not really avant-garde,

231

you know. In fact by today's standards pretty old hat. He did his stuff years ago, and even then it was largely derivative. You'd do far better getting tickets for the Royal Variety Show at the Palladium. They've got Arthur Askey appearing this year.'

It was a lame and vain attempt. She thought I was joking and went into peals of laughter. 'You're just jealous you're not coming. Wait till I tell Edith – she won't like it at all!' And smirking gaily she trotted off. I yanked on Bouncer's lead and we set off home in a cloud of gloom.

It was a facer all right. And I could visualize the whole grisly scene: Spendler at the lectern prosing on about his doleful daubings, interminable slides being shown of his 'bohemian' life in Salzburg before the First World War, earnest self-important questioning from the audience; but above all, graphic illustrations of *Dead Reckoning* and – crucially – *On the Brink*, which even Mavis could not fail to recognize. I saw and heard it all: Mavis's sudden screech of delight as 'her' picture appeared on the screen; the audience's amused scorn turning to sceptical wonder as she insistently pressed her claim; reporters swarming around brandishing notebooks and cameras; and then – horror of horrors – the police summoned by the Tate officials to interview the witness.

The moment I got home I launched myself upon the unread *Times*, hoping wildly that Mavis or her art tutor had somehow been mistaken and confused the name. But of course no such miracle. The announcement was only too clear: VENERABLE AUSTRIAN ARTIST, CLAUS SPENDLER, TO VISIT TATE GALLERY. The writer reported that the 'acclaimed' painter was due to arrive in London in a month's time to give a series of talks entitled *The Teutonic Muse and its Place in the Post-Expressionist Oedipal Psyche*. In the course of these 'probing reflections' Herr Spendler, the reader was assured, would make close

232

scrutiny of his own formidable output – with particular reference to the two works whose recent mysterious disappearance had so shocked art lovers the world over. (Nonsense! I thought. No one in their right mind lamented their loss, except of course the coteries of posturing humbugs or grasping spivs like Nicholas!)

The worst part of the article was where it stressed that the audience would be invited to submit questions and comments. And once again I began to visualize Mavis's excited reaction and hear those quavering tones as she described the way the picture had fallen into her hands at Pick's fête, and the happy coincidence of the two 'nice clergymen' being in her house at the very time that the dastardly theft had occurred! The horror dawned in all its gory detail and I felt sick to the roots.

Bed was the only answer, but it was hardly a palliative; and I lay there twitching and desperate, until worn out by anguish I drifted into troubled sleep. Some time later I awoke with a dead weight pinioning my knees and the room rent with bouts of rhythmic snores. Why Bouncer had chosen to visit the bedroom that night I did not know, but despite the noise his presence was vaguely reassuring, and I was able to drift back to sleep in comparative calm.

That of course did not last, for by early morning the fears and images had resurrected themselves, and it was with the greatest difficulty that I instructed a wooden-faced couple on the joys of marriage and the benefits of mutual support. Neither looked particularly supportive – nor indeed joyful – and I wondered how long their proposed arrangement would last. I also wondered whether I myself would have fared better – not to mention Elizabeth Fotherington – had I ever had the temerity to take a spouse. Might this whole dreadful business have been avoided with a consort at my side? Quite possibly. But then recalling some of the women I had encountered in my life, it seemed that boredom would have been a high price to

233

pay for safety . . . although at the moment a little of the latter was what I craved above all else!

I sighed, and returned my thoughts to the couple sitting opposite, who by now were looking not so much wooden as ossified. 'Marriage,' I said brightly, 'is a great adventure . . .' Their faces did not reflect my optimism.

As the days went by and Spendler's advent grew closer, I became increasingly desperate. My nerve crumbled with helplessness as I contemplated that dread rendezvous in the Tate Gallery and the appalling results which must surely ensue. Should I forewarn Primrose to flee the country before it was too late? Should *I* flee the country? Should Nicholas be alerted? . . . Damn Nicholas! Blow Mavis! And above all, bugger me!

I tried to lose myself in the daily maze of parish paper-work, but the humdrum lists and reports soon melted under the insidious memory of Spendler's grim and deso-late scenes. And always in my ear was the winsome voice of Mavis retelling her tale: 'And you know, it was such an amazing coincidence that I found our dear vicar and his friend downstairs in the hallway just at the *very* moment when the burglar must have been there too!' However, it wasn't simply the matter of the paintings that haunted my thoughts – but what it could so easily lead back to: the Fotherington Affair. If I was arrested and 'Benchley' inter-viewed, who knew what might emerge – or Ingaza let drop! It was one thing parrying March's bovine brain but quite another to confront the relentless probings of THE YARD. No! At all costs Mavis and Spendler could not be permitted to meet.

The prospect of a further elimination appalled me and I discounted the thought immediately. Such a recourse would be, to echo Maud Tubbly Pole, 'a stiff too far'. But what else? What else for heaven's sake! For days I vainly cudgelled my brain. Until with only three days to go I decided that, if nothing else, I could at least write my will and leave my modest means to a haven (if such existed) for persecuted clergy. I found some scrap paper, made the draft and went to bed.

For once the dreams were good. We were back in the war again, beset with bombs and barbed-wire entanglements and – joy of joy – Spendler's cross-Channel ferry torpedoed by enemy U-boats, and the Tate Gallery demolished by incendiary. What bliss, what ecstasy . . .

I awoke in a muck sweat, and prepared myself soberly for Matins.

Returning to the vicarage calmed but still without plan, I encountered Edith Hopgarden – or rather she made it her business to encounter me. She looked dolled up, and I wondered, perhaps unjustly, if she was on her way to meet Tapsell, although it did seem a trifle early for such assignations. But as long as it wasn't the organ loft again, I really couldn't care: more pressing matters gripped my mind. She confronted me, high-heeled and resolute, and I prepared for the worst. But rather to my surprise she started to smile – although, being Edith, there was a sharply sardonic edge to the gesture.

'Well, of course it couldn't last,' she began. 'After all, what could you expect?'

'Er . . . I'm not quite sure I understand.'

'Mavis of course. All that art nonsense she's been babbling on about. Simply a fad . . . I knew it would end in tears. And so it has!' she added with triumph.

'What do you mean?'

'Oh, she's in a frightful state,' she exclaimed scornfully. 'A lot of fuss about nothing, if you ask me!'

'I *am* asking you!' I murmured. 'What are you talking about?'

'They've had a monumental row, she and the art teacher; and Mavis has cancelled her term fees and flounced out.

Says she'll never attend a class again and that she had never really liked it anyway. If that isn't typical!' And she smirked in satisfaction.

For a moment my mind was blank as I tried to absorb the import of her words. And then wild hope and fearful incredulity whirled in tandem as I came to see their possible significance.

'Do you mean,' I asked cautiously, 'that Mavis has really walked out, that she's chucked it all in? What about those essays she always seemed to be doing, and ... er ... that London lecture she was looking forward to? Surely she'll attend that, won't she?'

'She's thrown the essays on the compost heap and told the tutor what she can do with the lecture,' replied Edith. 'Shown a bit of spirit for once – but it won't last of course.' And she sniffed confidently.

'But you think she won't go up to the Tate?' I pursued.

'Oh no, *that's* all off. Says she has no intention of spending her hard-earned savings on anything organized by Miss Rachel Prinkley – Spendlow or no Spendlow.'

'Spendler,' I said absently.

'Well, whatever his name, she's gone off him, and the whole silly charade. A good thing too: at least now we shall be spared her bleating on about spatial significances – whatever they're supposed to mean. I asked her once and she hadn't a clue. Typical!'

Edith tapped a smug and pointed toe on the pavement and gave a dismissive laugh. Then having apprised me of her friend's folly, she patted her perm, drew on her gloves, and marched off in a swirl of self-satisfaction. For once I felt sorry for Mavis.

42

The Cat's Memoir

I was sitting behind the sofa quietly savouring memories of the haddock recently liberated from Miss Dalrymple's shopping bag, when Bouncer thrust his head around the corner and grinned broadly.

'He's in a right lather now,' the dog announced cheerfully. 'Make no mistake!'

I consider this part of the room essentially *my* domain and do not take kindly to Bouncer's incursions. So regarding him coldly I said I was not in the habit of making mistakes and would he kindly remove himself forthwith. He promptly sat down on his haunches and began to chew the cushion that F.O. had carelessly flung over the arm. There was silence as I considered my next move. But curiosity (a trait common among cats of an intellectual bent) got the better of me, and reluctantly I asked what he was talking about.

'The vicar. He's pacing about and throwing pills down as if there was no tomorrow. It's the pictures again. That Mavis woman – I think she's told him something he doesn't like.'

I sighed. 'More thumping on the piano, I suppose. Never a quiet moment in this household ... And kindly get off my tail!' He shifted himself and sneezed explosively.

'Do you mind!' I protested. 'I have just groomed my fur and you have to start spreading your germs and damp everywhere!'

'It's the cobwebs,' he grinned, 'they're getting pretty thick down there. It's time F.O. rolled up his sleeves and did a bit of dusting.'

'And dogs might fly,' I said. 'The crypt isn't exactly his favourite place – except when he's got stolen goods to store!'

'Ah,' replied Bouncer solemnly, 'now that brings me back to what I was saying . . .' And he settled himself more solidly in the small space, while I shelved all thoughts of peace and haddock.

As a matter of fact, what the dog had to say was not without interest – albeit interest of a somewhat disquieting kind. The vicar occasionally takes him to Evensong – saves a walk later in the evening – and he told me that they were on their way home when the Mavis woman appeared and started to jabber her head off about going up to London for some talk given by a very old man called Spent. (At least, that's what the dog said his name was.) He said the vicar's agitation seemed to grow in commensurate proportion to the lady's pleasure. (No – one must be accurate. Bouncer's precise words were: 'The more the old bird squawked, the more he spluttered and twitched.')

Apparently, by the time they parted F.O. was in a dreadful state and seemed intent on getting home as quickly as possible. Needless to say that didn't suit Bouncer at all, and he made it his business to stop and sniff at every object they passed. He said he knew the smells by heart but it was a matter of principle, and he was blowed if he was going to be cheated of his evening exercise just because F.O. was desperate to get at his pills. The dog can be amazingly stubborn at times!

I asked what happened when they eventually reached the vicarage.

'Oh, he gulped the pills, fiddled around on the piano and then mooched off to bed. I went up later ... thought he could do with a bit of company. You can hear those bed springs right down in the kitchen! Anyway, I jumped up on the bed, soothed him down and he went off to sleep.'

'*You* soothed him down? That's hard to imagine!' And I gave a hollow mew.

He seemed to miss the point, and replied airily that it was a talent he had developed as a puppy and one not given to every animal, least of all to cats. Naturally I would have produced some choice riposte, but just at that moment F.O. came blundering in searching for lost documents. This happens with trying frequency, and it doesn't do to hang about as the experience is not unlike being caught in the Sack of Rome. So I shot out of the door and into the garden – but not before delivering one of my better protests. It sets the vicar's teeth on edge, but I consider it essential to register disapproval at such times: humans will take the most disgraceful liberties if their antics go unremarked.

Anyway, we had two days of tears and tantrums; and then, unaccountably, all was sudden radiance and bonhomie. Evidently something had happened to put him in a better mood. I asked Bouncer if he knew what had wrought the sudden change in our master. He replied that he didn't, but that it must have been something pretty good as he had been given an extra large marrow bone. When I pressed him to at least hazard an opinion, all he could do was smack his chops, extol the 'finer' points of the foul thing and ask if I didn't wish I had been given one too! One day I'll wring that dog's neck.

43

The Vicar's Version

Following Edith's departure, I walked home in a state of dazed and cautious delight. I say 'cautious' for experience has long taught me that things are rarely what they appear, and that chickens should never be counted etc., etc. However, my mind was certainly verging on optimism. But only when it came from the horse's mouth could I really be sure. Obviously further words with Mavis were required.

This was not a prospect I relished, and I wondered what would be the best line of approach. A telephone call ostensibly about some parish matter? A 'chance' meeting during one of her church floral sessions? Both were possible. But it struck me that if she was in such a state of disturbance as Edith had intimated, her resolution might be flagging and she might already be harbouring ideas of reconciliation with the scorned Miss Prinkley. Any such notions should be firmly squashed: it was imperative that Mavis's decision not to attend the Spendler lecture be final! Chance meetings or random telephone calls were not enough; only a full and formal session would suffice. She would have to be invited to the vicarage, plied with flattery and cups of tea, and firmly persuaded that the Tate Gallery was grossly overrated and that Herr Spendler's paintings far removed from the interests of one so discerning as herself.

Thus I telephoned and unctuously invited her to tea the following day. She accepted with alacrity, and I went out to procure scones and meringues from one of Molehill's better bakeries.

Preparatory to her arrival I had worked out a tactful means of introducing the topic – but none was needed, for she arrived promptly at four o'clock flushed and garrulous, and obviously only too eager to talk about her altercation with the art teacher.

'Do you know, Vicar,' she exclaimed, 'my last essay took such a long time to prepare, and I presented it in a charming folder which I had decorated with pink roses and gambolling gazelles. Everyone said how pretty it looked! But when Miss Prinkley handed it back she said that the significance of the cover had entirely escaped her, and as to the contents, did the words "vapid" and "banal" mean anything to me? Well, as a matter of fact they didn't, and I had to ask the gentleman sitting next to me. He seemed to take great pleasure in explaining the terms very loudly and at considerable length. It was all most embarrassing!'

'Oh dear,' I murmured, pushing a consoling scone in her direction, 'that seems a bit rotten! What was the topic of the essay?'

'Picasso's *Guernica*.'

'Ah ... ye-es ... I see.' And like Miss Prinkley, I too wondered at the cover's significance, but refrained from enquiring: there was quite enough sugar in the meringues.

'Well, Mavis, I'm sure you are not the first person to have trouble with Picasso,' I ventured soothingly, 'and that particular picture is notoriously tricky. Why, I remember when it first appeared, how difficult it was to grasp the full –'

'Oh, it's not difficult!' she protested. 'Not difficult at all. It's all about war, you see, and how dreadful it is – particularly in Spain.'

I nodded encouragingly. 'Well, yes, I suppose that is the general theme ... but, uhm, what about its style and treatment? How did you deal with that?'

'Oh,' she said airily, 'I skated over that, naturally. I mean, it's the *fundamental concept* that matters, isn't it?'

'Yes, I suppose . . . but the technique needs some –'

'What I wrote, Vicar, were my reminiscences of wartime here in England, and our Anderson shelter at the bottom of the garden, and Mother doing her fire watching and getting stuck on the roof, and those nice Canadian soldiers billeted next door coming to her rescue, and the nylons that they gave my sister, and her Californian Poppy scent, and the problem with the sweet-points and my ration book, and putting the sticky tape on the windows, and how in the nursing canteen we all had to knit scarves for Britain, and what fun it was when . . .'

I cleared my throat and asked if she had devoted the entire essay to this catalogue of quotidian memory.

'Oh no,' she exclaimed, 'that was only the first five pages. After that I talked about the Brotherhood of Man and how we should all be one happy family and be nice to one another, and that in my opinion if only women were allowed to rule the world there would be no more fighting and all that silly nonsense! It would be so simple really.' And she smiled confidently.

I poured her another cup of tea, digesting these philosophical pearls. 'Very interesting, Mavis. But I gather your tutor thought otherwise?'

She tossed her head dismissively. 'That Miss Prinkley – she's so high and mighty! Just because she's got some degree in Art History she thinks she's the cat's whiskers! Do you know what she said to me at the end of the class?'

I shook my head and contrived to look sympathetic. 'She said that over the weeks she had come to the conclusion that I was following the wrong course and wouldn't I feel much more comfortable in the basket-weaving group next door.'

'And would you?'

'Certainly not. I do have a mind, you know! And I told her so in no uncertain terms!'

'Goodness! What did she say?'

'She said it was a pity about that as I clearly had talents elsewhere, and that she knew several old baskets richly deserving of my attention.'

'Crikey!' I gasped.

'What?'

'Er – well, I never!'

'Yes. She's obviously got a peculiar fixation about baskets. I didn't really know what she was talking about but she looked distinctly disagreeable. So I decided there and then that I was wasting my time *and* my intellect on her boring course, and so I resigned immediately. Resigned!' And picking up her fork, she attacked a meringue with a savagery that I never thought to witness in Mavis.

There was brief pause as she munched, while I reflected upon Miss Prinkley and her problem with elderly baskets.

'Does that mean that you won't be going up to London to hear the Spendler lecture?' I then enquired hesitantly.

'Certainly not with that woman!' she exclaimed. 'But I *might* go under my own steam. After all, it seems a pity to miss such a *distinguished* artist, although of course I'm not at all familiar with London, so it would be rather an adventure, especially on my own!' And she simpered archly through the remains of her meringue.

For one fearful moment I thought she was going to ask me to accompany her; but the moment passed, and I said in firm voice, 'Simply not worth it, Mavis, not worth it at all. As I said before, Spendler's a has-been. Always was really. It's only journalists and, er, out-of-date art teachers who go on about him. The real cognoscenti know far better.' I gave a superior smile and passed her another meringue.

She took it thoughtfully, and then said brightly, 'Is that your considered opinion, Vicar?'

'Absolutely. You are far too sensible to waste your intellectual powers on that sort of thing!'

'Well . . .' she said, flushing demurely, 'I *am* rather busy, of course. I mean, there's always my poetry project . . .'

'Ah yes! Your *Little Gems of Uplift*,' I interrupted. 'How is that going these days? It was such a success last year – the Young Wives were enquiring about it only the other day. Mustn't neglect that, you know!'

She nodded in agreement. 'You're so right, Vicar. I mustn't let the patrons down. There's a lot to be done and no time to waste on that, that . . . old man and his – *footling* pictures!' She clapped a hand to her mouth delighted at her own daring.

'That's the spirit, Mavis!' I cried. And in an access of triumph I asked if she would like some sherry. She twittered and wittered, and then having expressed the fear that it might make her tiddly, accepted with a coy giggle – but not before eliciting my promise to attend the *Little Gems* event in the parish hall. There is always a price.

As we sipped sedately, I wistfully recalled the gun-cracking blast from Maud Tubbly Pole demanding her second treble Scotch . . .

44

The Dog's Diary

That bone was one of the best I've ever had – what the cat would probably call *bona rara* or some such, but what I call JOLLY GOOD! In fact, it's been so good that I've hidden it in one of my special places so I can go and visit it from time to time and pretend it's still got some meat on. The master had been pretty twitchy for a couple of days (that Mavis woman getting on his nerves) but all of a sudden he became normal again – well, as normal as he's ever likely to be – and came waltzing into the kitchen one morning grinning all over his face and dropped this bone in my basket. As I've said before, one of the *bonuses* of living here (yes, Maurice isn't the only one who can make jokes, quite good at them myself when I try) is that you never really know which way the wind will blow next. He's up and down like a rubber ball; but as I tell O'Shaughnessy, that's what keeps a dog on his toes all right!

Anyway, a day or so later, that Mavis person came to the house for tea, and they went droning on in the sitting room while I lay quietly under the piano. F.O. seemed fairly in control, as you might say, and kept smirking to himself, so I guessed things were going his way. I was pleased about that because what with one thing and another, and especially the rabbit business, things have been a bit bumpy recently and he could do with a rest. Well, they went on jawing, and then he gave her some brown stuff in a small glass and they talked some more – at least, she garbled and he just nodded.

I was just beginning to think that I might be getting a bit bored and that it was time I went to look for Maurice, when there was a sudden crash in the front porch which made the vicar nearly leap out of his skin, while the Mavis person squeaked like a demented mouse and spilt her drink all over the floor. It set me off too, and I had a good old airing of lungs! F.O. shouted at me and then lolloped off to see what the racket was about. I was quite interested myself, and not finding the Mavis much fun, followed him into the hall. There seemed to be a lot of scuffling and cursing going on, and then I heard him say, 'Oh my God, not you!'

Yes, it was the Brighton type – clutching a bottle in one hand and a suitcase in the other. It struck me that he wasn't entirely steady. But then you can't always tell with humans – they often walk peculiarly; something to do with them having only two legs.

Anyway, putting it mildly, F.O.looked none too pleased, and the two of them did a lot of jabbering and whispering which I didn't really understand; but by that time I needed to stretch my leg against a tree, and I was just beetling off to the pet flap in the kitchen and throwing a few barks over my shoulder for good measure, when the sitting-room door opened and the Mavis appeared, saw the Brighton type, and squawked: 'Why, if it's not the Venerable Benchley! What a delightful surprise!'

Don't know what happened after that as the need for a leak was getting urgent and F.O. gets ratty if I disgrace myself indoors, so I scooted off pronto to the garden.

45

The Vicar's Version

The tedium of Mavis was appallingly alleviated by the sudden arrival of Nicholas Ingaza. Unlooked for and out of the night, he appeared on my doorstep in a state of dishevelled and fearsome jollity. In vicious mood Nicholas is dangerous but manageable; amused and inebriated he is incorrigible. That he should be clutching a large bottle of brandy was, given his lurching stance, only to be expected. What was not expected, and distinctly ominous, was the accompanying suitcase which he deposited in the hall with a deafening crash.

I was just in the middle of saying that Mavis Briggs was in the other room and would he kindly return whence he had come, when over the din of the dog's barking I heard her voice behind me exclaiming, 'Why, if it isn't the Venerable Benchley! What a delightful surprise!' I shut my eyes and suddenly felt very old and tired . . .

'Who's she?' gurgled Nicholas.

'Don't you remember?' I hissed. 'The woman whose picture you nicked, the one who made you smell all those geraniums!'

'Oh Christ! She hasn't got any more with her, has she?'

'No, but she thinks you're an archdeacon,' I moaned.

'Better put on a good show then!' he replied in a bellowed whisper. And adopting a sickening leer and mincing gait, he advanced upon Mavis with proffered hand.

She took it eagerly and simpered up at him, scanning the spivvy suit and raffish tie. In my heightened state I doubtless only imagined her look of puzzlement, but muttered something to the effect that the Reverend had just returned from holiday and what a relief it always was to be able to relax in mufti for a few days! She nodded respectfully and continued to simper.

We returned to the sitting room where I noted Mavis's upturned sherry glass on the floor and its contents seeping into the carpet. She was clearly embarrassed and full of abject apologies, but before I had a chance to calm her down Nicholas took it upon himself to observe in tones of silky indulgence that that was *exactly* the sort of little upset he himself had *every* day with the altar wine, and that God didn't put us on this earth to cry over spilt alcohol, did he now? The words may have been somewhat slurred but were accompanied by a smile of such unctuous beatitude that Mavis was deaf to any such verbal laxity. And as for myself, recalling the amount of alcohol that Ingaza had always managed to spill over the floorboards of St Bede's, not to mention down his own throat, I rather assumed he knew what he was talking about.

She regarded him gratefully, which was unfortunate as it emboldened him to go further: 'In fact, my child,' ('my child' ? How *could* he!) 'far from crying over alcohol – spilt or otherwise – it is my belief that the good Lord likes nothing better than to see his creatures make merry with the grape.' ('Make merry with the grape'! Was he raving?) 'And so, as token of my gratitude to Francis who has been so kind in welcoming me to his humble abode, I suggest we spurn the sherry and instead partake of some of this excellent cognac I happen to have with me!' So saying, and continuing to smile winsomely at Mavis, he proceeded to wrench the foil from the neck of the bottle.

Mavis looked flustered and excited. 'Oh, I couldn't possibly!' she twittered. 'I mean, I've never had brandy before, except in mince pies of course, I don't think I could . . .'

'Of course you could – steady your nerves before going home. One for the road – as the heathen say!' And he laughed loudly in a wheezing falsetto.

'Actually,' I broke in hastily, 'I think Mavis *is* in rather a hurry. Perhaps this isn't quite the time . . . Didn't you say you had to meet Edith or somebody, Mavis?'

'No,' she said, looking fixedly at the brandy. 'No, I didn't.'

Reluctantly I got out the glasses. With a theatrical flourish, Nicholas splashed a large dose into one of them and thrust it towards Mavis.

'Rémy Martin – rather a good one, I think you'll find. A personal gift from the archbishop . . .'

'The *arch*bishop!' she exclaimed wide-eyed. 'Good gracious! How kind. Which one?'

'Oh . . . Durham, I think – or it could have been York. They're all much of a muchness really . . . one meets so many in my job, you know.' He spoke with a preening nonchalance. It was an absurd display and I thought sourly that no one but Mavis could possibly swallow it.

'Well,' she ventured, 'if it's from the archbishop, I suppose I *might* just sample a little . . .' and she raised the glass to her lips and took a tentative sip.

I was momentarily distracted by Nicholas offering me a cigarette, but when I next glanced at Mavis I realized that his absurdity was not the only thing she had swallowed: the entire contents of the brandy glass had disappeared – drained to the last drop, and I hadn't even started on mine! She looked quite well on it: pink and glazed and obviously waiting for a filler. With uncharacteristic generosity, Nicholas duly obliged. She downed it in two, an action which made even Ingaza's jaw drop open. 'Stone the crows!' he muttered. Crows wouldn't be the only ones stoned, I thought grimly, eyeing Mavis's once more empty glass.

The spectacle of his cognac going down at the rate of knots seemed to have a sobering effect on Nicholas, and the ingratiating leer was rapidly replaced by an expression of twitching alarm. As Mavis, grown suddenly expansive, began to drool over the cat who had just strolled in, he gestured frantically while at the same time mouthing what I inferred to be, 'Get her *out* of here!'

Receiving no response from Maurice, Mavis returned her attentions to the Rémy and its owner. 'What a delicious cordial!' she enthused. 'Very tasty indeed. Most unusual. It's nice to have a little treat now and again, isn't it, Archbish . . . I mean, Archdeacon?' And she giggled gaily.

'Yes,' said Nicholas drily. 'How are your geraniums?'

'My what? . . . Oh, oh yes, my geraniums. They're doing very well, thank you.' She toyed with the stem of her glass, looking at the bottle. Nicholas gazed fixedly at the cat.

There was a pause, and then clearing my throat I said briskly, 'My goodness, is that the time? We'll never finish things at this rate. No peace for the wicked, I fear! Such a shame, but I'm afraid the archdeacon and I have a mass of paperwork to get through. So boring!'

'Oh yes, frightfully boring!' exclaimed Nicholas eagerly, whipping out a fountain pen.

Mavis looked momentarily put out, but rallying quickly said, 'In that case, we must all have another little drop to give you strength! Shall I be mother?' And seizing the bottle she proceeded to top up the glasses. We watched mesmerized, and then dutifully began to sip. Needless to say, Mavis finished first. At which point I stood up, and taking her firmly by the arm and muttering about the paperwork, propelled her towards the front door. Effusive farewells were expressed and she toddled happily down the path.

I returned to the sitting room to find Nicholas slumped on the sofa, pale and silent. Eventually he said slowly,

'Well, if that's a specimen of your parishioners, no wonder you're a bit odd. Are they all like that?'

'They are not all like that. And I am not odd!'

'Uhm. If you say so . . .'

'Look here, Nicholas,' I exclaimed in irritation, 'you didn't have to come here at all. I mean, what are you *doing*, suddenly turning up with no prior warning? It's not particularly convenient, I –'

'Well, that's a nice welcome, I must say, dear boy,' he protested. 'It's a poor thing if a chap can't drop in on an old colleague once in a while to have a friendly natter. You see,' and he dropped his voice, grinning conspiratorially, 'you see, I've pulled off rather a good deal. Thought you might like to help me celebrate. Hence the cognac – or what's left of it after your friend got her paws on it!'

'She is *not* my friend, she is . . .'

At that instant there was a light tap on the window, and through the gloom the spectral face of Mavis appeared.

'God in heaven!' Nicholas yelped. 'She's come back for more!'

I sighed resignedly and went to the door.

At first I didn't understand what she was saying – something about a car, and what a problem it all was, and that she was very sorry, and would the archdeacon mind . . .

Gradually the breathy and brandied tones became clear. The 'problem' was Ingaza's cumbersome Citroën – sprawled up on the pavement and slewed right across my front gate; and thin though she was, even Mavis was unable to insinuate herself past either bonnet or bumper.

'Don't worry, Mavis. We can shift that quickly enough! I'll just get the Reverend Benchley to fetch his keys.' I went inside and explained the situation.

Nicholas groaned and levered himself off the sofa. There followed a lengthy and fruitless search for his car keys, accompanied by much tut-tutting – or rather its graphic equivalent. Finally he expostulated, '*I* don't know where the hell they are! Surely she can get out some other way. Haven't you got a back gate or something?'

'No,' I said testily, 'I haven't. Only a couple of holes in the hedge.'

'Well, shove her through one of those and then perhaps we'll get a bit of peace.' (Peace! If only! I thought.)

The upshot was that, gallantly assisted by the 'archdeacon' and myself, Mavis did indeed exit through the hedge. She seemed to relish the experience, emerging on to the pavement in a mood of dishevelled triumph; and declining my offer to accompany her home, disappeared into the night singing a hymn. Nicholas and I returned to the house and tidied up the remaining brandy.

We were down to the last quarter when, recalling the suitcase in the hall and the fact that I was evidently required to house him for the night, I asked him again what on earth he was doing in the area.

'Ah, wondered when you might get back to that,' he replied. 'As it happens, I've been in Cranleigh, doing a bit of business with my old chum there, and very productive it's been too!'

I sighed. 'One of your "contacts", I suppose.'

'Yes, and we've come to a nice little agreement. Very nice indeed. In fact, Francis, if you play your cards right I might do you a favour and cut you in on it.'

'*Cut* me *in* on it!' I cried. 'What do you think I am, some sort of shady racketeer? I leave that sort of thing to you, Nicholas!'

'Not entirely, dear boy. After all, you did – as they say in the trade – *finger* the goods.' He smiled blandly and smoothed his hair.

'Yes, but only because you . . .'

'Helped you out of a tight spot? Don't I recall a little police matter a few months back to do with a lady and some binoculars . . .' And he leered mockingly.

'Well –' I began defensively.

'Something pretty shady there, if you ask me. Never did get to the bottom of it.'

'Nonsense,' I replied uneasily. 'As I explained at the time, it was all an unfortunate misunderstanding and as usual the police had got a bee in their bonnet and wouldn't let it go. It was annoying, that's all.'

'If you say so, old man. If you say so.' The tone was suave, the look cynical.

The events of the evening had been more than tiresome; but now things were turning uncomfortable in the extreme. Ingaza was too damn sharp, and I sought desperately for a way of changing the subject.

'I say,' I ventured brightly, 'a pity all your smart cognac's gone. I could do with another drop. We'll just have to make do with something less exalted! I think there's still a bit left.' And getting up quickly but unsteadily, I went into the kitchen and spent some time rootling for clean glasses.

When I returned he was smoking one of his sleek Russian Sobranies. No offer came my way and I had to make do with a Capstan. Putting the bottle between us, I said jocularly, 'Now, who shall we drink to?'

'To *whom* shall we drink?' corrected Nicholas solemnly. He paused, and then raising his glass in mock gravity, announced: 'To His Lordship The Right Reverend Horace Clinker!'

'Good Lord!' I said. 'Whatever for?'

'Anyone living with Gladys probably needs all the help they can get.'

Whether the accompanying grimace related to my grocer's brandy or to Gladys, it was hard to know. Either way, it seemed to have diverted him from pursuing the matter of my 'shady past', and my own private toast was to the hope that things should stay that way, and so I nudged the conversation further in the direction of Clinker.

'Yes, I suppose she must be a bit of a trial . . . not the easiest of ladies. In fact, probably quite a blight one way and the other!' And I chuckled encouragingly.

There was a pause, and then he said languidly, lighting another Sobranie, 'But then of course he did have that grand night of passion . . .'

'With *Gladys*?' I exclaimed.

'No, of course not Gladys. Who do you think!'

I must have looked blank for he raised his eyes to the ceiling, and then fixing me with a cool stare said, 'Me, of course.'

Even as I reeled from the shock, I nevertheless experienced a curious sense of recognition . . . Funny the way things fall into place. The latitude Nicholas had enjoyed at St Bede's when Clinker had been acting dean had always been a source of mystery. But I had rather assumed it was on account of their earlier drinking sessions at Oxford when Clinker had been a young Classics don and Nicholas an undergraduate. By all accounts (principally Nicholas's) in those days Clinker's toping capacity had been prodigious, and I had vaguely assumed that this had been the cause of his leniency with Nicholas at St Bede's: some mad escapade from the wilder past which he feared might surface were his erstwhile bar crony not given the kid glove. Little had it occurred to me the exact nature of the escapade. It would certainly explain Nicholas's antipathy to the ghastly Gladys – although, I reflected, that was an antipathy universally shared.

'Ah,' I said.

Blowing a smoke ring in my direction, he gave a heavy-lidded smile, and with the old bantering tone said, 'Oh yes, I was quite a catch in those days – but then strangely enough so was Hor. Difficult to credit, I know, but life and marriage can play funny tricks: a pretty lethal combination really – Episcopal Office *and* Gladys!' And he gave a hollow laugh, while I tried to get my mind round the picture of Clinker being 'a catch'. It was difficult.

'Anyway, what's he up to these days?' he continued.
'Plays tiddlywinks.'
'Christ!'

The rest of the evening passed without interruption or, mercifully, further revelations – from either side. The brandy finished, I volunteered to do my Marx Brother act at the piano, but my guest seemed less than taken with the idea and so we decided to call it a day. Fortified with water and headache pills, I went to bed – trusting fervently that come the morning Ingaza's fertile curiosity would not lead him back to the events of the previous year.

46

The Vicar's Version

To my relief, the next morning nothing more was said about those earlier events, Ingaza being far too intent on downing copious cups of black coffee and consuming outlandish quantities of bread and Marmite. Eventually, having satisfied his cravings and thanking me profusely for my hospitality – in particular 'the female cabaret', as he termed Mavis's antics – he rescued the lost car keys from Bouncer's basket and took off for Brighton.

As I stood on the pavement his parting words had been, 'We must do this again, old mate. Peps you up!', an observation which made me return to the house feeling tired. However, no time for rest: there were two weddings in the offing plus a baptism and a burial, not to mention attendance at the Mothers' Union Discussion Day, a perennially gruesome event of much sound and fury – although whether anything was ever signified I could never quite make out.

Thus the week proceeded at a sprightly pace, and by the weekend I could have done with a breather. However, Saturday too was destined to be busy for I was due up in London at midday to attend the usual bi-monthly meeting in the Brompton Road. I hadn't really recovered from the last time, and it had more than crossed my mind to give this one a miss; but noting on the agenda an item proposing that such meetings be held at rarer intervals in future, I was eager to vote to that effect.

Mission accomplished – i.e. the vote having gone substantially in favour of the proposal – I fought my way back to Waterloo hoping to arrive in Molehill in time for an evening concert on the Third Programme.

The train was fuller than I had expected, and my hopes of procuring a compartment to myself were swiftly dashed. Fortunately I had managed a corner seat, which was the only advantage, for we sat crammed five aside and my opposite numbers were two large and garrulous women with two diminutive but loudly snuffling children. The snuffles were soon punctuated by guttural coughs, generally in tandem, and to shut out both noise and germs I contrived to insulate myself behind the evening paper. Since my neighbour already had his open this was not an easy manoeuvre, but eventually I was able to unfurl it to a readable degree, and somewhat squintingly began to scan the headlines. These yielded little of interest, being largely concerned with sport and the unremarkable views of some political has-been, and with subtle elbowing I managed to turn to the inside page and the crossword.

I was just about to embark on this when my eye was caught by the item next to it. This was a photograph of what I at first assumed to be a French onion seller – i.e. sporting the usual accoutrements of beret, push-bike, some odd smock-like garment, and a drooping Gauloise. No onions were visible, but since he was also wearing a distinct expression of Gallic pique I thought perhaps they had been stolen. My mild curiosity turned to incredulity as I started to read the accompanying article. ARTISTIC BONES IN HIS BELFRY ran the headline, and the ensuing words filled me with fascinated horror:

'Père Martineau, respected curé of the church of St Denis in the village of Taupinière close to Le Touquet, was none too pleased yesterday when gendarmes stormed his church, raided the belfry, and took from it two paintings found concealed under a heap of old sacks. It is understood that the French police had received an unknown tip-off to the effect that the missing Claus Spendler pictures, far from being on the other side of the world as has generally been assumed, might well be located in the curé's bell tower. One of these works, *Dead Reckoning*, has as its main subject a pile of starkly glittering human bones – or as the artist prefers to call them, *fragmenti mori*. Art experts called to the scene confirmed that there was a strong likelihood of these being the stolen items. When asked what he knew of the matter, Father Martineau replied – among other things – *"Sacrée merde!"* and *"Je m'en fous!"* He further added that since he had always hated the Austrians as much as *"les sales Boches"* why in the *"nom de Dieu"* should he wish to keep their *"peintures putrides"* in his belfry, and that Herr Spendler and the investigating officers could park the said items up their *"grandes fesses"*. After a night in the cells, the curé was released pending further enquiries.'

I stared unseeingly at the snuffling child opposite, who, possibly unsettled by my look of wild consternation, promptly began to howl. For once, however, the noise was of little concern, my mind being far too engaged with images of the uncovered plunder and a blaspheming French priest. The parallels of our situation were bizarre to say the least – though I doubted whether, similarly apprehended, I could have shown the same truculent élan as my Gallic counterpart. But then the French have a knack with these things.

I gazed into the darkness beyond the window-pane, cursing the quirks of fate and wishing, rather like the curé, that Spendler could shove his stupid *fragmenti mori* into some convenient recess. Last seen, the pictures had been in the grasping hands of Nicholas Ingaza as he 'rescued' them from my inadequate care. So what were they now doing near Le Touquet of all places? And who was this Père

Martineau? A genuinely dumbfounded innocent? Or simply another conniving cleric caught haplessly in Ingaza's slithery web? For one brief moment I felt a pang of comradely sympathy: after all, we were in a sense victims-in-arms. However, glancing again at the lowering figure in the photograph, I changed my mind. Apart from the dangling cigarette, I very much doubted whether the curé of Taupinière and the vicar of Molehill had anything in common other than their parish names . . . and of course the 'fingered' merchandise!

The rest of the journey passed swiftly but in a haze of frenzied speculation and worry. This latest turn of events would certainly account for the postcard earlier in the year lauding the gaming delights of Le Touquet's casino. Presumably Nicholas's visit there had been a sort of belt and braces reconnaissance jaunt in case the Molehill venture aborted – as it assuredly had! And if indeed he *were* party to the pictures' concealment, would the curé now rat on his English accomplice? Would Nicholas rat on me? After all, questions would surely be asked about the location of the goods prior to their arrival in Taupinière! I shut my eyes and groaned – an action which redoubled the howls from opposite.

When the train reached Molehill I irrationally but instinctively made my way home via the less frequented route. Quite what I was expecting I do not know – phalanxes of the Metropolitan Art Squad poised at every wall and corner? It is amazing the strength of the imagination in such circumstances! Thus, head down and keeping to the shadows, I slunk back to the vicarage, my mind in a turmoil of questions. *Where* exactly was Nicholas now: Brighton, Cranleigh – Bangkok? Was he perhaps holed up in some rustic outhouse in the Pas-de-Calais surviving on stale crusts and Calvados while *les flics* 'pursued their enquiries' in nearby fields? The possibilities were legion. Would it be safe to try telephoning his Brighton abode, or might there be a bug on the line? After much pondering I decided against it; better not anticipate things. My father's words came back to me: 'When in doubt, Francis old man, do damn all!' But it was all very well for Pa, he had never been faced with imprisonment – let alone the noose!

The next four days were agony. Nothing further appeared in the newspapers and not a word from Nicholas, but my mind was relentlessly plagued with lurid fears. I tried vainly to concentrate on parish matters, until eventually, unable to stand the tension any longer, I dialled the Brighton number.

I had done this only once before – also at a time of crisis – and, as previously, the voice that answered was not Ingaza's but the rasping tones of Eric, his East End associate.

'Oh yes,' he said cheerfully, 'you was that geezer what called before. I remember – some vicar friend from Nick's past. How are yer?'

'Very well, thank you,' I replied meekly, wincing slightly at the linkage of 'friend' and 'past' (the latter carrying unfortunate connotations of mammoth press headlines regarding a certain Turkish bath). 'Er, do you think I might speak to Nicholas if he's in by any chance?'

'Out of luck, old son. He's not here. Gone to see his auntie in Eastbourne.'

'Gone to see his *auntie*!' I gasped. 'What ever do you mean? He hasn't got an auntie!'

'Oh yes he has, old mate. Had her for a long time, ever since he was a nipper as you might say. Very fond of Aunt Lil he is, visits her reg'lar. Takes her to the flicks, and then in good weather they toddle along to the bandstand. He likes the cut of the conductor's jib!' And he gave a raucous laugh.

The idea of Ingaza having anything so domestic as an elderly aunt was somehow disconcerting. That he was in the habit of regularly accompanying her to the cinema and thence to the sedate joys of the Eastbourne bandstand was even more startling, and for a couple of moments I was literally lost for words. My silence prompted the voice to ask if I wanted to leave a message.

'No ... no, it's all right, thank you,' I replied, still shocked. 'I'll call again – tomorrow perhaps.'

'OK. Suit yourself, but I'll let him know you called anyway. Ta-ta for now.' And so saying he rang off.

I gazed down at the receiver, trying to picture Ingaza entertaining his aunt on the Eastbourne sea front. But I also started to picture the fulminating Frenchman in Taupinière ... What on earth did he think he was *doing* lolling in a deckchair listening to the band when the Spendlers were discovered and our futures in such jeopardy! Plainly unhinged!

I lit a cigarette and reflected. Maurice glided into the room and deposited his woollen mouse at my feet. Needless to say, this was not meant as a friendly offering, merely a cue to throw it across the room so he could flaunt his pouncing skills. I did as required, made a complimentary noise, and resumed my brooding.

Assuming that it *was* Nicholas responsible for delivering the pictures to Taupinière, who had tipped off the French police? Had the information come from England, and if so from what source, for God's sake? Was Nicholas being watched? Was *I* being watched? Or was it the work of some maleficent Frog cleric determined to do down his rival in the promotion stakes? But recalling the photograph and the article, I rather doubted this. Sourly saturnine and trenchant in abuse, Father Martineau seemed an unlikely candidate for imminent elevation.

The telephone rang: Edith Hopgarden wanting to know if I had decided on the venue for the Sunday School Treat, and if it wasn't *too* much trouble would I kindly give her some indication of the numbers. I produced a negative answer on both counts and went to bed. It had been a hard day.

Despite what I had said to Eric, I delayed telephoning again. Anxious though I was, the state of not knowing was marginally better than confronting the worst, and for the moment the luxury of ignorance suited me well. But I knew it could only be a matter of time.

And a short time it was. For four days later, just as Bouncer and I were leaving the church porch after the early service, I saw with a lurch of fear the familiar bulk of Ingaza's black Citroën parked a few yards from the lych-gate. There was a figure in the driving seat, and even from a distance I recognized the tilt of the slouch hat and the thin elbow draped casually over the sill as he flicked ash on to the gravel. As I drew closer, the arm gave a languid wave and he had the nerve to toot the horn.

'Don't do that, you idiot,' I hissed, 'people will notice! What are you here for!'

'Can't see any people, old chap. You obviously need to get your numbers up. As to why I'm here – well, I've been conducting some more business with my chum in Cranleigh, so thought that as I was in the district I might as well toddle over and see how Francis was getting on.' And he grinned sardonically.

'Francis was perfectly all right until he saw you,' I replied crossly. 'I suppose you do know the balloon's gone up! How could you possibly be parading up and down on Eastbourne sea front when all this kerfuffle was going on in France? They'll be on to your tail – *and* mine, at any moment!'

He looked entirely unperturbed by my protests and said blandly, 'Take it easy, old cock, you'll bust something if you go on like that.'

'I should think I will,' I exclaimed, 'and mainly thanks

to you! What on earth did you think you were doing palming those things off on the French priest? Looks a most unsavoury character, bound to shop you quicker than anything!'

'Oh, he won't shop me,' he replied blithely, 'I know too much. But you're quite right. It was a tactical error. Might have guessed Henri would balls it up. You're all the same: unreliable.'

'We are not all the same!' I snapped. 'I bear no comparison to that questionable type, and it was hardly my fault if Primrose made a mess of things by shoving *On the Brink* behind that other canvas . . . Besides,' I added, 'he's an RC!'

'RC or not, you've both got something to hide. With Henri it's gambling debts, among other things. Too fond of poker and Chantilly, hence his alacrity to accept my offer of a fat fee in exchange for a little co-operation – bit of a *quid pro quo*. With you it's something else. Don't know what, but there's something there all right!' And he laughed. I did not. In fact I went rather quiet and fumbled to light a cigarette.

'Here, have one of mine,' said Nicholas smoothly. 'Much better than your coarse weeds. Now, get in and I'll tell you what the score is.'

He proceeded to outline what he referred to as 'the current situation'.

Apparently he had known Martineau for some years and they had, he indicated, 'an arrangement of mutual convenience'. What this entailed I did not enquire and he did not enlarge. But it meant that when he was seeking a storage facility for the Spendlers he had always had the Taupinière connection at the back of his mind. In the event, however, he had selected Molehill: partly for its greater ease of access, but also on account of his earlier help to me. He had been sure I would jump at the chance to oblige an old pal (!) But after the débâcle of Mavis and the fête business he had reverted to his original plan, feeling that my involvement was more liability than boon.

'Yes, yes,' I said impatiently. 'But what the hell is going on *now*?'

'What is going on now, Francis, is that the whole heist has failed – i.e. the paintings are virtually worthless, Spendler discredited, and fortunately, with no evidence to disprove his defence, no charges are being brought against old Henri.'

'What do you mean?' I exclaimed. 'Those pictures are as hot as hell!'

'They were for a time,' he replied drily, 'but that is no longer the case.'

'Why ever not?'

'I've told you – their stock has fallen.'

'Yes, but why?'

'Because of that sod Higginbottom.'

'Who's Higginbottom, for God's sake!'

'Professor Sir Giles Higginbottom, *éminence grise* of the art world: narcissistic, toffee-nosed, opinionated, and unfortunately one who knows his artistic onions better than anyone else on the cultural scene. Of course, having little knowledge of cultural scenes you wouldn't have heard of him,' (I was stung by that, but felt insufficiently sure to dispute it) 'but I can assure you, when he speaks it's like the voice of God.'

'And I suppose he's spoken, has he?'

'Too right he has,' Nicholas said bitterly. 'Blown the pictures sky-high and declared Spendler a posturing charlatan.'

'Huh,' I grunted, still piqued by his allusion to my cultural ignorance, 'you don't need to be an art pundit to know that!'

He sighed impatiently. 'The quality of the stuff is immaterial, Francis. What matters is the value. And thanks to Higginbottom their value has dropped to bottomless depths: nobody wants the things, and I've lost a pretty packet!'

'But why has he spoken out now? I mean, the paintings have been missing for some months, and there's been quite a lot in the press about their importance and so on. Why didn't he slate them earlier?'

'Because for the last year he's been off the planet – i.e. walled up in some crumbling pile in the Outer Hebrides putting the finishing touches to his *magnum opus* on Chinese line drawings. Spendler and his poxy pictures were the last things on his mind. Now, however, amidst much rejoicing and acclaim the great tome is finally finished. And it would seem that as a light diversion from all his hard labours he has transferred his attention to putting the boot into Spendler. As a result the chap's reputation is in shreds, a number of fashionable critics have egg on their face and, as said, I've lost a hefty whack.'

For a couple of moments he looked sour in a way that only Nicholas can, but then he brightened, and said, 'However, all is not lost. In fact, fingers crossed, quite a nice little windfall is heading my way. Doubtless you'll be glad to know that negotiations with my Cranleigh friend are progressing *rather* well. Things on a much surer footing this time ... and fortunately, of course, Lil won't be involved.'

'Lil? Your aunt? What on earth had she got to do with it?'

'Oh, it was all her idea from the start,' he replied carelessly. 'And frankly, if she ever makes another dud suggestion like that she can kiss goodbye to the bandstand at Eastbourne!'

He must have seen my look of astonishment for he went on to say, 'Oh yes, bright old bird is Aunt Lil. Too damn bright sometimes, gets carried away ... sort of *folie de grandeur*. Anyway, one thing's for certain – she's not getting her thieving mittens in the Cranleigh pie!' And he gave a mirthless laugh.

I was too flabbergasted to pursue the matter, and instead asked who it was that had tipped the wink about the paintings being in the curé's belfry.

'No one of importance,' he replied, 'some racing crony that he had blabbed to in his cups. Foolish chap imagined he'd get a reward. Another of Higginbottom's casualties!' I began to warm to Higginbottom: clearly a thorn in the side of venality and humbug!

There followed a brief silence as I struggled to absorb the import of his account. And then I shifted in my seat and glared at him.

'What unspeakable folly!' I burst out. 'To think that I went to all that trouble to house those repellent paintings – risking life and limb in the belfry, lurking like a lost lemon in all that garbage at Pick's fête, enduring the vacuous chatter of Mavis Briggs, putting up with Primrose's tantrums, and above all having a heart attack every time I heard the words "art" or "Spendler" ... And now you tell me they are worthless and you've lost interest in the matter and are engaged in something else! Well, this time kindly don't drag me into your schemes, I really can't stand the strain! It's all been most unsettling, I –'

'Keep cool, dear boy, keep cool. Fret not – your secret's perfectly safe with Old Nick!' And he blew a conciliatory smoke ring in my direction.

'Secret?' I repeated suspiciously. 'What secret?'

'Well,' and he cleared his throat, 'you being a professional fence of course. What else could there be?'

I closed my eyes. What else indeed! What else, Oh Lord, what else ...?

I was too tired to sustain my anger and we parted on fairly cordial terms, Nicholas even suggesting I was in need of a little holiday and how about buzzing down to Brighton for a couple of days where he and Eric could show me some of the more exclusive delights. But my previous experiences had taught me quite enough about Brighton and I had no need for further acquaintance with its charms, exclusive or otherwise. And besides, neither was I over-whelmingly keen to encounter the so far faceless Eric. However matey they may be, some people are best kept disembodied and at a distance. Indeed, I reflected, when one came to think of it, probably most . . . It would save a lot of bother.

The next day brought much relief: I had a funeral to conduct. Funerals are my forte; and in all modesty I think I can say that at such times I rise to the occasion with a suitable mixture of panache and sobriety. Of course, one can never be sure of the deceased's opinion – but ever since I was a curate let loose on my first burial, people have been highly complimentary of my performance, and seem to leave the churchyard in a more ordered frame of mind than when they entered. Speaking for myself, I have always found the ceremonial of the Anglican obsequies a particularly soothing experience, and invariably return home with a feeling of a good thing done, and in a rare state of spiritual confidence. Baptisms are less felicitous: partly because, unlike funerals, one is never entirely in control of the subject.

However, that day it was a funeral and not a baptism, and after the recent trauma of Ingaza and the paintings – not to mention other nagging fears – I sunk myself into its sombre ritual with the same pleasurable ease as one lowering himself into the benison of a warm bath.

Bath over, I strolled home, took the dog for a run, and then after a sandwich supper played a little boogie on the piano. It was only when I was preparing for bed that I saw the letter. It had obviously arrived by the afternoon post and was still stuck under the flap of the letterbox.

At first I wasn't going to open it, thinking it might as well wait till the next day and be included with the rest of the post. But then in a moment of abstraction, I picked up the paper knife and slit open the envelope. A stiff white card with black embossed lettering emerged. I groaned, for it was the annual invitation to the Bishop's Palace for tea and buns in the Episcopal Chamber with the 'opportunity' to meet Clinker, various other church dignitaries, fellow clergy, the more zealous of the laity (which invariably included Mavis Briggs), and the usual assortment of chain-clanking aldermen. It is my experience of such functions that these latter are invariably the first to arrive and the last to leave. The 'county', on the other hand, attend late and bugger off smartish. My own tactic is to avoid Clinker (and even more so Gladys), home in on the sandwiches and remain firmly in the shadows. This of course does not always work but one has a good try.

Thus I retired to bed moderately calmed – albeit a trifle irked by the prospect of the impending 'festivities'.

47

The Cat's Memoir

The last couple of weeks had been a time of great turbulence – or as the dog would say, 'a right pantomime'. F.O.
seemed to oscillate between states of darkest gloom and
moods of absurd euphoria. I could not quite make out
what caused these switchbacks but they seemed largely
connected with that drooping Mavis woman and the type
from Brighton.

The latter's sudden arrival early one evening coincided
with a visit from her, and the combination of the two sent
the vicar spinning like a humming top. Bouncer had disappeared into the garden, and being curious to discover
what was going on I had gone into the sitting room. A
mistake really, for no sooner had I settled by the fire than
the Mavis person grabbed my tail and began yanking at it
in a most unseemly fashion; and then, emitting ludicrous
gurgling noises, started to tickle my ears. Well, naturally I
wasn't standing for that! So giving her a brisk tap with one
of my claws I escaped into the hall.

After about half an hour I observed F.O. and his friend
escorting the lady into the garden and bundling her
through a hole in the hedge. When I later remarked to
Bouncer that I thought this rather odd behaviour, he said
that in his opinion it was by far the best hole to have

chosen as the others were filled with nettles. He knows about these things so I suppose he had a point.

Anyway, having dispensed with the guest, the vicar and his companion returned to the sitting room where they proceeded to imbibe large quantities of kitchen brandy. The result was unaesthetic but at least it meant that they slept well, and the house remained calm until well into the next morning.

Eventually the visitor departed, and our master went up to London for one of his routine meetings in Knightsbridge, whence he returned with a fresh stock of his special peppermints from Harrods. Having almost depleted the previous batch, he had latterly been sparing in their consumption. The new ration, however, precipitated a reckless orgy of crunching and grinding, in the course of which he broke a tooth, and the house was strewn with sweet wrappings for days on end. He also brought a newspaper back with him which he kept reading and rereading, and judging from the attendant imprecations I concluded it contained something not to his taste.

Thus up and down we went for several days, until one morning Bouncer came trundling into the kitchen and reported that he had just seen F.O. and the Brighton type 'jawing away in that big black car'. Apparently he had been cajoled into accompanying the vicar to the early service and, when it was over, the Brighton type had appeared and they had started talking. Bouncer said he hung around for a while, and then getting bored came home. When I asked if he had overheard anything useful, he said that from what he could make out it had been the usual subject of the paintings. I replied that as long it was only the paintings and not the murder, things were probably all right. He agreed – but it made us think, and we sat for some time pondering quietly.

Then he suddenly turned to me, wagged his tail and gave a snort.

'I say,' he exclaimed cheerfully, 'I've been with O'Shaughnessy and we've made up a poem about you.'

'Really?' I said with interest, swishing my tail.

'Yes. Do you want to hear it?'

'By all means,' I replied graciously, and settled myself comfortably.

'Here goes then:

> 'There once was a cat called Maurice
> Who fancied a Tabby called Doris;
> When he put out a paw
> She cried, "Crikey!" and "Cor!"
> And buggered off fast to the forest.'

There was a silence while I regarded him bleakly. And then mustering my iciest tones, I observed, 'If you imagine, Bouncer, I should be likely to consort with a commonplace Tabby, let alone one called Doris, you are greatly mistaken. And you can tell that to O'Shaughnessy too.'

'Oh well, if you don't like it we'll try another one . . .'

'That will not be necessary, thank you. Your literary endeavours do not impress me.' And stalking out of the room, I launched into a spectacular sulk that lasted the entire day. It was very satisfying.

48

The Vicar's Version

I arrived a little late at the Bishop's Palace, having dozed too deeply after the one o'clock news and misjudged the time it would take to clear the Hog's Back. One can usually zip along at prodigious speed, but for some reason, that afternoon the road was endlessly clogged by hearse-like Morris Oxfords. Thus when I was ushered into the Episcopal Chamber things were already in full swing and my route to the sandwiches perforce circuitous.

There was the usual mix: hordes of soberly clad clerics of varying degree and rank, their be-hatted wives (of similar gradation), the predicted aldermen, fearsome delegates from the Townswomen's Guild, Mothers' Union, and Women For Peace (these last the most frightening of all), and worthy bevies of bustling laity. Among these – though perhaps not exactly a 'worthy' and certainly not bustling – I was surprised to see Mrs Carruthers.

She stuck out like a sore thumb, and a very colourful one too! Last seen she had been in her gardening clothes sporting hoop earrings of singular size. That afternoon she was dressed in vibrant green from head to toe – even down to the shoes, which, being patent leather, gave off a kind of electrical aura. Her green headgear was a taffeta concoction crowned by a scarlet feather. The earrings were also much in evidence but this time the diamanté had been replaced by shimmering jet. She looked not unlike some plump but exotic bird – an impression enhanced by the bursts of staccato shrieks emanating from her corner of the room.

There was quite a lot of noise coming from the opposite corner too, where Gladys was holding court with her usual assertion, and volubly declaiming Lord-knows-what to a couple of callow curates and the suffragan bishop. The latter looked bored, the curates cowed. Now and again she would stop her barrage and cast baleful glances in the direction of Mrs Carruthers who was hugely enjoying herself in the midst of an audience clearly entranced by the quivering feather. I just caught the last part of a sentence:

'. . . well, dears, if you fancy a few gnomes – better come round to me. I've got every flipping gnome under the sun!' There followed the usual screech of jangling mirth, and I thought wryly that Clinker would cop it that evening, and wondered what had prompted him to invite her. Defiance? A sudden desire to live dangerously? Either way, glancing at Gladys, I feared the storm clouds were fast brewing.

As I hovered in the corner, trying to manipulate my well-filled plate with one hand while balancing a teacup with the other, I caught sight of the bishop jawing intently with – or rather at – a diminutive cleric by name of Fiskins. The latter was looking tired, and I wondered for how long he had been standing thus buttonholed. Not for much longer as it happened, for at that moment Clinker looked up, and catching my eye started to move in my direction. This was disappointing as I was enjoying the sandwiches and didn't want distraction, least of all from Clinker.

He prefaced his greeting with a loud clearing of throat and gave me a look which I can only describe as shifty. He seemed strangely ill at ease and I had the impression that he wanted to say something but was reluctant to begin. Diffidence from Clinker was almost as unnerving as the usual bombast, and I wished that he would go away and leave me alone with the salmon and cucumber.

273

'Ah, Oughterard,' he commenced, 'thought you might be here, gives me an opportunity to, uhm . . .' He paused, staring fixedly at the empty plate in his hand. I wondered irritably whether he was expecting me to offer a titbit from my own carefully chosen fare. He began to clear his throat again, while I steadfastly sipped my tea and waited.

At last he said, 'Well, Oughterard, they have *decided*. And you . . . er, might as well hear it from me before they send you the letter . . .' (What letter, for God's sake! What dire decision had been taken? And in any case, who were 'they'? Canterbury and Co. demanding my resignation? The Mothers' Union declaring me *persona non grata*? Some Church body for overseas affairs sending me to join Rummage in Swaziland?) I must have looked nervous, for Clinker suddenly rallied, and in the old hectoring tones exclaimed, 'Oh, for goodness sake, man, stop looking like a startled rabbit and listen to what I am telling you! The Powers That Be in their questionable wisdom have, for some reason best known to themselves, decided to make you a . . .' He paused as if groping for the word. '. . . have decided, Oughterard, to make you a *canon*.'

I could see from his sour expression that it wasn't a joke, and in dazed wonder fumbled for an appropriate response.

'Well, I never!' I said weakly.

'Yes, thought you would find it mildly preposterous – as any sane person would. Still, it's done now and we'll have to make the best of it. One good thing: it's non-stipendiary. You won't be required to *do* anything – at least, not of any consequence.' And he seemed to brighten. As did I.

But then he frowned again and added grumpily, 'Pretty ironic! They turn down my candidate, Rummage, for the archdeaconry and then appoint you as canon! Some very peculiar people getting on the selection boards these days. Fisher's losing his grip. Anyway, we'll talk about it later.' And whipping one of my sandwiches and muttering something about loose cannons, he moved off to quell Gladys.

I stood in a state of blank perplexity trying to absorb the

startling news and wondering, like Clinker, what I had done to merit such elevation. As I pondered, my eye was distracted by a nearby tray on which reposed a solitary cream cake. It looked particularly enticing – smothered in jam, and with cherries augmenting its oozing cream. But as I started to move towards it I saw Edith Hopgarden making a similar beeline. Undeterred, I stretched out my hand and took it smartly. First pickings for the new canon! I thought.

On my way home I bumped into Savage, and told him my news. 'Cor, that's pretty good, Rev!' he exclaimed. 'Suppose they'll be making you Pope next!'

'Unlikely,' I said. 'That's the other lot.'

My encounter with Savage resulted in further bombardment with his wife's fairy cakes. A consignment was delivered the next day 'to celebrate the Rev's leg-up' and wishing me well in my new 'cannonade'. I was touched by this kind thought but rather doubted whether I should be able to generate the explosions evidently envisaged by the Savage family. However, the gift was certainly appreciated, and Bouncer and I spent a happy hour squabbling over the butter-cream and the meticulously applied silver balls. The cat looked on with a sour expression.

In the course of this pleasurable consumption I pondered the reasons for my advancement. Who on earth had recommended it? Certainly not Clinker! And on what grounds? It was puzzling. However, the answer was not long in coming, for the second post delivered a peremptory note from Archdeacon Blenkinsop:

'Gratifying to know that there are some members of the Church who still take their diocesan duties seriously. Your handling of the Rummage absurdity was exemplary, and I only wish others would heed my precepts as efficiently as you did: the Church would be a more stable institution. We no longer live in sober days, Oughterard, but I like to think my views still hold sway in certain circles of influence! Congratulations on your appointment.'

Bugger me! I thought. Bully for old Blenkinsop. Just goes to show – pomposity has its uses!

A day later I received the official letter cordially inviting me to take up the post of Honorary Canon – in recognition of my dedicated contribution to parish stability (i.e. being bland and uncontentious) and of my solid services to the diocese (i.e. toadying to Blenkinsop). It irritatingly over-emphasized the lack of remuneration for such office, but assured me that other than delivering an annual sermon to the diocese, no further duties would be required beyond those already being 'so suitably discharged'. In the conclud-ing paragraph there was mention of my being allocated a stall in the cathedral, and on ceremonial occasions being permitted to embellish my cassock with a scarlet cummer-bund . . . So that was something to look forward to.

That evening I telephoned Primrose and told her my news.

'Your brother is now a canon,' I announced. 'Canon Oughterard. Do you think it sounds all right?'

'It doesn't matter what it sounds like,' she replied. 'What are you paid?'

'Well, money doesn't really come into it . . .' There was a snort of impatience from the other end, and I added defensively, 'But I can wear a red sash and have been given a personal stall.'

'In the Gents, you mean? What will they think of next!'

I explained carefully that the stall was not in the Gents but in the cathedral chancel and that it would have my name on it.

'Just make sure they spell it properly. You know how illiterate these people are!'

'These people' was one of Primrose's favourite terms of disparagement and was applied frequently and broadly. So broadly in fact, that it was impossible to know the precise category to which she referred, or indeed how wide its boundaries – the general point being that whoever they were, they deserved disapproval.

Nevertheless, as a celebratory gesture she graciously offered to buy me a large whisky the next time I went down to 'do the garden', but added darkly that perhaps in view of my new status I should decline the spirit and stick to ginger beer. I said that I did not think that was part of the contract.

We then got on to matters artistic, i.e. the Spendlers, and I was able to tell her that things were all but cleared up, and thanks to Professor Higginbottom, the artist was scuppered and our reputations no longer imperilled. To which she replied that as long as I was her brother an imperilled reputation was par for the course. I forbore to ask after the chinchillas, and we ended our conversation amicably.

Initially I felt rather awkward with my new designation, but people in general seemed receptive (apart from Clinker of course), and since it made no undue demands on my normal routine, I gradually became attuned to the idea. Indeed, there were occasions when I derived a certain pleasure: when sporting the scarlet cummerbund for instance or being treated to sudden bouts of cringing deference from Tapsell. These latter would not last but at least provided short-term entertainment. Edith, of course, remained rock-like in her hostility. Guilt is an intractable business, and being caught twice by your vicar in a compromising situation might well fuel resentment. Though she was lucky, I thought ruefully, to have only an illicit liaison to cope with.

The following weeks passed very pleasantly – and indeed, not without a little gaiety, the redoubtable Miss Dalrymple having organized quite a racy, not to say lavish, drinks party in my honour. There were French cocktail onions, bowls of mock caviar and, instead of the usual

Mateus Rosé, *real* pink champagne! Halfway through, and presumably prompted by the pinkness of the champagne, Colonel Dawlish was so bold as to open a book on the topic of my first canonical address. This gave rise to much speculative merriment, and people kept sidling up and asking in lowered tones for a private 'tip'. Naturally I hadn't a clue so they didn't get far. However, it did occur to me that perhaps an appropriate theme would be the evils of insider trading.

Thus a good time was had by all – except for one. Owing to the toll taken by one of her frequent colds, Mavis Briggs was unable to attend. Regrets were sadly expressed, and we were denied hearing a medley fiom her poetic *Gems of Uplift* – an omission which was possibly the high point of the evening.

The difficulty with the canonical sash was Maurice. He liked it. And when I got home that night it was to find him sprawled on my bed, head thrust beneath its scarlet silk, and tassels firmly gripped between his paws. The grey woollen mouse lay jettisoned on the floor, obviously discarded in favour of richer pickings. He was snoring.

The problem was how to disengage sash from cat. Maurice is a tricky customer at the best of times, but when possessions are threatened the ensuing scene can turn spectacularly sparky. It would be a manoeuvre requiring considerable tact and I approached it with some diffidence. But as with Colonel Dawlish, suddenly emboldened by the pink champagne I took a chance, gave him a quick prod, and without hesitation whipped the thing from under him. It worked a treat, and apart from a brief howl of surprise, Maurice did nothing except stare at me in glazed indignation. I gave his tail a friendly tweak and reminded him he was now sharing the house with a canon and he had better jolly well show some respect. He closed his eyes and resumed snoring.

49

The Vicar's Version

The days sped towards Christmas, and with a slight pang of unease I realized that the Elizabeth Fotherington Memorial Event would soon be upon us.

This was a ceremony I had instigated the previous year, principally as a means of allaying police suspicion of my involvement with Elizabeth's end – a sort of smokescreen device which, on the face of it, had proved successful. And it had certainly been popular in the parish. The central part – the awarding of the Fotherington Chorister Prize – had produced enormous local interest, inflated the Church Spire Fund, and enhanced our choral reputation. The special anthem composed by Tapsell and the choirmaster, and set to words by the seventeenth-century lyricist Herrick, had been universally approved.

But there had been a deeper reason for the ceremony's genesis, buried yet subtly compelling: some sort of expiatory necessity, nagging and as yet unresolved ... It was something that would have to be dealt with one day. One day.

However, my immediate task was the upkeep of standards, i.e. a repeat of the previous year's success. Reputations were at stake – St Botolph's and Elizabeth's – and I was intent on preserving both. So I briskly rounded up Tapsell and the choirmaster Jenkins, and with a bit of canonical bullying heavily laced with grovelling flattery, reminded them it was high time that rehearsals were afoot. In fact they needed little urging. Both are prima donnas and each was eager to reap the last year's plaudits and get his photograph in the newspaper again.

Thus having set in motion the two protagonists, I had to get myself organized. The earlier occasion had been highly demanding: emotionally, for obvious reasons, but intellectually too, as it had been my place to select the words of the anthem, a task that, given the circumstances and not having much literary expertise, I had found perplexing in the extreme. However, my choice of the Herrick poem had seemed to please, and for a good fortnight after the event Molehill's two bookshops were inundated with requests for 'that nice seventeenth-century chap'. Curious the way good reputations can spread via dubious routes.

But this second time around things were less difficult, and the only matter that really presented a problem was my address from the pulpit. Somehow it had to fit the occasion. But how? The matter would obviously require very careful thought, and to that end I poured out a large glass of my precious Talisker (kept for special occasions), lit a cigarette and sunk into my favourite armchair.

I suppose that like the Scholar Gypsy I was expecting the 'spark from heaven to fall', and p.d.q. at that! It didn't of course, and an hour later, with the ashtray littered and the malt reduced by a fair third, I was no further on.

There came a slight scrabbling at the door and Bouncer nosed his way in. He sauntered over to the piano stool, regarded it for a moment, looked at me, and then made to cock his leg. Since I had seen him in the garden only a few minutes earlier, I knew very well that this was no sudden emergency and shouted at him to stop. He lowered his leg, wagged his tail, and came slinking over. There are times when I think that dog goes out of his way to wind me up!

He settled meekly at my feet and stared up with that kindly yet quizzical look which is at once reassuring and faintly unnerving. I stared back, wondering what on earth was going on behind those doggy eyes. For a few moments we sat quietly in a state of mutual regard.

And then with a start, and nearly upsetting my glass, I realized what my theme would be: God's creatures: their comfort and companionship, and their benison in times of angst and strain. That was it, I would dissert on Man's best friend: his wise jester and clownish sage; solace of the bereaved, safe confidant and loyal mate . . . Yes, that was what Molehill's worthies would hear from the pulpit – an encomium upon the dog, the cat, and other four-footed helpers! I laughed in relief and ruffled Bouncer's cobwebbed ears. I think he thought I was barking.

As might the reader. After all, on the face of it there seemed little to link the animal fraternity with the deceased; and given the nature of the occasion I was going to be hard pressed to justify my theme. Had animals held a particular place in Mrs Fotherington's affections? Not as far as I was aware, unless of course you counted the waspish Maurice whom she had persecuted with unrelenting sentiment. Still, I recalled, there had been the wretched canary, and she had certainly indulged Bouncer's greed by feeding him titbits at that fateful soirée (memory of which still sends a chill down my spine!).*

Yes, I decided, there was ample material on which to peg my thesis. In any case it is always good to embellish people's qualities, however limited. Indeed, one might say the greater the limitation the greater the need . . .

And thus supper over, I embarked eagerly on the task of eulogizing the role of domestic pets, while at the same time conferring upon Elizabeth attributes of the most tenuous kind. Regarding the latter, I think I rather over-egged the trifle, as for days afterwards people kept coming up to me and remarking how little they had realized what an *incredible* rapport Elizabeth had established with our four-footed friends and that her sensitivities in this sphere should be an example to us all! Even the *Molehill Clarion* ran a brief article to the effect that I had paid 'shining tribute to a great animal lover', and prefaced its report with the slightly unsettling headline, THE LADY'S SECRET: CANON

* See *A Load of Old Bones*

CONFIDES. However, generally it was all very gratifying – although a whiff of cynical dissent did waft over from the direction of Colonel Dawlish.

He accosted me one morning, shook my hand warmly and said, 'Nice piece of rhetoric, Oughterard. You're getting better. I always told 'em you'd get into your stride eventually. Made an interesting change from the usual sort of thing. About time the ox and the ass got a mention. Mind you, all that stuff about Elizabeth being a protector of furry beasts was a load of my eye – as well you know!' And he grinned sardonically.

'Well . . .' I began weakly, 'there was her cat – and the canary . . .'

He snorted loudly. 'Oh, come off it, Canon. She may have drooled over those two creatures, but fundamentally she was terrified of anything on four legs. You should have seen her with my Tojo – ran a mile rather than get near him!'

Since Tojo was a wholly manic West Highland with a propensity for duffing up both humans and fellow terriers, I had some sympathy for Elizabeth. However, before I could say anything to that effect, the Colonel added slyly – and rightly, 'Admit it. You used a weak case on which to peg a strong argument!' And whistling merrily he sauntered off.

Well, I mused, if that was the only objection I wasn't doing too badly. And with that comforting thought I took a gentle potter in the church before returning home to lunch and a nap.

When I awoke, the telephone was ringing. To my surprise (consternation?) I realized it was Eric, Ingaza's chum.

'Wotcha, Rev!' he began affably. 'Thought we'd just give yer a tinkle to see how you was getting on. His Nibs would of phoned himself but he's in bed with a chill. Leastways, that's wot he *says*. If you ask me, he's swinging the lead – trying to escape his Auntie Lil. She's been playing up no end since all that picture stuff and it's getting on his fins!' An explosion of mirth came hurtling down the line.

'Er, good afternoon, Eric,' I said wonderingly. 'How kind of you to enquire. So sorry to hear that Nicholas is laid up. The occasional rest does us all good!' And I laughed nervously.

'Well, funny you should say that 'coz that's wot we was phoning about. "Get on the blower," Nick says, "and tell Francis I meant wot I said about him coming down to Brighton. Looked peaky when I saw him last. Could do with a bit o' the old ozone!"' Another rasping chuckle, and I adjusted the receiver to a more convenient distance. Peaky? Of course I looked peaky. Who wouldn't in Ingaza's clutches! The paintings danced before my eyes.

'That's very kind of him,' I said, my mind racing at breakneck speed, 'the only problem is that things are a bit hectic just at the moment, what with a fresh spate of christenings and funerals, the verger on holiday, and, er, problems with the pews – damp rot, you know . . .'

'Cor, you don't 'arf lead a merry life. Better take a break soon or yer may crack under the strain of it all!' More guffaws. I refrained from saying that I thought I had cracked a long while ago; and instead joined faintly in the merriment.

'Anyhow, Nick says that congrats are in order. You've been a good boy, so he says!'

'Sorry, I'm not quite sure what you –'

'You being made a canon or whatever. Goin' up in the world, cuttin' the old *moutarde*!'

'Ah, yes – yes of course. Thank you. But, uhm, how ever did Nicholas hear about it? News certainly travels fast!'

'Oh it does, old son, it does. S'matter of fact it was his other Surrey pal. Nose like a bleedin' ferret, that geezer!'

I might have guessed. The Cranleigh Contact!

He went breezing on. And then being persuaded that I really couldn't manage a trip down to Brighton, bade me a fond goodbye – but not before saying that come the spring the pair of them would probably be taking a little jaunt north and thus passing quite close to Molehill . . .

I had intended going into Guildford that afternoon in quest of some new socks and handkerchiefs, but after my discourse with Eric suddenly felt fatigued and decided to give it a miss. I wandered over to the piano, played a few scales and then toyed with a little Cole Porter. But it was a lacklustre performance and after ten minutes I gave up and resumed my chair.

I pondered why they had invited me to Brighton. Was it really for the pleasure of my company? Surely not. There must be some darker purpose! What dubious game was Nicholas playing now – and more to the point, what role had he cast for me?

I stared at the small sepia photograph of my father on the mantelpiece, and from the distant past heard his brisk and crackling tones: 'Now don't mope, Francis! Moping gets you nowhere. Be bold. Be brave – and kindly stand up straight!'

As a gesture, I dutifully uncrossed my legs, straightened my shoulders, and reflected on more of the parental diktats: 'Never sell yourself short, boy. Capitalize your assets – and what's more, *nil illegitimi carborundum*!' I smiled wryly. He had been proud of that one – the only 'Latin' he had known – and he would bark it out with force and frequency. 'Daddy's one bit of scholarship,' as Primrose used to say.

But I suddenly brightened. Despite everything, his words were not without point – and in terms of my present situation were surely pertinent. I *had* been guilty of fruitless moping, and yes, was rather allowing the *illegitimi* to grind me down. Enough was enough! (Well, more or less

284

at any rate.) As to selling myself short: it was, I supposed, just possible that Nicholas was without ulterior motive and was genuinely concerned with my welfare. Could the invitation to Brighton be really free from strings, and my company on the promenade all that they sought? The concept presented some difficulty but I flirted with the hope nevertheless.

Calculation of assets, let alone their capitalizing, was also quite difficult. But as I reviewed the events of the last few weeks I realized that things could be a lot worse, and that all was not as yet lost. For example, I was still in the clear re the ghastly Fotherington business; the picture nightmare was apparently resolved; Ingaza held at bay from Molehill until at least the spring; I had received promotion (albeit of a nominal kind); and for some curious reason I seemed to be gaining favour in the community. There was also the additional benefit of having the war-blinded Savage as my friend – not to mention the comfort of his wife's fairy cakes. Few assassins could ask for more.

I pondered Nicholas's suggestion of taking a break. Perhaps he was right and I really did need a little holiday: somewhere quiet and undemanding where I could recharge my batteries, or, to quote some American professor I had once heard lecturing on the wireless, get 're-energized'. Though whether the 're' part was entirely applicable, I wasn't sure. Energy has never played a great part in my life, and even during my 'missionary' phase, its display was largely a triumph of will over instinct. Still, given the present circumstances some sort of electrical surge might be no bad thing!

I brooded on the logistics of getting away – and the locations. In spite of Ingaza's possibly well-meant offer, Brighton was definitely out. Apart from anything else, the thought of being dragged into Aunt Lil's orbit was too awesome to contemplate. There was also the prospect of Eric . . .

No, I would need to go somewhere soothing, beautiful, and as remote from the south coast as feasible. The Scilly Isles perhaps – but Clinker went there. The Shetlands? No need to be excessive. Connemara and the place of my namesake? A glorious area, but overlaid with memories of fraught family holidays and Pa's fishing fiascos.

Perhaps somewhere with religious links ... Walsingham? Not with that east wind! St Columba's Iona? Remote all right, and by all accounts with a distinctly spiritual 'something'; but it necessitated a rough and questionable boat trip and I doubted if my stomach would stay the course. Besides, the very name sounded a trifle stark ... whereas *Lin-dis-farne* held a soft, emollient note: a sound redolent of peace and soporific ease. And even as I murmured it to myself I could see 'bare ruined choirs', hear the lapping of gentle waves, the cry of the curlew, and the misty monkish orisons ...

Yes, that was where I would go, to St Wilfrid's own land, and soon! My imagination was gripped, my resolution firm, and I rushed to the telephone and dialled the number of the Reverend Pick.

'I say, Pick, you wouldn't like to oversee my parish for a few days, would you? There wouldn't be much to –'

'No,' came the firm answer.

I took a deep breath and smiled winningly down the phone. 'Oh, come on, Theodore, be a sport. I just need to get away for a spell to recharge the old batteries – you know the sort of thing!'

'Not really,' came the reply. 'My leaves of absence are always planned well in advance. I am not one for leaping about at the drop of a hat.'

'Well, neither am I,' I replied hastily, 'it's just that I've been under a bit of pressure lately and could do with some *time out* – as our American friends would say!'

'I suppose in plain English that means you want to skive off.'

'Oh, come – that's putting it a trifle brutally! Besides, you might recall that I was quite useful at your fête this year –'

'How about next year?'

'Oh yes, absolutely. That's on!'

There was a pause. And then in a tone which for Pick sounded almost bright, he said, 'Well, tell you what – I'll lend you Barry. It's time he got from under my feet. He can easily take a few services at your place – even do some house calls. In fact, come to think of it, if he were to arrive in time for Matins he could stay on till well after Evensong – *every* day.'

I thanked him for his most selfless offer, and in response to further insistent probing assured him of my presence at the wretched spring fête.

First hurdle over. The second was Primrose. Would she board the animals? Probably not. But nothing ventured . . .

To my amazement, and in view of the chinchilla fracas, Primrose was vaguely agreeable.

'Well, if you must you must, I suppose. But a week is my absolute maximum: the dog's all right, but I wouldn't be able to stand that peculiar cat for any longer! Yes, bring them down . . . and then while you're here you could also give the garden a good going over.'

'Yes,' I replied meekly. 'Of course I could.'

Celebration all round! Much to do: maps to be consulted, accommodation booked, the motor prepared, parishioners notified. But first of all a grateful gin, a couple of gaspers, and this time a really good go on the keys! I summoned Bouncer in readiness for the performance. He came in toting his rubber ring, pottered over to the piano, and sat down with a look of benign expectancy. I raised my hands, poised for a spate of sparkling arpeggios . . . and then dropped them in my lap as the doorbell shrilled.

The dog barked and I cursed. However, thinking it might be Savage bearing fresh fairy cakes, I went into the hall hoping he might have time to share the gin, and along with Bouncer, enjoy the music. So beaming genially, I flung open the door.

Samson, not Savage, stood in the porch.

'Good evening, sir,' he intoned nasally. 'Was just passing. Thought you'd like to hear the news.'

'Oh yes?' I said jovially. 'Has one of my raffle tickets come up trumps? Or have you won the police prize for best salesman?'

He looked at me without expression.

'No, sir. No, I don't think either of those apply ... You see, they've opened it again.'

'Opened it? Opened what?' I asked, still smiling.

'The Fotherington case, the murder in Foxford Wood – they've reopened it. Just thought you might like to know, seeing as how you were a close friend of the deceased ...'
And this time, it was he who smiled.